## PRAISE FOR *WELCOME TO NIGHT VALE: A NOVEL*

"This is a splendid, weird, moving novel about families, the difficulties of growing up, and the deep-seated vulnerabilities involved in raising children. It manages beautifully that trick of embracing the surreal in order to underscore and emphasize the real—not as allegory, but as affirmation of emotional truths that don't conform to the neat and tidy boxes in which we're encouraged to house them."
—NPR.org

"*Welcome to Night Vale* lives up to the podcast hype in every way. It is a singularly inventive visit to an otherworldly town that's the stuff of nightmares and daydreams." —*BookPage*

"Fink and Cranor's prose hints there's an empathetic humanity underscoring their well of darkly fantastic situations. . . . the book builds toward a satisfyingly strange exploration of the strange town's intersection with an unsuspecting real world."
—*Los Angeles Times*

"The charms of *Welcome to Night Vale* are nearly impossible to quantify. That applies to the podcast, structured as community radio dispatches from a particularly surreal desert town, as well as this novel." —*Minneapolis Star Tribune*

"The book is charming and absurd—think *This American Life* meets *Alice in Wonderland*." —*Washington Post*

## PRAISE FOR *IT DEVOURS!: A WELCOME TO NIGHT VALE NOVEL*

"Different from other mystery novels . . . as captivating and light as any mystery novel can be but explores one of the most complex issues: the conflict between science and reason on the one hand and, on the other hand, religion and cult."

*—Washington Book Review*

"Compelling . . . A confident supernatural comedy from writers who can turn from laughter to tears on a dime."

*—Kirkus Reviews* (starred review)

"(A) smart exploration of the divide—and overlap—of science and religion . . . A thrilling adventure and a fascinating argument that science and belief aren't necessarily mutually exclusive."

—Tor.com

"Very clever. . . . With a gripping mystery, a very smartly built world (a place similar to our own world but at the same time distinctly other), and a cast of offbeat characters, the novel is a welcome addition." *—Booklist*

"A mysterious, must-read exploration of the Great Unknowns, with a touch of Carl Sagan and Agatha Christie."

—Marisha Pessl, *New York Times* bestselling author of *Night Film* and *Special Topics in Calamity Physics*

# THE BUYING OF LOT 37

## ALSO BY JOSEPH FINK AND JEFFREY CRANOR

*Welcome to Night Vale: A Novel*

*It Devours! A Welcome to Night Vale Novel*

*Mostly Void, Partially Stars: Welcome to Night Vale Episodes, Volume 1*

*The Great Glowing Coils of the Universe:*
*Welcome to Night Vale Episodes, Volume 2*

*Who's a Good Boy?: Welcome to Night Vale Episodes, Volume 4*

## ALSO BY JOSEPH FINK

*Alice Isn't Dead: A Novel*

# THE BUYING OF LOT 37

## Welcome to Night Vale
## Episodes, Volume 3

## JOSEPH FINK AND
## JEFFREY CRANOR

HARPER PERENNIAL

NEW YORK • LONDON • TORONTO • SYDNEY • NEW DELHI • AUCKLAND

HARPER PERENNIAL

Illustrations by Jessica Hayworth

HarperCollins books may be purchased for educational, business, or sales promotional use. For information, please email the Special Markets Department at SPsales@harpercollins.com.

FIRST EDITION

Library of Congress Cataloging-in-Publication Data has been applied for.

ISBN 978-0-06-279809-1

19 20 21 22 23   LSC   10 9 8 7 6 5 4 3 2 1

To the cast and crew of *Welcome to Night Vale*

# CONTENTS

# FOREWORD

AFTER AN EYE EXAM, MY OPHTHALMOLOGIST, DR. SWENSON, WILL TURN her monitor so that I can see the image on screen: my own retina, reflecting the beam of her pen light in a ghostly green, run through with a pattern of blood vessels as unique as my fingerprint. This is my favorite part of an eye exam because I get to see the inside of the seeing part of me.

Listening to *Welcome to Night Vale* often provides a similar thrill. Joseph Fink and Jeffrey Cranor manage to establish and defy listener expectations within the span of a single sentence—sometimes more than once. I myself am a writer (I got to write "Niecelet," Episode 113 of *Welcome to Night Vale*, in fact), which means I generally know how words work, I know how pacing and sentence structure function, and I'm familiar with the mechanics of absurdism. So laughing out loud in my car while listening to a Night Vale episode is akin to working at a haunted house and still falling for the jump scare every night. It's hard to surprise a person waiting to be surprised. And yet they do it all the time. Experiencing my brain scamper off in the wrong direction then spin around, confused and delighted by a bizarre turn of phrase, feels like I'm learning something about my usual habits of thought; I get to peer inside the thinking part of me. I know a lot of Night Vale diehards are devoted to its characters—they fall for Tamika's moxie, Cecil's baritone, Old Woman Josie's angels, Carlos's hair—but the language of Night Vale is my favorite character. I'm a sucker for the *language* in which all these figures are described—I think I like the window as much as the view.

The first time I ferreted my way into the vicinity of Night Vale was backstage at the Town Hall theater in New York. I'd been asked to serve as The Weather for the evening and was excited to perform in such a grand venue—brass railings and red velvet seats and chandeliers chandeliering in that way unique to big theaters or old hotels. I listened to the show over the backstage intercom and snuck around to steal glimpses of the attendees sitting out in the darkness—hundreds and hundreds of rapt faces. Some of those faces were painted, some were hidden behind mesh panels (costumed, I'd learn, as the Faceless Old Woman Who Secretly Lives in Your Home), some of them hung like moons below cotton Glow Clouds rigged with working LED lights. Until that point, I'd spent most of my musical life as a hip-hop artist, touring the club circuit, sometimes playing a big festival stage. I'd performed in lovely rooms before, but this was something entirely different. The fans reveled in every inside joke, dissected every reference, knew every grain of desert sand in Night Vale. I didn't know the term *world-building* then—it's not a phrase that's bandied about in the halls of the rap academy, but it was plain that Joseph and Jeffrey had made a complete, functioning human culture where people could actually live—at least for the span of a ninety-minute live show. I could not wait to tell my rap crew about this.

But, of course, if you're a frequent visitor to Night Vale, you know how hard it can be to tell someone about the show in a single, quick description: *It's like the surrealism of Joe Frank with the whimsy of Lisa Frank. No, it's like Voltaire meets David Lynch. No, it's like*

*Carl Sagan meeting his younger self and playing a rousing game of solitaire. Sometimes it balances right on the edge of sense and it runs on puréed imagination, and the tone is often sarcastic but sometimes brutally earnest, and it's fun to feel your mind careening around on one ice skate, trying to keep up. Here, I've made a pie chart.*

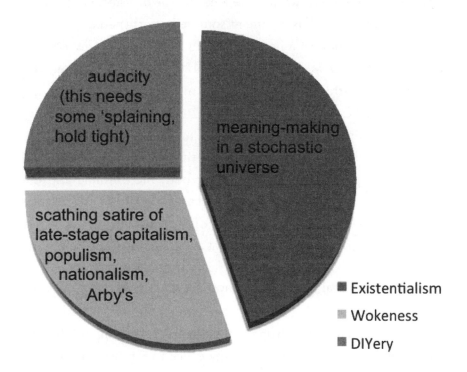

I have one comment about the writing of *Welcome to Night Vale* that neither Jeffrey nor Joseph are likely to appreciate. So if you, dear reader, *are* Mr. Fink or Mr. Cranor, I will now kindly ask that you skip this section—just skim until you hit the series of wingdings and then merge right back in.

Okay, what I'd like to talk about is the inclusivity of the characters of Night Vale. The people (and sometimes nonpeople) who populate Night Vale come in every permutation of size, sex, shape, ethnicity—almost all the kinds of bodies you can imagine and many you cannot. I brought this up with Joseph once, on stage at one of his tour stops, and the compliment I'd intended, about having constructed such an inclusive universe, was very swiftly shot out of the sky. He said something like, "The actual population is actually varied. You don't get extra points for writing characters that represent the real world—it would take a conscious decision *not* to write characters that way." His comment sounded smart then and it looks smart typed out now. But here's the thing: I write fiction myself and, looking at my past work, I don't remember making a conscious decision to write straight characters with mostly European-sounding names. But that's exactly what I'd done. It was a decision that somehow simply slipped past the sentries of my conscious mind. I have since returned to old stories to correct that mistake and I owe Jeffrey and Joseph a debt of gratitude for both the example and the standard they set in that arena. (Also, let's just pause to acknowledge and lament the complete insufficiency of the word *inclusive*, which is academic and sort of flaccid and not at all reflective of the indelicate, electric business of being alive in a sea of other living things.)

⬥ⱆ●ⱆ▢○ⱆ  ♌ᑲⱆ&⊡  ꙑⱆ■♦●ⱆ○ⱆ■✒ (Welcome back, gentlemen.)

The data analyst who helped me create the stunning pie chart in this foreword has just leaned into my office to remind me to make good on the promise to explain the term *audacity* as it appears in that graphic. (Thanks, Marela.) In this instance, it does not refer to a "willingness to take bold risks," but rather to the open-sourced audio program Audacity. Until very recently, each episode of Night Vale was recorded (by Cecil) through a USB microphone and then edited in Audacity. This fact blew my mind. Audio software is like word-processing software; a few programs completely dominate the market. No matter which ones might perform best, most of the documents you create, read, or receive are probably in Word. To find out that *Welcome to [expletive deleted] Night Vale* was created in

Audacity was like peeking into the kitchen of a Michelin-starred restaurant to discover that the chefs were not flambéing their fare in Le Creuset cookware, but were gathered around a microwave—no, a hotplate—no, a Bic lighter held beneath a pane of foil. It was genuinely amazing to imagine that a culturally important thing was produced by such simple and universally accessible means.

Which brings me to one of the most exciting ideas in Night Vale's constellation of conspiracy theories. Could it be possible that this time—this one time—the good guys who work hard and give thanks and consult their consciences before corporate sponsors—could it be that they win? For me it's easy to root for the Night Vale team and to celebrate their assorted successes because they try so damn hard and they bring their friends with them and they take real, artistic risks. And to makers of anything, in any discipline or trade, that model is a welcome one—even if you've got to defy space-time and march through an endless desert to see it up close.

—Dessa,
written on October 2, 2018,
in room 405 of a very fine Milwaukee hotel

# INTRODUCTION

"The Librarian" was our first touring live show for Welcome to Night Vale and also the first moment I knew I had to make a dramatic change in my life.

We began our second year of the podcast with millions of downloads each month, but downloads don't pay the bills. In August of 2013, we printed five hundred Welcome to Night Vale T-shirts and put them up for sale on our website. Within two days, they were completely sold out plus about one hundred more oversold. We had to take the store offline.

For the first time, Welcome to Night Vale made a little bit of money, and it was the first sign that we might be able to make writing a podcast our full-time job. But I wasn't confident we could sustain five hundred shirt sales every week.

Joseph quit his job selling green energy on the streets of New York almost immediately. I had a full-time job as database manager for the non-profit cinema Film Forum. Arts administration was a fulfilling career I'd had for sixteen years, and this one in particular was a great job. I liked the people there, it paid well with benefits, and it was a true nine-to-five gig, leaving my nights and weekends free to make art, which historically had been a hobby, not a job. Jillian and I were in our tenth year of marriage and had just bought our first home the year before. I was not ready to depart stable employment for an artistic endeavor that had grossed about one thousand dollars over its first fifteen months.

We did a few live shows in the autumn of 2013, two in San Francisco at the Booksmith ("Condos," as featured in Volume 1), and two in Brooklyn at Roulette, which all sold out in under two minutes, and it occurred to me that we should actually organize a live show tour.

I had to miss the San Francisco shows because I didn't have vacation days left, and I had no idea how I would fit a touring show around my job, but it was clear that there was a demand for people to see Cecil in-person telling these stories.

We had no booking agent, so I just used my party planning knowledge to book our first tour.

1.  Rent an appropriate venue.
2.  Send out invites (in this case, put tickets on sale).
3.  Figure out what you'll do at said event.
4.  Show up and do the thing.

We found theaters in Seattle, Portland, San Francisco, Los Angeles, San Diego, Las Vegas, and Phoenix for performances over a two-week span in late January 2014. We took the money we had from T-shirts, our other four live shows, and our bank accounts and paid out about twenty-five thousand dollars to these venues and put tickets up for sale. We sold out twelve of the fifteen shows (mostly within an hour of putting them on sale).

We said "Hurrah!" But then we panicked and said, "What the hell are we going to perform once we get there?" And "How are we going to get around?" And "How do you tour even?"

Joseph and I started by writing a script based on the first thing that came to our mind: "What if the Librarians in Night Vale escaped?" Boom. Done.*

I put together a pretty basic touring budget. We booked mostly Airbnbs, and save for the flight from Portland to San Francisco, every other leg of the tour was drivable. So we did what any fancy touring artists do: we rented a Chrysler Town & Country minivan from Budget.

By early December 2013, we had our West Coast tour locked and loaded, and we were already planning another month-long tour of the East Coast and Midwest for March, and I knew I had to quit my job.

Surely you're thinking, "Which you did quite quickly, because getting to do national tours for a show you wrote is a dream come true!"

Oh, heck no.

I spent a week trying to figure out if I could manage Night Vale as a business while still keeping the security of my day job, and I learned that the number of hours in a day is inflexible. Jillian was trepidatious but supportive. We had just bought an apartment in Brooklyn two years earlier, and she had gone to part-time work the previous year in order to focus more on her choreography. My salary enabled us to do both of these things. Now it was I who wanted to leave full-time employment for uncertain artistic pursuits.

Truth be told, I actually didn't. I didn't want to at all. It was Jillian who told me to write out expected earnings for the next two tours, and we realized we could live off that for at least a year. If Night Vale fell apart in that time, we would rethink our future, but perhaps it is worth the risk for an opportunity like this.

So I quit my job at the end of 2013 and met the crew in Seattle to start the tour in mid-January, serving as de facto tour manager, something I had no idea how to do. I had several nervous fits trying to figure out how to order and ship merchandise, as well as learning that (apparently) people like to eat food around dinnertime. I ordered us a pizza in Portland, and the delivery guy showed up side stage mid-show and announced to a performing Cecil Baldwin (and our audience), "Pizza's here!"

While waiting in the airport to fly to San Francisco, I was in a mental fog caused by imposter syndrome and fear of flying. I had spent the morning crying and didn't feel like talking or looking at anyone. At the airport bar, Cecil noted that I looked not so good. I said I was getting a cold, which I wasn't, but I would rather lie than burden people with my anxieties. Cecil said, "Oh, me too. I just bought some Emergen-C to try to stave it off. You want one?" I said yes. He handed it to me, and without thinking, I put it directly into my mouth, like it were a lozenge.

The table went silent, and I looked up to see Meg, Joseph, and Cecil staring straight at me, eyes wide, not knowing what to say. I was trying to play it off like, "Oh, I know you're supposed to dissolve these in water first, but it's totally fine to just suck on them." But what happened was a bunch of pink foam dribbled out of my lips and Meg started laughing. Then I started laughing, and Joseph and Cecil. It was an embarrassing catharsis and I felt great for the first time on the road.

By the end of the tour, we had met two people who would change our touring course forever for the better: Lauren O'Niell of Booksmith, who became our tour manager for the next tour and laid the groundwork for future touring; and Andrew Morgan, our booking agent.

As Night Vale entered its third year, we were touring The Librarian to Europe and Canada and even making inroads toward an Australia/New Zealand tour.

As of January 2019, Meg is now our full-time tour director and live show emcee and is the best at both jobs. Our touring has become the lifeblood of Welcome to Night Vale as a business and as an artistic endeavor. We have performed more than three hundred shows in seventeen countries, in some of the most amazing venues on earth (London's Palladium Theatre, New York's Town Hall, and on the main stage of the Sydney Opera House).

We learned so much from "The Librarian." That first tour was the most stressful two weeks of my life to that point, knowing I'd left a comfortable job I did well for a career I'd never trained for. But seeing Night Vale fans en masse, in person, across the country is a pleasure that never stales. And that first tour was also the most exciting two weeks of my life to that point. Driving the West Coast of the U.S. with three dear friends (and essentially work spouses) doing what we loved and learning so much about each other.**

—Jeffrey Cranor

---

*By "Boom. Done." I mean we spent weeks trying to write a script that was seventy minutes long and was fun for a live audience, in a way that a podcast cannot be. In "The Librarian," at the end of this volume, note that the segment just before the Weather about the escaped librarian entering a theater was the first scene we wrote. Joseph was inspired by William Castle's *The Tingler* to instill a euphoric thrill among the audience, a stirring anticipation that something, indeed, was lurking under their seats. I loved this scene live. It never failed to cause audiences to shift in their chairs, laughing uncomfortably through the whole bit.

**The most notable learn-about-each-other moment came in our drive to Vegas when the four of us each took a 150-question Sorting Hat quiz to figure out which Hogwarts house we belong to. Each of the four landed in a different house—Joseph: Gryffindor; Meg: Ravenclaw; Cecil: Slytherin; and to the surprise of no one, me: Hufflepuff.

# EPISODE 50:
# "CAPITAL CAMPAIGN"

## JULY 15, 2014

### COWRITTEN WITH ASHLEY LIERMAN

WHEN JEFFREY AND JOSEPH INVITED ME BACK TO WRITE ANOTHER EPI-sode after "Summer Reading Program," I was both excited and a little intimidated to come back to the world of Night Vale, after its huge and well-deserved boom in popularity. I also knew, though, that if I had another story I wanted to tell in this setting, it would involve Night Vale Community College. Being a librarian led me to write "Summer Reading Program," but I've always been a college or university librarian, not a public one, and I feel most at home with the humor and horror of higher education. In fact, back in the early days of the podcast when the creators sought fan contributions for a potential book (which unfortunately never became a reality), I submitted a piece called "Minutes of the Night Vale Community College Faculty Meeting," which was what led to my being invited to write an episode in the first place—and later became an episode in its own right, during a hiatus of the regular podcast.

So I was eager to return to the community college, and play around with some more of its possibilities. I did struggle for a

while, though, to think of what foible of campus life could be wor-
thy of reporting on in the community news and would at the same
time have the potential to build up into an appropriately dramatic
crisis. Finally, I found myself delighted by the idea of a fundraising campaign that resulted in the donation of a lot of unwanted,
disruptive animals instead of cash, and ended up pursuing it. In a
throwaway aside in "Minutes," I had introduced Mrs. Sylvia Wickersham, an eccentric alumna with a penchant for gifting the college useless, animal-centric facilities, and I decided that bringing
her back as the culprit of my unfortunate capital campaign would
be a perfect fit.

Unfortunately, this plan had one small drawback—that I've
never worked with college development at all so I have no idea
how a capital campaign is actually run. Would it be announced like
this? Would it be opened up to the general public? Do community
colleges even hold capital campaigns? No idea! Let's just say that
idiosyncratic college fundraising practices are the absolute least of
what's weird about Night Vale, and chalk any mistakes up to that,
okay?

Another issue was that in my original draft of the episode,
the problematic animals in question were deer. After all, when
thinking *Night Vale*, who doesn't also think *deer*? When editing
the episode, however, Jeffrey rightly pointed out that there had
been a lot of deer in the show and this might be overkill, so he
suggested replacing them with another animal while keeping the
story's same basic structure. I agreed and suggested rabbits, which
seem similarly benign and innocuous at first glance but, even on
their best behavior, would be really alarming when more than six
thousand are running around a college campus. Jeffrey did a bit
of editorial work on this episode in general—all to the good, in
my opinion. Overall, I think some of its strongest moments are his

additions—most notably the ultimate fate of the bunnies, which I found particularly morbidly hilarious. If I had to pick a favorite bit of this episode that I contributed myself, though, I would say it's the conservative dry cleaner eating his plastic hanging bags. Something about it just tickles me.

—Ashley Lierman

Home is where the heart is. We found it one day in the sink. It hums things late at night, but they are not songs.

# WELCOME TO NIGHT VALE

If there's one thing I've learned as a proud citizen of Night Vale, it's that horses are incredibly susceptible to suggestions from government satellites. But I've also learned that Night Vale is a community that cares about education. Night Vale is a community that fears education. Night Vale is a community that allows education to happen the way terrified campers allow bears to eat their food. Education is important, say whispers with no obvious source we all hear every night.

College graduation rates in our little town are above the national average. We bravely continue to promote literacy in spite of the terrible dangers associated with books. Our truancy rates have significantly declined due to the Sheriff's Secret Police's program of humane, low-fatality taserings.

So I know we can count on all of you to support the Night Vale Community College Capital Campaign, which was launched this past Monday to fund the establishment of a new science center for students. Science, I especially believe, is very important.

College President Sarah Sultan announced, "In our present, rapidly changing technological environment, it is more important than ever to encourage students to consider study and careers in all the sciences. Except astronomy," she added, pretending she was coughing. "Nobody cares about astronomy," she said obviously under a cough.

Reporters stood quiet and confused about how President Sultan could make such an announcement, as she is a smooth, fist-sized river rock, and has no visible mouth and likely no internal organs, muscles or passageways that can create a human-sounding voice.

"Telepathy," President Sultan said without a cough. "It's telepathy, you guys," she said in all of our minds.

Fundraising opportunities like these can make a huge difference to small local colleges, so please, Night Vale, consider making a contribution. As always, you can give to the capital campaign by burying your check, cash, or credit card donation in warm, wet earth and whispering, "I know what you did. I do not forget."

I've gotten a lot of calls and emails and telegrams and sympathetic glances the past couple of weeks from people who are wondering if Carlos the scientist has returned from the otherworld desert he is trapped in. And here I remind you that he became trapped there while saving our city from treacherous, dark forces. I remind you he is a hero. I remind you that my boyfriend is a hero.

Sadly, Carlos is still in the desert, the same desert our new mayor was once trapped in. Fortunately, as Dana discovered, cell phone batteries last forever there, and there's pretty good Wi-Fi despite there being just vast amounts of sand and, apparently, a mountain.

But if our mayor can make it out fine, I think a scientist can, too. Scientists are always fine.

Listeners, I've been seeing all the reviews for that new restaurant, Tourniquet. Sounds like executive chef LeSean Mason has created a real culinary hit. It's almost impossible to get a reservation there. I tried to get a table (for . . . for just one, of course) and the nearest available date was not for another two months. And even then, it wasn't a reservation for Tourniquet, but for Applebee's.

Actually, you know what? I think I've been looking at the Applebee's website. It's very easy to misspell *tourniquet*.

Anyway, Gia Samuels's review in the latest issue of the *Night Vale Daily Journal* mentioned Tourniquet sous chef, Earl Harlan. And that surprised me. He was a childhood friend of mine, and I had no idea he was a professional chef. It also surprised me because he was dragged away screaming by the herd of mute children at last year's Eternal Scout ceremonies. Very few ever survive Boy Scout courts of honor, especially not those dragged away by the mute children.

So, it's good to see Earl back home and safe, and likely returning to his volunteer duties as Scout Master. I hope one day I can get a reservation to his fine restaurant. Let me see. Nothing. Oh wait. Yes! Yes! I got one. I . . . oh no. No, I'm on the Applebee's website again. Never mind.

An update on the progress of the Night Vale Community College Capital Campaign. Thanks to the generous donations of Night Vale citizens, the campaign has already reached 30 percent of its target goal.

A particularly notable gift was made by local eccentric recluse and proud alumna Mrs. Sylvia Wickersham. The college fundraising staff was caught off-guard by this donation, as no one has heard from or seen Mrs. Wickersham in over a decade. Also the gift was a fine porcelain vase filled with two dozen English Angora rabbits.

College representatives expressed their gratitude for Mrs. Wickersham's generous and super cute contribution, of course, but would like to remind the greater community that it is preferred that donations be made via cash, check, credit card, spinal columns, or other common negotiable currencies.

"Money," college representatives added helpfully, through the narrow crack of a slightly lifted manhole cover on Main Street. "You know, the kind you use to procure goods and services, when you still have a physical form?" they added in spray-painted bubble graffiti on the side of an abandoned warehouse near the train tracks.

More on this, as there is more on this. Night Vale, our new leader is almost here!

This Friday is inauguration day for new mayor, Dana Cardinal, who used to be an intern at this very radio station. Dana may, in fact, be the most successful intern this station has ever had. So few of our interns have ever gone on to do anything important.

Inauguration of new mayors includes a swearing-in ceremony that takes place behind a thick velvet curtain. The curtain is raised a few inches, and all the press and public are shown a few shuffling feet and hear loud, high-pitched shouts. The mayoral swearing-in ceremony is the one point in Night Vale's political calendar where

citizens may voice their opinions and beliefs without risking reprisal
or imprisonment. They are, in fact, encouraged to shout even the
most forbidden beliefs and thoughts during the ceremony, openly,
and without fear.

The event will take place in an undisclosed location two hundred miles from downtown Night Vale, and will be exactly two
minutes long.

Former mayoral candidates the Faceless Old Woman Who Secretly Lives in Your Home and Hiram McDaniels, who is literally a
five-headed dragon, have both declared this a botched election and
are filing for a recount by shouting their complaints into the side of
a canyon wall they think might be Hidden Gorge. No one can tell
exactly where Hidden Gorge is, which is how it got its name: *Gorge*.

It doesn't matter. I'm ecstatic for our new mayor. It'll be weird
having a former intern as a leader, but I just think she'll do a wonderful job. Congratulations, old young friend.

I've just been informed that Mrs. Sylvia Wickersham has made
another large donation to the Night Vale Community College Capital Campaign: this one consisting of one thousand live and extremely fluffy rabbits.

The Capital Committee is beginning to have difficulty finding
space on campus to house her donations. What foliage existed on
campus has been immediately devoured, several of the botany program's greenhouses have been broken into and ransacked, and many
of the rabbits have reportedly entered the student center, refusing to
wait in line before ordering at the snack bar and taking way more
napkins than they need.

In an effort to make the most of this impressive endowment, the
Capital Committee is currently discussing the possibility of repur-
posing some of the rabbits toward Residence Life operations.

English Angora rabbits are well known for their thick, soft, silky
wool so the College's Student Housing Office feels this presents an

opportunity to make new blankets and rugs and hats and blindfolds for students, as well as winter cloaks for the coyote-faced advisers that lurk about the Student Programs Office.

Representatives have attempted to contact Mrs. Wickersham to discuss the possible redistribution of her generous gifts, but without success. More curiously, when attempting to visit Mrs. Wickersham's home, Committee Members were informed by her neighbors that they have never actually seen Mrs. Wickersham but they often have dreams of her.

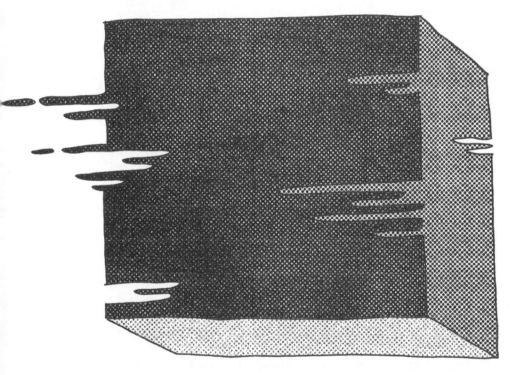

"I mean she never looks like herself," each of the neighbors stated. "Generally she appears as a hovering green box that pulses with light, and her voice sounds like an oboe playing a whole note, but, like, in this dream kind of way where I totally know it's her," they concluded.

Some Committee Members raised questions about how an incorporeal dream being could donate wild animals, and also if maybe she could stop doing that. Those members were quietly removed from the room by other Committee Members.

In any case, Night Vale, let us hold Mrs. Wickersham in our thoughts and of course dreams, and hope for her safe return. Or, possibly, for an end to her rabbit donations. Both would be nice, but let's not be greedy, Night Vale. We all take what we can get in this life, you know?

We take what we get.

Bad news from the Night Vale Community College, listeners. A donation of five thousand English angora rabbits in the name of Mrs. Sylvia Wickersham has just arrived at the College's fundraising headquarters. It's uncertain how they found their way there, as said headquarters had already been relocated to the underground Emergency Fundraising-Related Disaster Bunker, constructed in the 1970s by Dr. Erliss Badermyer, the Community College's all-time second-least-popular president.

As of last report, the rabbits have invaded and taken over control of fundraising headquarters: using dedicated telephone lines to make personal calls, uttering insensitive remarks about the body types of students and staff, and tilting the vending machines in clear violation of safety labeling.

Simone Rigadeau, the transient who lives in the Earth Sciences building, says these are typical behaviors for this breed of rabbit and that she is not surprised. She also repeated her claim that the world ended more than thirty years ago before grunting some French cuss words and disappearing into a small round hole in the wall.

The 6,800 rabbits—more rabbits now than students—are running amok throughout campus. They have disrupted lectures and shown flagrant disrespect for faculty. They have joined academic and social organizations and engaged in irresponsible drinking. There are even reports that these vulgar, cuddly rodents broke into the College President's office, and licked viciously on President Sultan for several minutes before her administrative assistant could free her.

Listeners, this is an urgent situation. These rabbits—well, all rabbits, really—are a menace, and they now have access to all the advantages of higher education. I advise you to lock your bookshelves, eat your diplomas, and place any vulnerable stones or rocks in your home on high, inaccessible shelves. If you see a rabbit, do not attempt to engage it in debate on post-structuralism, semiotics, gender politics, or sporting events.

Even as I speak to you, college officials and the Sheriff's Secret Police are desperately searching for Mrs. Wickersham, hoping to mitigate some of the damage that is being done. I hope that they find her, Night Vale. I hope that the rabbits do not find us. I hope that we all find something, or someone, that can keep the light on a little longer against the endless, pressing dark.

And in the meantime, I take you now to the weather.

**WEATHER: "Ghost Story" by Charming Disaster**

We have received information that agents of the Sheriff's Secret Police broke down the door to Mrs. Sylvia Wickersham's neo-Victorian home on the east side of town. Their search of the house found it completely empty and uninhabited, with the exception of a small, green tree lizard sunning itself in the front parlor.

The Sheriff's Secret Police grabbed the lizard and were on the verge of eating it, as none of them had had lunch that day—I mean some raisins and a few roasted almonds, but that's not really a full lunch—and lizards are a complete protein. But the Capital Campaign Committee stopped them.

"This is Mrs. Wickersham," said a Committee Member.

"This is Mrs. Wickersham?" said the Secret Policeperson.

"Yes," the Committee Member said, explaining further that Mrs. Wickersham was a high-level donor to the college. At certain levels, donors receive benefits like mugs or tote bags or names carved into bloodstones. At higher levels, donors receive very special benefits like being able to invade the dreams of their neighbors, or having all of their belongings taken from their home, or being transformed permanently into a tree lizard.

"Most of our benefactors choose a Gila or skink or chuckwalla," the Committee Member said, quoting from the College's own fundraising brochure, as the lizard form of Mrs. Wickersham dangled and squirmed above the Sheriff's Secret Policeperson's gaping purple maw.

"Mrs. Wickersham takes a lot of pride in her alma mater," the Committee Member explained, "and she has donated so much to the college. None of it has ever been money, but she is a valued donor to the community," continued the Committee Member as a brass band somewhere else in the world and completely unrelated to this story played eighth notes quickly, but softly.

"Why did you make a big fuss about it and call us here?" said the Secret Policeperson.

"Oh that," said the Committee Member, shrugging. "It was good publicity for our Capital Campaign."

The Sheriff's Secret Police coaxed the tree lizard into a comfortable vivarium filled with fresh reptile bark, wrote *EVIDENCE* on the side of it in Sharpie, and removed it to an undisclosed location near the microwave in the Secret Police break room.

In her absence, Mrs. Wickersham's next of kin was found to legally be her dry cleaner, Ben Burnham, who was amenable to the idea of retracting Mrs. Wickersham's donation. More specifically, what he said was, "Yeah, sure, whatever. What do I care? All the colleges're just factories for little socialist robots these days anyway. Beep boop, free healthcare for everybody, beep boop, I'm a robot." He then began to, without breaking eye contact, eat the plastic hanging bags on his desk, starting from the top and working his way down.

The rabbits have been removed and redonated to the Night Vale Petting Zoo. This worked out well, since until today the Night

Vale Petting Zoo has only ever housed emaciated wolves. But now, thanks to Mr. Burnham's donation (on behalf of Mrs. Wickersham) of nearly eight thousand cuddly rabbits, those wolves will not be hungry again for months.

Despite all interruptions, the Night Vale Community College Capital Campaign has actually surpassed its undisclosed goal, and construction of the science center is slated to begin this coming summer. The Capital Committee would like to extend its thanks to everyone who donated. A community that cares for education, after all, is a community that cares for its future—with all the fear and respect and awe that the future is due. Knowledge may be terrible, but we can only prefer it to ignorance. Light may be terrible, but we can only prefer it to the dark.

Stay tuned next for a reality that cannot possibly match expectation.

And as always, good night, Night Vale. Good night.

**PROVERB:** Soccer is also commonly known as football, Canadian baseball, American football, violent jogging, and World War II.

# EPISODE 51:
# "RUMBLING"

## AUGUST 1, 2014

### GUEST VOICE: DYLAN MARRON (CARLOS)

My introduction to the wonderful world of Night Vale and fictional courtship with my favorite small-town radio host ran parallel with something else: falling in love off-mic with my favorite human, a human named Todd.

Before I was invited to join the cast as Carlos, when Night Vale was just a cool town my friends had built in the minds of many, Todd and I happily listened along as fans. We texted each other after hearing the pilot episode and remarked how cool it was that folks across the world could witness an interracial queer couple falling in love set against the backdrop of a sleepy desert town as we, ourselves, an interracial queer couple, happily fell down that same lovely and infinite hole.

Our stories didn't always align on the calendar, but the connective lines could still be drawn. Carlos and Cecil moved in with each other first, but then Todd and I beat our fictional partners to the altar. It was never a competition, but a synchronized double date through time and space that transcended the planes of fiction and life.

In "Rumbling," we find Carlos still trapped in the desert otherworld while Cecil is missing him back home in Night Vale, or as we might say colloquially in *our* pedestrian world: long distance. In this way, the podcast served as a precursor two years before Todd and I became a long-distance couple ourselves, like so many modern partners who refuse to trade relationship for career often do.

Joseph and Jeffrey are especially skilled at writing about love. Their representation of love is not always direct, but rather refracted through the weird-but-deeply-accurate funhouse mirror that is *Welcome to Night Vale*. In this episode they perfectly capture the obstacle course that is long distance in their own Night Valean way. It is at the same time mundane and profound, while communication across distance is alternately casual and urgent. All of that is present here.

To get out of this strange otherworld Carlos must reach a door while Todd is tasked with getting a diploma. The scientist bravely weathers shaky ground while the student finds balance on compounding deadlines. The fictional boyfriend struggles with poor cell phone reception and the real husband struggles with . . . poor cell phone reception (don't worry, we use Wi-Fi when available).

Both Carlos and Todd are swamped with work they're fascinated by, while still emotionally tethered to their partners back home. They are in two places at once. "There is a lot of work for me to do here," Carlos tells Cecil through the receiver, "and, the only person who I truly care about isn't in this desert anyway." Substitute *desert* with any other location and you've captured modern romance.

Now, to be fair, Carlos can't reach Cecil without an elusive portal that connects their two distinct worlds. Todd and I, on the other hand, have Amtrak. But missing someone is missing someone, whether they're conducting Important Science in a parallel dimension or studying law on a campus two states away.

Come home soon, Carlos. Cecil misses you.

Come home soon, Todd. I miss you, too.

—Dylan Marron

Look! Up in the sky. It's a bird. It's a plane.
It's a cloud. It's a moon. Also, some stars.
There are so many things in the sky.

## WELCOME TO NIGHT VALE

New Night Vale mayor (and former intern at this very station) Dana Cardinal announced today that she wants to open the Dog Park for public use.

Said Dana—or I guess I should start saying Mayor Cardinal—"Dog Parks should be used for dogs and owners to exercise and play. A Dog Park should be a fun gathering place for citizens to meet and socialize, not a secretive patch of municipal darkness full of conspiracies warning signs."

Only moments into her announcement, the City Council entered the press room, walking in synchronous steps, hips together, teeth apart, blocking the view of reporters and photographers, and unplugging the mayor's microphone. The Council shuffled away to the Council Chambers, taking the mayor with them.

Twenty minutes later, Mayor Cardinal re-emerged, wearing several large, ivory rings and a long cerulean cape. She announced that dogs are not allowed in the Dog Park. People are not allowed in the Dog Park. You may see hooded figures in the Dog Park. But not for long, as there are now plans to reinforce the fence around the Dog Park.

Oh, listeners, guess who we've got on the phone line now. I'll give you a hint, he saved Night Vale a few weeks ago by shutting out a great terror trying to invade us from another world.

**CARLOS:** It wasn't just me.

**CECIL:** He's also my boyfriend. And a scientist. And I miss him.

**CARLOS:** I miss you, too.

**CECIL:** That's right. My boyfriend is a hero. Please welcome to our show Carlos, the scientist.

**CARLOS:** You're too much.

**CECIL:** Listeners, Carlos had to stay behind in whatever strange desert otherworld, which was very brave of him even though he's now very far away from people that love him. Any luck getting back through to Night Vale?

**CARLOS:** Not yet. Oh! But I've been exploring this strange rumbling noise here. It's the same rumbling noise we heard when that terrible light was coming into Night Vale.

**CECIL:** Are you safe? Is everything okay?

**CARLOS:** Actually there it is again. When we shut the doors the rumbling and the unbearably bright light went away. This empty desert with the mountain and the lighthouse and the large wandering army all seemed so normal, you know? But last night the rumbling returned.

There it is again. I need to grab my instruments.

**CECIL:** I can't hear it.

**CARLOS:** I'll call you back.

**CECIL:** No. Carlos! I—

[*Carlos clearly has hung up.*]

Every time, I never know when you'll call back.

Well, speaking of the town being safe, our neighboring town, Desert Bluffs, ran a full-page ad in the Sunday extra-large imagination edition of the *Night Vale Daily Journal* this week that said, I imagined, "Thank you for having us, Night Vale. Best of luck in your future."

I can't tell if that's an exclamation point or a question mark there. What a weird font. It's like someone put paint or some other thick liquid on the tip of a sharp finger and then handwrote this ad. It's just like that.

Then at the bottom it has a photo of your face, dear listener, and the same finger-painted lettering that reads "BLESSINGS FROM A SMILING GOD."

Wow, where did they get that photo of you? Although, honestly, it's not a bad photo. I mean, you look just adorable when you're sleeping.

I know this farewell ad may seem like a kind gesture, but good riddance to those monsters. No one is happier than me to see us run Desert Bluffs out of town.

Meanwhile there has been a lot construction noise (bike horns, seesaws, parrot shrieking, etc.) from the old StrexCorp headquarters at the lip of Radon Canyon. Several tall beings with wings who all introduced themselves as Erika were seen hanging around outside, while a Sheriff's Secret Police representative ran frantically between onlookers putting her hand over each person's eyes and shouting, "You're not seeing anything real!"

Well, I for one am excited to learn what these of course completely nonexistent angels plan to do with the huge, malevolent corporation they purchased.

Oh, also I stopped by the office of station management. Seems our community radio station was purchased back from StrexCorp by our original owners, whom I have never met or seen and who until recently had run this radio station for centuries.

It's nice to have all these familiar faces back, or not faces. More like muffled screams and chattering echoes and pulsing orange lights surrounding dark stone doors that are never in the same place you remembered them being. Just a quick stroll past the new old boss's office brought me back to the good old days as I crumbled to the floor, struck numb and blind with flashes of hideous daydreams, a history's worth of deaths that were not my own.

How great to be back to the way we were. The good old days. The fearful, terrible, deadly good old days.

Oh, my phone's buzzing.

**CECIL:** Hello, Carlos? Are you back on the line?

**CARLOS:** Yes. So there's a lighthouse here in the desert. It's on top of a tall mountain. And there's a blinking red light on top of this lighthouse. And this blinking red light always blinks. That's what it does. But now that the rumbling has returned. . . . Can you hear the rumbling from your end, Cecil?

**CECIL:** No.

**CARLOS:** It's very loud. But when the rumbling happens the blinking red light stops blinking. It just stays on.

**CECIL:** What do you think that means?

**CARLOS:** I don't know. I've talked with some of the army of men and women and others who roam about this desert and they look frightened. They have never seen the blinking light stop blinking. It is what a blinking light is supposed to do, and fear is what happens when a thing that has always behaved one way does not behave that way at all. They run and hide now when they hear the rumbling and see the static red light up on the mountain. I, too, am starting to feel scared.

**CECIL:** Carlos, remember how you got into that desert in the first place? You went through a door in a house that did not seem to exist. Have you found any of those doors yet?

**CARLOS:** Not yet, no.

**CECIL:** Carlos, look for those doors. There must be at least one left somewhere.

**CARLOS:** I'll start looking very soon. But listen, Cecil, I'd really like to figure out this rumbling–slash–red-light thing. I'm a scientist. I need to discover slash understand things. It's what I do.

**CECIL:** But couldn't you look for the door while you figure it out?

**CARLOS:** I'll look for the door some tomorrow. For sure I will.

**CECIL:** Well, it's not that I—

**CARLOS:** The rumbling's gone. Do you hear that? I've got to run. I need to find Doug.

**CECIL:** Who's Doug? Carlos, who's Doug? Carlos?

Okay. Well, I guess let's just have a look at today's horoscopes.

LEO: Need a penny, take a penny. Have a penny, take another penny. Pennies are worthless, but go ahead and take them all. Build a great fortune only to have its great copper weight crush your lifeless pauper body.

VIRGO: Don't shoot the messenger, Virgo. It's noisy and will alert others of your crime. Lure the messenger inside. Make sure no one saw him come in. Choose something quieter than a gun— perhaps suffocation or an accidental fall. Really plan these things out. Stop being so trigger-happy, Virgo.

LIBRA: Do you believe in ghosts? You don't? Well won't YOU be surprised when you wake up in the middle of the night tonight? Scream loud enough so the neighbors can hear you.

SCORPIO: You are respected by your peers. You are a great thinker and leader. You—What is this? This is definitely not the right reading for a Scorpio. Must be a typo. I bet the stars meant to say: "You should hear what they're saying about you. Very funny things, Scorpio. They're saying very funny things at your expense, you jerk." Yep, that's definitely what the stars meant to say.

SAGITTARIUS: The best revenge is living well. The second best is tasteless, slow-acting poison. Maybe it's more of a tie. Either way, you got wronged and you need to set things right, Sagittarius.

CAPRICORN: 'Tis better to have loved and lost than to never have loved at all, which is better than to have never loved at all but also somehow lost a love, thus creating a paradox. Paradoxes are bad, Capricorn. Be careful, or logic will destroy you.

AQUARIUS: Your boyfriend is trapped in an alternate desert dimension. It is difficult to say when he will return. Perhaps take up drinking while crying in a quiet room. Wow. That's a very specific and painful horoscope. Thanks for nothing, stars.

PISCES: A train leaves a station traveling west at forty miles per hour. Another train leaves a station traveling east at sixty miles per hour. These two trains left on different days in different years in different countries. How long until the passengers acknowledge their own impermanence?

ARIES: I think they saw you, Aries. Hold still. They cannot see you if you do not move. Ssshhh. Don't move. Don't move. Donnnn— —Nope they saw you. So long, Aries.

TAURUS: Someone misses you a lot, Taurus. And even though you have nothing but endless time, trapped out in a nightmarish desert hellscape, you have a hard time making a phone call longer than ten minutes. Maybe call a bit more than you do, Taurus. Yep. That's just some astrological advice, from the stars.

GEMINI: You know those eight spiders a year you eat in your sleep? Well, they add up. And they are all organizing a pretty dramatic escape. Very soon, Gemini. Very soon.

CANCER: The ocean is vast, you convince yourself, walking alone between the trees. The sky is endless, you mutter repeatedly trying to finally lull yourself to sleep. Matter can neither be created nor destroyed, you contemplate despite not understanding the first part of the statement. What's on the Food Network tonight, you say aloud to a stranger you have known for years.

This has been today's horoscopes.

Ah, he's calling in again. Carlos?

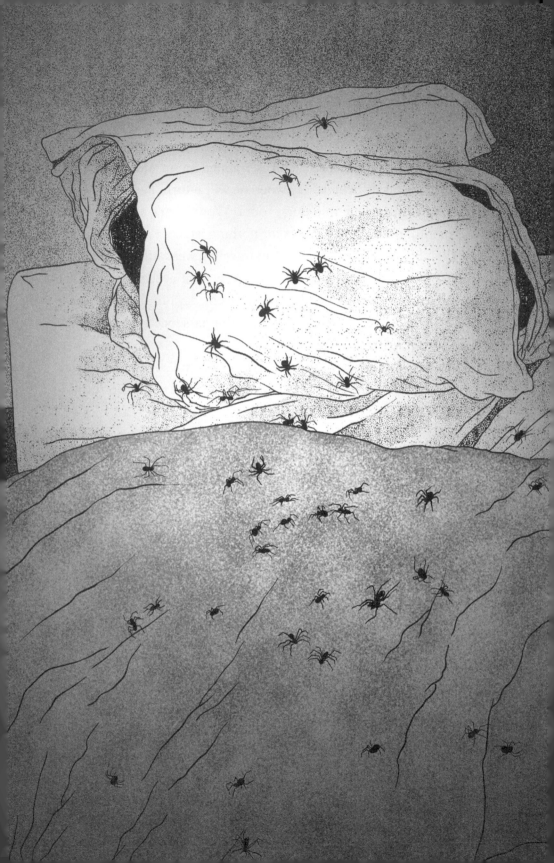

**CARLOS:** Cecil, the rumbling has started again. The mountain is moving. Up and down, like breathing. There are creaks and groans in the earth, in the stones, that together sound like a growl. An undulating snarl of something much bigger than anything that should ever be able to snarl.

Cecil, this is a strange place, and considering where I've lived for the past couple years, that says a lot. I know Dana used to be trapped here and she has told you about it. I mean I used to wonder how she could call and text you from this place for an entire year with no cell towers or power outlets. But I've been here for weeks and I have three bars (only 4G but still) and 97 percent battery, which was the charge I had when I came through the door in the house that doesn't exist.

In a temporary peace between the rumblings, I walked with some of the desert army toward a small patch of discolored sand. We found a swath of damp dirt, just a handful of red mud, and in that mud were several tiny white bones—looked like long legs and short wings of a creature I can't even imagine. I look forward to figuring out exactly what this is. I'll be able to imagine it then.

**CECIL:** Carlos, I don't think it's safe there. I want you to—

**CARLOS:** Cecil, nothing and nowhere is safe. But there are things greater than us. Greater than all of this. (You can't see but I just made a big, sweeping hand gesture to indicate everything in the universe.) And there are people who must learn about it all . . . how it all works and why. This is what we call science.

**CECIL:** I know what science is.

**CARLOS:** And I am a scientist.

**CECIL:** I understand. It's just that I miss you and . . . oh my, the building is shaking.

**CARLOS:** You can feel it? You can feel the rumbling? Oh, this is exciting. Wait, this is new. The ground is moving very quickly. There is a large lump, churning the sand up and down. I'm leaning out over this ledge to get a better view of this fantastic event, and ow———

**CECIL:** Carlos? What happened?

**CARLOS:** I got hit. What is that? Is that a rock? Ow!

**CECIL:** Carlos!

**CARLOS:** Cecil. The rocks are coming down. They're coming down the side of this hill. I need to take cover. I need

[*thump/rattle/click*]

**CECIL:** Carlos? Carlos?

Listeners, while the earth still shakes, take shelter. This does not feel like one of our government-scheduled earthquakes, but if I were you I would still do as the Earthquake Safety Mascot, Duncan the Brown Recluse Spider, always says: "I'm small and I hide a lot, so it's easy to be safe!"

And with that, I take you now to the weather. . . .

**WEATHER:** "Echo in the Hills" by Carrie Elkin and Danny Schmidt

**CECIL:** Carlos, are you there? Carlos?

**CARLOS:** I'm here.

**CECIL:** Are you okay?

**CARLOS:** I'm fine. A scientist is always fine. Doug was really helpful.

**CECIL:** Who is Doug?

**CARLOS:** He's one of the members of this great masked army. He must be a captain of some sort, given his size and the respect he appears to garner.

As the rocks and boulders came down, Doug picked up a large flat stone and held it above us. The rocks bounced off his makeshift shield. Unfortunately, I dropped my phone. I smashed the phone something good. I thought I lost you for a while there, Cecil. I was despairing that my one way to reach you would be lost for who knows how long. But then, you know what? Something really amazing happened. Something tremendous. The phone healed itself.

**CECIL:** That's great.

**CARLOS:** It is great. But phones don't just heal themselves. This is another scientific mystery I can't wait to get to the bottom of.

**CECIL:** Where's Doug now?

**CARLOS:** Oh, I don't know. He's probably back at the encampment. They're a nomadic army. Sometimes they are here, sometimes not. I don't really have time to make new friends. They're nice people, but there is a lot of work for me to do here. And the only person I truly care about isn't in this desert, anyway.

I do not know what the rumbling is. I do not know why some doors work and others do not. I do not know why my phone never loses battery power and can heal itself. I do not know how long it will take me to pursue this knowledge, but I do know two things.

**CECIL:** What's that?

**CARLOS:** I love you.

**CECIL:** I love you, too. What's the other thing?

**CARLOS:** You just said it.

Cecil, I have to go. Be patient with me. We have our phones, we have our voices, and you have the best voice of them all.

**CECIL:** Thanks for being on the air with me. We did almost the entire show together.

**CARLOS:** We can still do things together, even in absence. I'll be back again soon.

**CECIL:** Find that door, Carlos.

**CARLOS:** I will, but first I need to see if the red light is blinking again or not.

**CECIL:** Bye, Carlos.

Listeners, I wish I could tell you where the rumbling came from, and that we are safe from it. The Sheriff's Secret Seismology Team announced that today's rumbling, which caused quite a bit of structural damage and knocked out power for one-third of the town, did not register at all on the Richter scale, which is a thing seismologists use to assign two-dimensional numbers to complex, multi-dimensional physical events.

But, the upshot is we are all alive for however many two-dimensional numbers we have left.

Stay tuned next for the sound of future becoming the present becoming the past in no time at all.

And as always, good night, Night Vale. Good night.

**PROVERB:** Everything that happens happens for a reason. Except ostriches. What the hell, man?

# EPISODE 52:
# "THE RETIREMENT OF PAMELA WINCHELL"

## AUGUST 15, 2014

It's difficult to write political satire in a political climate as absurd as the current. When we created the character of Pamela, it was a great deal of fun to have a politician who could not stick to a topic, whose thought processes were impossible to follow, and who fundamentally seemed to exist in a different universe than the rest of us. This concept became less fun later on.

We still have deep affection for the character of Pamela, as evidenced by us making her a major character in our recent novel, *It Devours!* She is, unlike some politicians, entirely well-meaning, even if the way she goes about her life can sometimes become threatening, or even terrifying. One game we have when writing her scenes is finding more and more strange ways for her to end her press conferences, including riding off on a steed and disappearing in a cloud of smoke.

This episode also represents the beginning of Intern Dana's transformation into Mayor Dana. It is a difficult transformation. She is young, and has no experience in politics, and also once killed a double of herself, or maybe she is the double, and she killed the original of herself. She isn't sure. Either way, she is carrying all the existential and identity crises of the young, plus a few more added by the strange nature of Night Vale, into a pivotal role of power, and it is not an easy process. It is a process we are continuing to explore, even now, in the podcast. Dana is one of the characters who absolutely makes up the beating heart of Night Vale, someone who does not always do well, but always means well, and who believes strongly in this town she is forced to try to run.

On a separate note, we often get asked for visual details about the characters, most especially Cecil. And we rarely give them. But that doesn't mean we never give them. We have mentioned in the past specific outfits that Cecil wears, and in this episode we make canon that he always has in his hand his Lil' Reporter's Big Book of Big-Boy Note Taking. What I find especially interesting, given how seemingly voracious the fan appetite for canon visual details has been, is that the few specific details we've given are generally ignored. I rarely see a Cecil cosplay that includes his furry pants or the notebook he has carried since he was five years old. Not to say I never see those. Sometimes I do and I get really excited.

I think that this is one of those times where what people think they want and what they actually want are very different. They think they want us to describe what Cecil looks like. But what they actually want is for us to confirm what they already think Cecil looks like (generally people prefer their Cecils to be much more suave and a snappier dresser than our Cecil). And so I'm happy to do that: whatever you think Cecil looks like is 100 percent correct. Please feel free to ignore the few details we've given, because, genuinely, the details you've come up with are going to be far more enjoyable for you.

—Joseph Fink

Pound for pound, Pamela Winchell probably has some of the most quotable Night Vale text just because she is so insane. She's insane by Night Vale standards (and that's even before you incorporate the brilliant whirlwind who is Desiree Burch playing her in the live shows). Pamela's tether to reality is just so thin!

In the early days of Night Vale, playing off of headlines and tropes, trying to figure out what bits were bits, having this insane mayor made sense. So you get her claiming that she's a bunch of birds inside a sack that looks like a person or whatnot and then speaking nothing of it ever again.

There's also kind of a dark psychosexual undercurrent to a lot of what Pamela says as well, but it's all so random that you can't quite pick it out. She has a purpose to serve—she likes to give press conferences, standing in front of a bunch of people and controlling the scene, as so many government mouthpieces seem to enjoy. But I think you'd be hard-pressed to find examples of Pamela Winchell at home, outside the spotlight, to determine whether she's actually insane or whether she's putting on a show.

Desiree Burch, who plays her on tour, performs standup comedy and award-winning solo shows, where she speaks candidly about race, body image, feminism, and sexuality. I feel safe on stage with Desiree because, even though she could literally pick me up and snap me like a twig, I know there is method to her madness.

One of the great fears of a life of great fears, perhaps the last great fear, is the fear of no longer being useful. Even more than death, even more than pain, as Americans we fear this loss of category, of self, of self-definition. What's a person to do once they have been made redundant? Then come the two most terrifying words a person can hear: What next?

When I was at a theater talkback with the cast in Washington, D.C., a member of the audience asked one of the actors, "What's your favorite role?" Without blinking, one of my castmates said, "The next one." Mild nods of semi-comprehension from the audience. But the octogenarian Shakespeare Patron pressed further: "Oh, so you're excited about the next show that you are working on after this one?" To which the veteran actor replied, "No. Just the next one. Whatever that may be, because it means there's a next one."

And if you have ever wondered what being a freelance artist is truly like—always remember that the sweetest gig is the next one.

—Cecil Baldwin

**Now is your chance. Well, that was it. It's over. Did you do it? Have you achieved what you wanted? No? Ah well.**

## WELCOME TO NIGHT VALE

Former Mayor Pamela Winchell called an emergency press conference today to announce that she is enjoying her retirement immensely, and she could not be happier to no longer be mayor.

"More happiness is not possible," she wailed. "Happiness is a fool's day dream."

She was then reminded by reporters that she is no longer mayor and so shouldn't be calling emergency press conferences, especially when there are none of the usual emergencies happening, like seeing an interesting butterfly, eating a very good sandwich, or being disappointed that it is two o'clock already.

I sought a statement from current mayor Dana Cardinal, who is, of course, a former intern and dear friend of mine. I found her at the end of a dark hallway draped with rotting black cloth and thick with cobwebs, where she was sitting on the mayoral throne and contemplating her hands.

"I thought it would be different than this," she said, "but it's exactly what it is."

I asked her specifically her thoughts on former mayor Pamela Winchell continuing to call emergency press conferences.

"Oh," Mayor Dana said, and then again, "Oh," and then, "She can do that if she wants. I'm too busy these days to do press conferences anyway. Tell you what," and then she did tell me what, which is that she is naming Pamela Winchell the Official Night Vale Director of Emergency Press Conferences.

When informed of this news, Pamela made swiping, dismissive gestures with her hands, saying, "I don't need her permission. I'll call them if I want. Anyway, I'm retired." She was crying. She smiled and she cried. "I'm retired," she continued, "but that's very, very nice of her. What a wonderful woman. I'm going to call an emergency press conference to let people know what a wonderful woman the new mayor is," she concluded.

And now a word from our sponsors.

Today's sponsor is the concept of itching.

Listeners, are you looking for an action that will pass the time but also is mildly irritating? Searching for a way to have your body express reaction to material it is allergic to? Want to express confusion in the most stereotypical manner possible?

I am just thrilled to be here on behalf of itching. Itching has been with humans as long as there have been humans. Longer than that even. Why, beings have been having to scratch themselves almost as long as they've been being.

It can be fun! It mostly won't be. But if it's your thing or if it's in a spot that's easy to reach, then it can sort of be fun. I'm not saying it will definitely be fun. It probably won't be.

The concept of itching. For a free sample, just think about it. Oh, there you go. See, you're experiencing it right now.

This has been a word from our sponsors.

Pamela Winchell called an emergency press conference to announce that while she thanks the current mayor for her generous offer, after some thought and discussion with a couple of helpful advisors, she simply is too busy being retired to accept. "I'm just too busy fishing," she said, wildly waving a fishing rod around, slapping it on her podium and narrowly avoiding catching several reporters with the absurdly oversized hook as they ducked and scrambled out of reach. "See?" she continued. "I'm fishing right now. This is what fishing looks like, I'm pretty sure," she concluded, cracking the thick, leather fishing line like in that popular and heartwarming series of adventure movies about a wisecracking archaeologist who comically destroys countless important artifacts under the hilarious misapprehension that they belong in his museum rather than in the religious sites of the cultures that made them.

As the reporters ran from her dangerous, flailing fishing line she shouted, "This concludes my emergency press conference about my complete retirement from emergency press conferences. Please assemble again in three hours for an emergency press conference that will update you on my retirement status."

She then took hold of a rope dangling from the hastily painted blue backdrop that we all assume is the sky and was lifted up through a door, shaking the flimsy particleboard known as the sky as she went.

In other news, Strexcorp Synernists Inc., a company which until recently had something of an outsized effect on our town, is now under the control of beings who call themselves angels and who do not legally exist. The existence of the company itself is therefore something of a moral/ethical question, the kind that philosophers consider in their secret black-market philosophy meetings.

Despite all the difficulties in discussing its very concept, Strex and its new owners have gone about making what they say are constructive repairs to a town damaged by its recent battle with a force that seemed (but was not) greater than our own.

For instance, they gave Teddy Williams of the Desert Flower Bowling Alley and Arcade Fun Complex the funds to hire contractors to renovate his building and cover over lane five with asphalt, thus trapping beneath it the tiny civilization that is still declaring war on us.

A so-called angel said in a statement: "I have donated a coffee table made of human bones to charity and will use the money I save on taxes to invest in the Desert Flower Bowling Alley and Arcade Fun Complex because angels (if we were real) would certainly love to bowl. Or, whatever," the creature added.

Meanwhile, I've been getting regular calls and Snapchats from Carlos—you know, my hero scientist boyfriend—from the desert otherworld he is very temporarily trapped in. He'll be back super soon. He says that he has found a cactus, only it's not a cactus, only it is. He says it's difficult to explain and that he really wants to explain it. This is what he is for, he said. To explain a world that defies explanation. He sent me a photo of the cactus but it only appeared on my phone as an error box that said EVEN IF YOU COULD, YOU WOULD WISH YOU HADN'T.

Well, it sounds like he's having fun out there. That's good.

Pamela Winchell called another emergency press conference to show just how well she's doing without the need to call emergency press conferences.

"Retirement is great," she said. "I've taken up bird watching." She then showed off this new hobby, in the process demonstrating a deep misunderstanding of both the concept of *birds* and the concept of *watching*. The resulting fire wiped out the podium and, indeed, the entire press conference gazebo, sending both Pamela and the attending reporters fleeing in every direction.

"See how wonderful being retired is?" she shouted behind her as she sprinted away, smoke-fueled tears streaming from her sunken eyes. "I love being retired. It's the best," she concluded, as the fire spread to several nearby structures despite the earnest lectures and head shaking from Night Vale's brigade of brave fire-disapprovers.

Oh, listeners, I finally got a chance to eat at Tourniquet, Night

Vale's hottest new culinary nightspot. I mean, I didn't get to eat their food, or sit at any of their tables, reservations are still just too hard to get. But I did make a PB&J at home and ate it quickly in their front waiting area as the maître d' glared at me implacably, as he does to everyone, due to the fact that he is a large idol carved from volcanic rock.

But despite the less-than-ideal visit to the restaurant, it did give me a chance to say hello again to Earl Harlan. Now, it was a big surprise for me, my childhood best-friend Earl Harlan working at this restaurant after being dragged away by mute interdimensional children, not to be heard from again for a year and a half. It was a big surprise for me obviously because I had no idea he had any interest in cooking, let alone the skills to be a sous chef.

Well I invited him to come on the show some time and give all of us a few cooking tips. I don't know if he'll take me up on it, but we might be lucky enough to get a peek into the mystical, nearly forgotten art that is cooking. Won't that be dangerous and probably illegal!

Despite pleas from local, regional, national, international, and interstellar authorities, Pamela Winchell has continued to give emergency press conferences to publicize her deep enjoyment of retirement and to decline the new mayor's standing job offer to give emergency press conferences.

Her press conference about tropical fish care resulted in a deadly flash flood that swept through Old Town Night Vale, washing away everyone's piles of cool stones they had found.

Her demonstration of coin collecting crashed several world economies, in the process breaking a ten-year peace treaty that had ended the previous Blood Space War.

And her demonstration of mass poisoning, unfortunately, went without a hitch.

Even as her press conferences have become much more fatal than usual, she has increased their frequency considerably, sometimes having two conferences so close together that they actually occur simultaneously, Pamela speaking in a rapid back and forth to two different groups of reporters as she shows two different cataclysmic methods of retirement she has recently been taught by her mysterious team of advisers.

More on this story as Pamela continues to create it.

And now, some "life hacks" that will allow you to parse and reprogram the code of life, thus changing the very fabric of your being in a clumsy and likely horrifying fashion. Also a handy way of organizing your entire existence through a complex system of binder clips and toilet paper rolls. Let's get started.

Life hack one is . . . um . . . listeners. Intern Maureen is waving to me frantically from the control room. More frantically than she does at all times about the general terrifying nature of life. She is mouthing something. Flannel fissure? Animals whiz beer? Oh! Oh . . . no. She's mouthing "Pamela is here." Listeners, it seems that Pamela Winchell, her press conference gazebo burned down, has chosen the steps of the community radio station as the site of her next retirement demonstration. Given the effect of her previous demonstrations, this could spell doom for our little station and our little lives. I must . . . I must try to talk to her. I will, listeners, I will make her listen.

And while I make her listen, I will also make you listen, to the weather. [*running from microphone*] Pamela! Stop!

**WEATHER: "Here I Land" by Nicholas Stevenson**

Well we have returned, as we always do, all of us, unless we don't, as we sometimes don't, all of us.

Many people who have had Night Vale community radio mean something in their lives rushed to the front steps of the building to save this vital part of our little town. The crowd held most of the population of our beloved burg. In this modern age of media, there is of course no medium so close to the common heart as community radio. Leading the crowd was Mayor Dana, who pressed Ms. Winchell further to accept her offer of the official position.

But Pamela was unswayed. She, in fact, was standing rigidly, her eyes rolled to the whites, her fingers splayed, booming RETIRE-MENT, RETIREMENT in a voice not her own. A great wind gusted up from around her body, whirling through the crowd and sweeping Intern Maureen away into the distance. To the family and friends of Intern Maureen. Etcetera. Anyway . . .

"Pamela," we cried, unified under threat just as we are often at odds through peace. "Pamela. Do not retire. We need you," we cried. "Specifically, we need you to stop demonstrating your retirement. Definitely stop doing that right away," we said in unison and in fear.

But Pamela would not hear us. We had given up all hope and were casting about for other things to give up: dreams, aspirations, and then, digging further, anticipated muscle pains, pre-grief for loss that hadn't happened yet, post-grief for losses long ago, and further still, until we were ready to give up that shifting, shivery spark that is our human heart itself. But then. But then . . .

Well, I don't remember what happened next. There seems to be just a gap in my memory, much longer and deeper than the usual gaps that we all develop in our memories to protect us from forbidden information we might have heard or hooded figures we might have accidentally brushed against in the dark of our rooms just before we turn on the lights. But fortunately, being a reporter, I had my Lil' Reporter's Big Book of Big-Boy Note Taking, just like I've had since I was five years old and the prophecies were first revealed that I was destined to be the voice of our little community.

I always make notes in this book, even if I'm not aware of it. See, just now I wrote down "said 'always makes notes in this book, even if I'm not aware of it.'" Wow. Very accurate and I'm not even holding a pen. Anyway. I can just consult my notes and see how this situation was solved.

Okay. It appears here that a man in a tan jacket, holding a deer-skin suitcase, approached Pamela's podium. "Fear not," he said, perhaps a tad melodramatically. "I can relate to what she's going through," he continued. "I think I can talk her through this."

"You look very familiar," we all shouted back, still in unison. "But I don't believe we've ever met you before. Who are you?"

But the man in the tan jacket was already skittering, spider-like, up to Pamela and whispering into her ear. No one could hear what he said, according to my notes, but Pamela seemed to immediately respond to his voice, stopping the mass destruction of her retirement activities and listening intently, occasionally nodding and saying, "Uh huh. Uh huh."

And then, miracle of miracles, she stepped away from the podium.

"Mayor Cardinal," she said. "I would be happy to accept the role of Director of Emergency Press Conferences. Thank you, and I am no longer retired."

She then asked everyone to meet her tomorrow at 7:00 A.M. sharp in the newly rebuilt Press Conference Gazebo for her first official emergency press conference in that role.

As for that mysterious man, he of the tan jacket and deerskin suitcase, he turned to the audience and started a lecture about the place he is from, frequently naming it and even pointing to it on a map, but any time the name of the place should appear in my notes, the writing has been violently scratched out to the point of tearing through the paper. And then just blank pages until a few minutes ago when my notes resume.

So! That's what happened. Or at least, according to my notes. It's entirely possible that during that memory gap I decided to use my notebook to try out a first foray into realistic fiction, and that something else entirely happened. Who knows which fictional version of the fictional past is true?

And so, listeners, now that we are safe, let us take a moment of deep sympathy for Pamela Winchell.

One of the great fears, among a life of great fears, perhaps the last great fear, is the fear of being no longer useful. We find a role in life, and we do that role to the best of our ability for as long as that ability is there. But all of us, even me, dear listeners, will someday hit a point where we no longer are able to do that thing that we define ourselves by doing. And more than the fear of injury, more than the fear of death, this is the fear that looms. The loss of self. The self that is the self we imagined we were our whole lives.

But we were never that self, not really. We were only a series of selves, living one role and then leaving it for another, and all the time convincing ourselves that there was no change, that we were always the same person, living the same life. One arc to a finish, not the stutter-stop improvisation that is our actual lives.

Worry less about the person you once were, or the person you dream you someday will be. Worry about the person you are now. Or don't even worry. Just be that person. Be the best version of that person you can be. Be a better version than any of the other versions in any of the many parallel universes. Check regularly online to see the rankings.

Pamela Winchell was mayor. And now she is not. But that does not mean she is not anything. She is still Pamela. She is still a human being. And now she is also the Director of Emergency Press Conferences.

We look forward to the Pamela that is, and whatever Pamela will come after.

Stay tuned next for a world so possible that its very possibility feels constricting.

And, of course: Good night, Night Vale. Good night.


**PROVERB:** Most people think pit bulls are dangerous dogs, but biologically speaking, most pit bulls are just three shih tzus wearing a trench coat.

# EPISODE 53:
# "THE SEPTEMBER MONOLOGUES"

## SEPTEMBER 1, 2015

**GUEST VOICES: MARA WILSON (FACELESS OLD WOMAN), KATE JONES (MICHELLE NGUYEN), HAL LUBLIN (STEVE CARLSBERG)**

ONE OF THE JOYS OF PLAYING THE SAME CHARACTER OVER TIME IS WATCHING him get fleshed out and seeing his relationship with the audience change. Jeffrey and Joseph's writing informs everything I do on stage and I hope that, in some small way, what I do provides some inspiration to them. Steve has become a more complex and fleshed out character, and in the last five years he has had two watershed moments: "Old Oak Doors" and "The September Monologues."

My first live show after "The Debate" was in San Diego back in early 2014, and I vividly remember talking with Joseph, who said he had been thinking a lot about Steve Carlsberg and that maybe Cecil wasn't always the most reliable narrator. That information helped fuel my on-stage performance—after all, even if Cecil hates Steve, that doesn't mean that Steve has to hate Cecil or think he is a bad guy—I went on playing him as happy-go-lucky, with those delicious moments of darkness the boys would write into my live-show bits.

In "Old Oak Doors," we saw the protective side of Steve emerge. He became the hero, and it became apparent to the audience for the first time that maybe Cecil's issues with Steve weren't entirely Steve's doing. I saw a difference in how the audience reacted when I came on stage after those shows. People began to relate to Steve, to care for him, to feel that he was misunderstood, but, of course, many still felt that Cecil's disdain was justified.

Then came "The September Monologues," where you learn the root of their tumultuous relationship, but from Steve, not Cecil. I love that the source of their conflict comes from a shared love for Janice and what each feels is best for her. The script is heart wrenching, and I only recorded two takes of it; the writing was so clear and visceral and funny and sad that it made it simple for me to perform. Strong writing is like that. Steve changed for me after "The September Monologues," because I knew that he was someone burdened with terrible and complete knowledge, living in a place where knowledge is forbidden. I'd always played him as happy-go-lucky, but now I include this layer of sadness and pain that comes from knowing the truth and it's always bubbling below the surface.

And for the record, I think Steve's scones sound delicious.

The way Cecil and Steve's relationship continues to evolve is such a joy because I think ultimately they have a lot more in common than either one knows. The disdain is still there, but it has been joined by grudging love and, maybe, a little respect. Like most relationships we have, it's not as simple as pure love or pure hate. There are dimensions and shades of gray and that's where Steve and Cecil are right now.

One thing I can tell you for sure is that Steve doesn't have to fight as hard to get those on-stage hugs anymore.

—Hal Lublin

The wind out of the desert is changing. I feel it.
You feel it. A shiver in the midday heat. A crackle
in the television broadcast. A shift in your immune
system. It is September and something is different.

**CECIL:** It is September and the days have gone sinister, from first eyes open to last slow breathing. It is September. And so, listeners, dear listeners, Night Vale Public Radio is proud to introduce . . . the September Monologues . . .

**FACELESS OLD WOMAN:** Chad. Can you hear me? My mouth is half an inch from your left ear and I'm whispering. You will feel a heavy warmth there, like air from a swamp. That means I'm talking to you, Chad. I'm right behind you.

Listen, Chad. How long have we lived together? Your whole life. That's the answer. Not that you'd know it. Because I do it secretly. Thus my name. The Faceless Old Woman Who Secretly Lives in Your Home. Oh, also I don't have a face.

Chad, I am getting away from the point. You are the point.

Is this how you want to live your life? Shuffling from one trivial moment to the next, never letting anything add up to anything else? Chad, it's not my place to say, I know. My place is hiding behind the boring button-up shirts in your closet, my thin, gnarled fingers almost brushing your hand each time you reach for one of these milquetoast frocks on your way to another unsuccessful night trying to find someone who will make you more than you are.

Chad, do you know how many flies live in your apartment? I do. I know all of their names, and I tell them where to lay their eggs. So listen, Chad, do not get on my wrong side. My fury is vast and murky and expressed through a papier-mâché gaped-mouth figure that I left behind your cereal boxes this morning. Not that you'll find it. You never eat breakfast. A good breakfast is the start of a good day, say the tablets we found in that ancient crater last year.

But I'm not here to lecture you, Chad. I'm here to understand.

Like: What's with all the candles? Your room is strewn with clothes like your dresser got sick from overeating, but suddenly you're buying nicely scented candles and arranging them carefully in the living room? That doesn't seem like you, Chad.

And the fabric. That rich, red fabric that you bought and . . . are you sewing that fabric, Chad? That doesn't seem like you either. Your other hobbies involve watching, or consuming, and now, here you are, doing. What does it mean?

I have uncovered many secrets, Chad. Do not think that you are going to be able to keep anything from me. I know what is behind the old VHS copy of *Cliffhanger* in your media center. I know about the way you talk to your horse figurines. Yes, I know about the horse figurines. And I know about the dreams, Chad. I put my faceless head very close to your face at night, as you sleep. If you opened your eyes, I'm sure it would upset you. So fragile and yet so certain, your belief in the sanctity and privacy of home.

But what about the amulet you hid in the bag of lettuce, deep in your fridge? Why the amulet, that ancient, cracked painting of a screaming goat set upon gold and ebony? I couldn't lift it, Chad. I tried with my bony, skin-taut arms that have a surprising animal strength, those arms that have been so close to you so many times, but that you have never seen. I tried to lift it, Chad, and I couldn't. Why wasn't I able to lift it?

This is me, as part of your life, trying to understand that life. And you, drinking beer with your friends, drinking beer by yourself, drinking beer before work by yourself, smiling with your friends and smiling at your work and sitting dead-eyed and silent for hours in your living room, wearing a polo shirt and khaki shorts, crying without making a sound or moving, a silence of tears down your slack, boyish face. Chad, this is you and I'm trying to understand.

I've stopped googling *bees* and I've starting googling your name, over and over. I can't find trace of you anywhere. Who are you, Chad? I thought I understood. I do not understand.

And now, you are rising from your easy chair, still weeping. You are putting on the long red robe and lighting the candles, arranged throughout the room in a pattern or shape that I do not recognize. You are raising up the amulet and you are speaking. No, shouting. No . . . intoning. This is not a language I understand. I understand every language. Your very speech is outside of my reality.

What I saw next, Chad, was beyond me. I have seen death, in its many heaving forms. I have seen the low-flying ships that hide on the horizon, in front of the setting sun, and I have seen the misshapen silhouettes of their pilots. I have seen the websites you visit. But, Chad. What I saw in that moment. What you summoned in your living room. What you brought to us here in this little town, my town, the town I secretly live in, the town in which I am, at least in my view, presumptive mayor. What have you done?

Chad, this is all to say, that I am the Faceless Old Woman Who Secretly Lives in Your Home, but not your home, Chad. Not anymore. Because something else is living there now.

Oh, Chad. Something else is living there now.

**CECIL:** The air is different. Or, no, it's not. It is the way we are breathing that is different. The breathers, all of us, have changed. We've gone . . . funny. You know? Just . . . funny. Words can't capture it. But I have only words. So. Up next, more words. After that, words. Words and words and words. Words that form . . . the September Monologues.

**MICHELLE NGUYEN:** Nobody's made a good album in years.

Michelle, you say. Michelle Nguyen, that's not true, you say. Well, you're right. Very little of what I have to say is true. Some of it is, though. Make of that what you will.

No, don't. I don't trust you to make anything good.

Hang on, there's a customer.

*[off mic]*

Welcome to Dark Owl Records. You! YOU! Why are YOU here? What do you want from me, you—

*[on mic]*

Nevermind, they left.

We sold a pretty decent record the other day. It was a Beach Boys album. Everyone thinks the Beach Boys are the best. And fine, fine, they contributed a lot to American music. You can hear their influence on people like Cole Porter and Joni Mitchell and Mozart, but I'm so sick of everybody thinking they KNOW music just because they buy a Beach Boys album.

I begged the guy not to buy it. It was, of course, the one with most of their big hits on it, like "The People Under the Floor" and "I'm Being Followed" and "Tracking Device Inside My Skin" and, no doubt, The Beach Boys' most famous song "Hand Me That Hammer, Madame Dentist."

He bought the album, anyway. But I broke it into pieces as I handed it to him. And then I told him the store was closed and he wasn't allowed to leave. He's still somewhere in the basement.

A couple of people came looking for him, but I covered my eyes with my hand and sat silently so they couldn't see me.

Point being, there are still a few good albums in the world, but not many.

[*pause*]

Oh, you know what I ordered for the store last week? It should arrive any day. If you're a true lover of folk music, you'll be just as excited as I am for this.

I ordered twenty-five copies of Woody Guthrie.

They're scale replicas of his body in his most recognizable pose, holding a guitar in one hand and an aquarium full of mice in his other two hands. These replicas are three-to-one scale, so there's no room with our low ceilings. I'll have to keep them outside of the store in people's lawns and next to highway overpasses and such. But they're just great.

Oh. Wait. Nevermind.

Folk music is over. It's done. Came and went. Stop listening to folk music. The Guthrie replicas are now 70 percent off. Please don't buy them, though. Folk music is dead.

You want to know what music I'm listening to right now? Joy Division. Not "Unknown Pleasures." Everyone's listened to that album. That album will never be talked about by me again. No, I'm listening to a different Joy Division album. It's a pretty recent album that was never actually released because they never wrote it or recorded it or produced it. But I managed to get a copy of this album and I listen to it almost daily, in private so it is not ruined by other people having heard it or talked to me about it.

It's a good album. I cry when I hear it. I cry when I think about it. I'm crying now. I'm sure it doesn't sound to you like I'm crying, because you can't comprehend my crying. You can't see me or hear me crying because you don't know me. You don't truly know me. This Joy Division album truly knows me in a way no other human ever has.

And so that's a complete list of music I like.

Looks like the coroner is here again.

[*off mic*]

Hello, Linda. We got the new Panic! At the Disco album in.

[*whispered into mic*]

I've been selling her blank CDs for years now and telling her that's Panic! At the Disco's aesthetic. That they just release completely silent songs with no titles on albums with no tracks or cover art and no name. It's really funny. Except for their new album really did come out, and it's called "Quit Fabricating Our Musical Career, Michelle." So I'm a little freaked out by that. But also, I think I'm really impacting the future of music.

[*normal voice*]

We here at Dark Owl Records pride ourselves on that. Impacting the future of music. Also the past. We impact the past of music. I'm wearing a hat right now.

So know that.

I hate Panic! At the Disco.

I've never actually heard their music, so I don't really hate them so much as resent them. Or rather, resent what they stand for. Or rather, resent what I believe that they stand for. Or rather, resent my perception of other people's projections of what they stand for. Or rather, myself. I hate myself is what I'm trying to say.

We have that in common, I think.

Panic! At the Disco is probably fine if you were to ever listen to their music. Lots of people buy lots of their music. Of course lots of people buy lots of ridiculous things: overpriced coffee, minivans, dogs, furniture, towels, medicine. You name it and some idiot will buy it.

[*off mic*]

Linda! Is that a Public Enemy cassette? Don't touch that. You do not have hip-hop access here.

[*on mic*]

We have a pretty good hip-hop collection.

[*pause*]

That's not true. It's just that one cassette. And it's broken.

Anyway, T-shirts and posters and trance music are all 50 percent off this weekend at Dark Owl, so come visit the store.

Wait. Nevermind. We're closed until further notice.

You're not allowed in here, anyway. Not with that tattoo. Who has a Woody Guthrie tattoo these days?

**CECIL:** It will all be over soon. And then something else will take its place. Like waves, says the common metaphor. From dust to dust, says a simplified version of a complicated philosophy. "Hm-mmmmmm," says the Big Bang, still echoing quietly through everything it created. Let us return, one last time, before it, you, or anything else ends, to the September Monologues.

**STEVE:** There are glowing arrows in the sky. You can't see them. I do.

There are dotted lines and arrows and circles. The sky is a chart that explains the entire world, but you can't see it. I know that.

The world makes sense. I believe that. I do. It has to. Otherwise, it wouldn't make sense. And that would be the worst thing that could possibly happen.

No one listens when I talk. They hear, but they don't listen. Even now maybe your attention is drifting. Why pay attention to me? Why pay attention to Steve Carlsberg? There he goes again with his theories and explanations. But I see them. I see the arrows in the sky. I understand what is happening.

Night Vale is a weird place. No one else sees that, I guess. But I do. It's not like other places. I've never been other places, but I know. I know what other places are like. I've read books. Don't tell anyone please. Don't tell anyone that I've read books. I have to maintain my position and the respect of my peers. I am a member in good standing of the PTA. I bring scones and they are always the first item in the potluck to go. I take great pride in that.

My . . . brother-in-law? stepbrother? brother outside of the law? . . . I can never get those terms straight. Well he just brings store-made hummus and wheat-free pita chips. Every time. I make scones with my own hands, from scratch. Sometimes I put in a zest of orange, sometimes I don't. They are not always the same. Nothing is.

People pick at the chips and the hummus. They want to be polite. Often they are not.

We all, all of us, so often fail at what we want to do. That's okay. As long as we understand our failure. As long as we see it.

I see my failure to help my community the way I would like to help it. I would like to guide it somewhere new, but the only person who listened to me was that man on the Desert Bluffs radio, and then, well, then all the rest happened.

The world would be better if more people saw the dotted lines and arrows in the sky. I can look out my window and see them. I am doing that now.

Listen, I love my wife. And she loves her brother. And we both love our daughter. And my . . . brother-in-law? (half-brother? double-brother? hm) loves his niece. So that counts for a lot. That counts for most of it. I don't hate him the way he hates me. How could I? I understand him. He hates me because he doesn't understand me at all. He cannot see the dotted lines. He cannot see the arrows.

I first met him at the wedding. He's busy, or he says he is. He does always seem to be at the station. Or, at least, he used to be.

This last year's been good for him I think. It has softened him a little, in the right places, although not at all toward me. But I never expect that.

He was very nice when I first met him.

"Welcome to the wedding," he said grandly, which was odd since he actually arrived after me. But it was nice gesture anyway, and I accepted it with a handshake and a hello.

"It's an exciting day, isn't it?" I said. "Here, try a scone."

I had made scones. It seemed right in the midst of a formal celebration like that to have a little touch of home, to remind people of the lifetime of simple gestures that this grand celebration was meant to launch.

"Oh," he said. "This is just scrumptious. This is the best scone I've ever had."

He hasn't said anything like that in some time.

We chatted for a while. I don't remember what about. Maybe the weather. No, definitely the weather. I remember it was the weather because we had to stand in awkward silence for a bit as we waited for the music to stop playing.

But then it all turned.

"How about those secret agents?" I asked, indicating the black suited women and men lining the back of the room, taking photos and writing down everything that everyone said.

"Ah," he said. "Yes, well," he said. He was raised in the Night Vale tradition of silence and with a belief in the power of hierarchy and bureaucracy. I had been raised that way too, but it didn't stick, because I could see the arrows and the dotted lines and the circles. Laid out across the world, I could see clearly how things were, the way that it all was organized, and for whose benefit.

"Sure," I said. "Those agents from—" Oh well, this next part is complicated. People always just refer to them as being from a vague yet menacing agency and, while they are certainly menacing, there's nothing vague about them. I explained to Cecil then exactly what branch they're from, who specifically they report to, and whose desk those reports ultimately land on. People can die for knowing these things. But I've always known it. I could always just see it, how it all really was laid out.

As I talked, Cecil's face changed. It twisted into a grimace.

"I won't have you teaching Janice lies like that," he howled. And I'm sorry for using such a melodramatic verb, but he really did. He howled. And then he refused to speak to me again.

During the ceremony, he tried to object, on the grounds that I knew and spoke aloud forbidden knowledge and dangerous truths. Which is actually a mandatory reason to cancel a wedding according to the laws of Night Vale, but his sister talked him down.

Since then, though, he has never trusted me. It's because of Janice. It's because I want Janice to understand the world the way I do. I want her to see the arrows and dotted lines, to know the world, not just repeat what has been told to her.

My brother-in-law, as you might imagine, disagrees.

"SHE WILL LEARN ONLY WHAT SHE IS ALLOWED TO LEARN IN SCHOOLS," he explains to me regularly and loudly. "DON'T POISON HER WITH EDUCATION."

I don't know. Maybe he's right. It's not like knowing has made my life easier. Quite the opposite. Quite the opposite.

But every time I look up, I see them. Glowing arrows in the sky. Dotted lines and circles. A great chart that explains it all.

And I ask you. How can I know all of this, how can I understand, and not try to explain? How can I see the dotted lines, so bright and tangible, and deny them?

I have to try. Even if it means that everyone, even my wife, even Janice, grows to hate me. The truth is more important than all that. It has to be. Or else why would it shine so clear above?

CECIL: Well, that's it for the September Monologues. We've said so much. What more is there to say?

PROVERB: [*the sound of static, rising in volume and suddenly cutting off*]

# EPISODE 54:
# "A CARNIVAL COMES TO TOWN"

## SEPTEMBER 15, 2014

### GUEST VOICE: DYLAN MARRON (CARLOS)

TROPES ARE HELPFUL LITTLE THINGS FOR SIMPLIFYING WRITING. YOU have four characters in your scene? Great. Let's make one the wise-cracking loudmouth. Another the cold-hearted CEO. Another the caring minister of a small rural church. And the last is a basketball-playing golden lab.

Easy. Dialogue should just come pouring out of you now.

Of course, left unexamined, tropes can become, at best, clichés and, at worst, stereotypes.

So much of Night Vale's humor and politics comes from inverting tropes. We look for an archetype or scenario that feels ubiquitous enough that we can make a joke about it without a long setup (e.g., "The town opened a new Dog Park. No one is allowed in the Dog Park.")

Here of course, we have the classic idea of the scary carnival coming to a small town. What sort of evil will this carnival bring? What horrors lie behind the fun-house mirrors? Did you hear about the boy who rode the Gravitron and never spoke again? And on and on.

There's a lot here to work with.

But examining this trope led me to thinking about xenophobia. That outsiders will come into your town, state, or country and they will harm you or change your way of life. Fear of foreigners is the heartbeat of social conservatism.

It felt more relevant to examine this part of that trope, to make the carnival coming to Night Vale a completely normal carnival. But it's Night Vale that's weird. It's Night Vale that is filled with evil and fear.

For Night Vale (and for our real world, too), the truest horrors can be found from within, not from without.

—Jeffrey Cranor

The secret to a long life lies in how
acutely you perceive time.

# WELCOME TO NIGHT VALE

A quiet caravan of flatbed trucks rolled into town last night. The
trailers were unmarked, except by age and neglect. The trucks parked
along Bandera Street, in an abandoned lot in the heart of the up-
and-coming Abandoned Lot Neighborhood.

People we do not know emerged from the trucks and began to
unload tall lights and heavy speakers. Perhaps many of you were
jostled from slumber by the faint pulsing of music that sounded like
music you know, even though it was music you had never heard.
Perhaps you woke unaware there ever was sun, confused by your
own consciousness, hearing the echoes of these unknown choruses,
and found yourself singing along, mouthing familiar words placed
in an unfamiliar order.

We do not know what these trucks have brought or what those
within them intend. All I can say is you should not go near that
abandoned lot on Bandera Street until we find out more. Which
might take a while. It's a very busy day. We can't investigate every horrifying fleet of unmarked trucks. We've got more important
things.

Like this voice mail from my boyfriend.

**CARLOS:** Hi Cecil.

I made so much progress today! Doug and some of the other members of the army of warriors who roam this otherworld desert took me to the top of the mountain, to the lighthouse up on it.

(Oh! I'm still stuck in the desert otherworld. How are you? I miss you.)

Anyway, they showed me the photos on the walls inside the lighthouse. One of the warriors, whose name is Alicia and who is not a woman or a man and who is Doug's partner and who has a dog and who is trying to make a new currency based on sand, walked me through the pictures. They were photos of living rooms and parks and lawns. Photos of Night Vale. I asked if Alicia took these photos, because they were good photos, colorful, well-composed, and alive.

Alicia shook their head "no," and the other warriors in the room pointed quietly back to the photos and I saw that they were literally alive. The people and all the other things that were not people moved in the photos. Blades of grass in the breeze. Small bees spiraling. A man refusing to smile. All within the confines of rough driftwood frames. Inside the lighthouse, you can see anywhere, although you cannot go to any of those wheres. And as I leave this message, I can see you, Cecil. I'm watching you shave. It's cute how you pull your nose up like that, but you missed a spot.

I'm sorry I haven't had time to go looking for the doorway back to your dimension. I'm learning so many things though. I promise. I promise to return soon. This desert otherworld is just so scientifically interesting. Maybe the most scientifically interesting community I've ever been.

I love you. I'll try calling you again tonight. Is it even nighttime there? I've lost all sense of time.

**CECIL:** So . . . I don't know. All of that, and such. And now, the news.

The foundation is finally being laid for the new Old Night Vale

Opera House. Old Woman Josie was on hand for the ceremony. In fact she brought her own cement mixer and poured it herself. Several creatures claiming to be angels, wearing yellow and orange triangles—the logo of StrexCorp, now, of course, owned by these same creatures—were on hand to assist, but Josie kept slapping their many hands away when they attempted to help her with the heavy mixer and the strenuous work.

"I'm fine, Erika. I have this. Go get me some water," Josie said, wiping her shriveled brow with a green handkerchief. "I ain't that old," she said before adding "Hey you forgot to record *Castle* last night. Make yourself useful and double check the TiVo before I get home tonight."

One of the supposed angels, all of whom are named Erika, pointed out that *Castle* is in reruns and she could probably download the episodes she missed from iTunes. There was a long pause as Old Woman Josie stared at Erika in silence, concrete churning its dull pulsing hum, onlookers forgetting to exhale, a single drop of sweat rolling down one of Erika's seven cheekbones. And then Josie said, "Okay. Whatever. Is the *Chopped* marathon on tonight?" and continued her pour.

The angel-like beings claim that StrexCorp is Night Vale's first angel-owned and angel-operated company. They claim this proudly and even placed it on their brochures and signs, despite the great risk of arrest and imprisonment for the felony of acknowledging the existence of angels.

Completion of the new Old Night Vale Opera House is scheduled for this coming spring. Many town residents are excited and confused over the return of this cultural landmark, as none of us know what an opera is. "Is it a type of deli?" asked one bystander, who shielded his eyes and asked not to be identified before dissipating into a black cloud and joining the rest of the cowardly air molecules.

"I heard opera is a virus you get from kissing," said another by-stander who was clearly former mayor Pamela Winchell wearing a fake mustache and clumsily altering her voice.

Nobody but Old Woman Josie and her mysterious friends know what opera is. Hopefully we'll all find out soon, Night Vale. Hopefully it's a good thing.

I have my doubts, though. I am sometimes more doubt than man.

The strangers at the abandoned lot have begun unloading the fleet of trucks, removing large metal cases from the trailers and assembling gargantuan machines covered in rust and the faint echo of bright color.

Residents of the Abandoned Lot District, who usually just talk hopefully about a day when they'll be allowed to finally build homes, have reported hearing organ music and smelling deep fryers. They saw carnival workers carrying bags of strange candy and leading packs of unfamiliar, loping animals into the lot.

Many of the strangers wear large wigs and bright, painted faces. They carry foolish hats and mangled balloons.

Listeners, I know what this is and it is not good! A carnival has come to our city, Night Vale. I do not even know how you can protect yourself from this wicked cultural affront to our community.

I reached out to the City Council, but I just got their voice mail, which was the Council saying in unison: "We're not here anymore. Good luck with whatever that is in the abandoned lot. If you'd like to scream or cry in horror, please do so at the tone."

So at least their voice mail is the usual one, but I don't think we'll get much help from them.

Night Vale . . . I have only ever heard of carnivals. I never thought I would ever have to actually see one. No one knows what they will do in the face of catastrophe until they are in that face. And here I am, still not knowing what to do. A carnival! Oh, all the mysterious lights in the sky! I do not know how this carnival found us nor what they intend. But I am certain it is not good.

It is rumored that our neighbors in Pine Cliff once welcomed a traveling carnival. Pine Cliff is now inhabited only by ghosts, but I don't actually know if that was related to the carnival at all. They might have been that way already.

And you know, there is a certain sweetness to the hastily as-sembled rides, to the thought of eating air-blown pastel sugar, your boyfriend winning you a stuffed animal at the bird-mocking booth. Exchanging known quantities of fiat cash for meta-fiat paper cou-pons. Oh, it sounds just . . . it sounds just dreamy—

No! These wicked magicians of the midway. They must be using mind control to draw us in. Do not fall victim to—holding hands hotly under the cool lights, the undulating swirl and discordant fugue of the merry-go-round about us. Carlos! Ah, Carlos! Let's go to the carniv———

No. Stop it. Cecil. No. Night Vale, avoid the carnival. Hide in your homes.

This Thursday at the Night Vale Public Library is the twice-annual Cleaning of Books. The Sheriff's Secret Police Super Secret Special Forces Unit will be on hand to subdue the librarians, who regularly attempt to not only undermine our city with dangerous books but also sink their sharp claws and pincers into library visitors before flying them off to eat or toy with or whatever it is they do to their victims.

The Cleaning of Books is our way of double checking that the librarians are keeping a clean stock of municipally approved books, such as the biography of Helen Hunt and all four of Dean Koontz's novels. Librarians are well-known for sneaking in books by dangerous authors. In 1988, two (TWO!) copies of *Pride and Prejudice* were found in Night Vale. No one knows quite how many people read these copies, but the ensuing riots inconvenienced hundreds and led to the current cleaning schedule.

Not everyone is in favor of this practice, though. New mayor Dana Cardinal issued a public rebuke of book cleaning.

The mayor admitted that while "books are pretty dangerous" and she "doesn't recommend them for everyone," we should concentrate more on protecting ourselves from the librarians themselves, who are the real danger.

Teenage book lover and heroic militia leader Tamika Flynn also offered her protest of this important event, saying, "Books and libraries are dangerous, which is exactly why we should protect them. Librarians are conniving and vicious monsters but they also know how to recommend a good read. Their methods may be violent, but we must be willing to face great challenges in order to achieve great things."

Tamika continued, "We will grow soft without books, Night Vale," as she waved her favorite copy of Helen DeWitt's *The Last Samurai*, onlookers shielding their eyes from the forbidden tome.

I don't want to disagree too much with young Tamika. I respect her leadership and her vast knowledge of books, but not everyone is cut out for reading difficult literature. Perhaps we could split the difference. We could select just a few people in town who are allowed to read challenging books. That way the masses don't have to be exposed to complex ideas and a small committee of trustworthy people like Tamika can tell us in a gentle way what those books say, very quietly so we don't have to hear them. It'll be all the fun and simplicity of an intellectual oligarchy, but without all the awful reading.

Intern Maureen has returned to our studio. She was swept away a few weeks back by an enormous gust of wind, and we thought her lost. We held services for her at the rec center. Her whole family was there. Many of her friends from Night Vale Community College came, or at least I assumed they were friends from school. They all had human bodies with coyote heads and they were eating armadillos out of a duffel bag. Huh. *College kids.*

Well, we were all glad to see Maureen come home safe. Or most of us. Her family seemed disappointed, this being the second time they've mourned her death in vain. They seemed emotionally exhausted, not angry. They told her this is the last time, Maureen. This is it. No more.

Anyway, today at work, Maureen's been doing research into carnivals, and according to her, carnivals need money to operate. If we do not want a carnival in town then we should just not give them our money and the carnival will go away.

Maureen has also handed me a report saying, oh my . . . Night Vale, the carnival grounds have been completed.

A forty-foot tall wheel with empty compartments spins lazily in the hot sun as broken speakers sing cacophonous platitudes over simplistic chord progressions. Carnival workers are brandishing hammers next to a tower inscribed with ascending numbers and topped with an alarm bell.

Night Vale residents have gathered near the grounds but are not yet entering. A group of the carnival workers with white faces and bulbous noses and large shoes have opened the gates to the carnival grounds and are cooing and beckoning our citizens to enter. These masked interlopers wish to sway you with broad toothy smiles, but they are nightmares, Night Vale. They are lies incarnate.

Remember that we are a great town. We are a great town that does not back down to grave danger. Are we not the same town that defeated a smiling god and a fascist corporatocracy and once! once! survived a street cleaning day??

I said earlier that I did not know what to do in the face of a catastrophe, but I was wrong, Night Vale, I was wrong. When I think only of myself, I am scared. But knowing I am with you, I am not scared. We are in this together. I have a community I can trust and love. There is no need to be frightened of treacherous outsiders.

Outsiders . . . wait, how did these outsiders get in? Night Vale is not so easily found, so how have they so easily found it?

Oh! Oh! The carnival gates have opened. All of Night Vale is there. Only I sit contained in my booth, helpless as usual. The carnival workers smile wider and wider and wider and wider. Breath is heard, loud and wet and without an obvious source, and the birds are gone. There is a fearful infinity of an instant.

I take you now, uncertain of what this next instant will bring, and none of you near a radio anyway, to the weather.

**WEATHER:** "Bremen" by PigPen Theatre Co.

The carnival has left. Night Vale citizens resisted entering the metal gates. They formed a semi-circle around the opening and shouted INTERLOPERS while pointing, as is our friendly, mandatory way of welcoming strangers.

Soon the painted people backed away, closing themselves into their miserable flatbed corral. They disassembled their mechanical monstrosities and drove them away.

Night Vale, en masse, waved fists and sticks and farm tools and cactuses and animal parts. Our citizens chanted curses upon the carnival.

The carnival employees, in their haste, left behind several artifacts of their attempted threat to our sanctity, our sanity. We found clear plastic bags filled with cheaply produced dolls. There was a large styrofoam-stuffed green and orange squirrel.

As the trucks drove away, proud and vigilant Night Vale civilians set the squirrel ablaze, that unholy totem of that unholy carnival. With the sun long gone, presumably scared away by the unexpected visitors, the happy fire of victory shone out to meet the taillights of the retreating trucks.

Witnesses heard the carnival perpetrators saying things like "run!" and "get out of here!" as they made their way to their trucks. Shouts of "what the hell is this town?" and "where the hell are we?" and "this is definitely not Modesto" and "I think they're going to kill us, Stacy, run!" were the verbal white flags, signaling our triumph as a town, as a proud community that stood for itself once again.

And intern Maureen, who is. . . .

Maureen, you look upset. Are you upset? Is everything okay?

Maureen does not look happy, listeners. I'm not sure why Maureen is not happy about today's victory she helped bring about. You are part of this, Maureen. This victory is also yours.

[*pause*]

Maureen, do you not love victory over outsiders who mean us harm?

Maureen, do you . . .

Well, Maureen left the control booth. She just got up in a huff and left. Huh, teenagers, I guess.

Stay tuned next for people arguing about sports. Not on the radio, somewhere else. Somewhere and soon people will be arguing about sports. I don't know what's happening next on the radio. I never do.

And as always, good night, Night Vale. Good night.

**PROVERB:** Say what you will about dance, but language is a limited form of expression.

# EPISODE 55:
# "THE UNIVERSITY OF WHAT IT IS"

## OCTOBER 1, 2014

THIS EPISODE REPRESENTS A COMMON PHENOMENON IN LONG-RUNNING stories. It's a setup for an idea that ultimately just drifted away or transformed or was set aside to maybe pick up in the future. My idea here was that throughout this year we would get different origin stories for the character of Carlos, and they all would be contradictory. This would be the first one, and then there would be another that told a completely different life story, and so on. And what happened was I wrote this one, and then I just didn't write another. I don't have a good reason for that. Other ideas became more prominent, and we followed those instead. I think this idea about Carlos could have been an interesting and fun one. But I think the ideas we followed instead are also very interesting and fun. Ideas are easy, and when you're a working artist you generally have way more ideas than you'll ever be able to execute. So you come to value the good execution of an idea, rather than the original idea itself. After all, any number of other ideas would have worked just as well, given proper execution.

What's with the name "The University of What It Is"? I have no idea. Like so much in Night Vale, it's a phrase that my brain locked onto and wouldn't let go of until I had written something with it. Once I had written something with it, I was free, since it had left my brain and gone off to all the listeners' brains instead. Thanks for carrying it for me.

This episode also sees the official debut of the character Jackie Fierro, owner of the local pawnshop who would, about a year later, be one of the main characters of the first *Welcome to Night Vale* novel (available at your local independent bookseller or library!). One of the strangest things about writing a book versus a podcast for us was the lag time between writing and release. With a podcast, we were used to writing a story and then having it out to the world in a matter of weeks or days, depending on how on top of script writing we were. This continuing process of write-and-immediately-release is immensely satisfying.

But with a book, you basically have to be completely done with the thing a year before it comes out. Which means by the time you're getting in front of crowds and talking about it, you've half forgotten what was even in it, since you've written a novel's worth of podcast scripts and live shows in between. Another effect of this is that there is a temptation that had to be resisted to build on plot elements we just wrote into a book within the podcast episodes that we wrote after. For our brains, this is a logical continuation of what we had recently been writing, but for the listener, it would be references to plots they won't be able to experience for more than a year. And so I would have to settle for introducing the character of Jackie, whom I had already written hundreds of pages about, as though she were new to all of us. What other elements of the podcasts are secret references to works we've already written but won't be able to release for some time? Who knows? (We do.)

—Joseph Fink

Oh, Cecil and his moveable emotional boundaries! He's so loveably adorable . . . but then you remember that he is literally broadcasting his relationship therapy to the entire town, and then it seems less adorable and more, oh what's the word . . . presumptuous? Indiscreet? Creepy?

So Night Vale citizens, confused by these outsiders who have come to their town to locate Carlos, are about to attack the representatives from the University of What It Is. This puts Cecil in quite the moral dilemma. As a native Night Valean, Cecil has been taught to fear and mistrust outsiders, but he's fallen in love with an outsider who is well on his way to being an insider (if he weren't trapped in a weird desert otherworld, that is).

So when does one stop being an outsider and start becoming a citizen? Is it dependent on legal status or social status or both? Or does it just take time?

In a way, these are the questions that America is asking itself right now. There's something about Cecil that's so innocent, it's like walking into a Cracker Barrel gift shop. It's like seeing things the way Anglo-Americans once saw themselves—Cecil in a weird way is a throwback to the best part of that belle époque Americana.

The America-as-remembered.

Tall-Tale America.

"Back in my day, we had to walk to school in ten feet of snow. Uphill! Both ways!" America.

Once while on tour with Night Vale, we pulled into a breakfast joint somewhere in rural Middle America, Kansas maybe? It had been a long day of driving, and we had more to go after our lunch break. I looked up at the quaint, antique barn-turned-comfort-food-cafeteria and saw three old ladies seated around a table in the second-floor window. They reminded me of the applehead dolls we made every fall back in Appalachian Tennessee.

And they stared, unblinking, stone-faced, at us as we got out of the van, stretched, and made our way across the gravel parking lot. I waved up to them. Nothing. I nudged whoever was next to me and pointed up to the three Midwestern biddies who were giving us interlopers the once-over. They never broke eye contact. They said nothing to each other. They just stared. Were outsiders that unusual there? The Night Vale crew can be boisterous and we certainly wear our hipster-artsy uniqueness like a badge at all times, but seriously . . . we can't be *that* unusual, right?

The too-apt twist to the story is that once we headed up to the second floor to get seated, there was nobody there, just the friendly cafeteria staff. We were the only customers in the place, and there was only one staircase up to the second-floor dining room.

Rural American stoicism or something more . . . sinister?

[*Cue Night Vale theme.*]

—Cecil Baldwin

**Let me be brief. Let us all be brief. Let us, briefly, be.**

# WELCOME TO NIGHT VALE

Listeners, I received a call today from a Dr. Sylvia Kayyali, who introduced herself as working at the University of What It Is. I told her I had never heard of that particular learning institution (actually what happened is the name led to a comedic back and forth: "What *what* is?" "What It Is" "The University is what?" "No, no, of What It Is" and so on) but eventually I accorded her the usual treatment of any academic person of importance, which was a bellowing lecture about the dangers of education followed by a tense, suspicious silence.

Taking advantage of that silence, she jumped in and explained that the University of What It Is was concerned about one of their faculty members, who had taken a sabbatical to investigate some probably fantastical rumors about a strange town in the desert and then had never returned.

I told her that I didn't know of any strange towns, just the pleasant burg we call home.

"Well," she said, "I'll keep trying then. If you hear from a scientist going by the name Carlos, please let us know."

As you could imagine, listeners, I made all sorts of noises when she said that, but she had already hung up and had left no call back number. My phone screen just showed a picture of a beach during a bad storm with a shivering human figure off in the distance, again and again nearly but not quite swept away by the pounding surf. I think that's an area code of . . . what? Idaho? I don't have these things memorized. More on this as I aggressively investigate.

Well, it's time again for one of our audience's most requested segments. I assume. I've never actually asked, but I can't imagine anyone having a different perspective from my own, so I assume this is what listeners are most focused on. It's time to check back in with Khoshekh and his floating kittens.

Khoshekh, the cat floating exactly four feet off the ground in the men's room here at the station, is doing great. Nothing to report. He's a healthy kitty going through his third molting of the year, and his fur-cusp is as radiant and sticky as any cat's has ever been. He loves to be petted, and the petting is completely survivable with the correct antibiotics.

His kittens are, of course, also floating in fixed locations in the same bathroom, and are being cared for by their various owners. Larry Leroy, out on the edge of town, has especially taken after one of the kittens, who he has named, confusingly, Larry Leroy. "Oh, Larry Leroy is just the best," Larry Leroy said, in what was either an expression of affection or extreme egotism. Either way, he's being a great dad to that little cat, and we wish Larry Leroy and Larry Leroy the best.

And now, a word from our sponsors.

Traditionally, when cooking a steak, there have been a few basic rules to follow. For instance, using a form of meat that is recognized by both the current culture and the human body as food. Following basic food safety procedures so as to prevent illness. Not intentionally bleeding on the finishing steak.

But that's just traditionally. Here at Outback Steakhouse, we say: No rules. Just right.

Absolutely no rules. Food safety? Pfft. Federal law? Ugh. The laws of physics? What are you, a narc?

It's weird here. The steak floats. Sometimes the steak is and also isn't, simultaneously. Sometimes the steak is a chair, and we point at the chair and we say, "That chair is a steak." And we make you eat it.

That is the one rule. If we say something is a steak, you have to eat it, no questions asked. I know we said there are no rules, but that itself is a rule and so is void. You want your philosophy non-contradictory? Go to Sizzler.

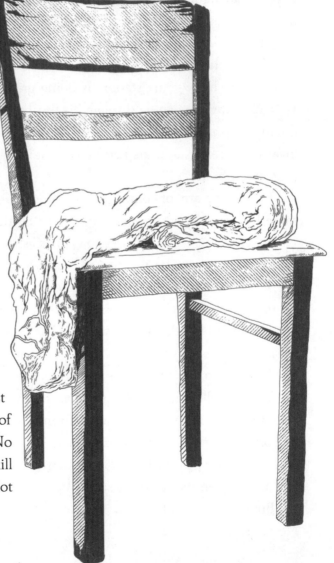

In the bathroom where most places have a sign saying EMPLOYEES MUST WASH HANDS we just carved LAND OF THE FREE directly into the wall. There isn't even a sink in there. Heck, our bathrooms are just sealed vaults full of poisonous gases. No rules. We might kill you. We've killed a lot of people.

Outback Steakhouse: "Do What Thou Wilt" shall be the whole of the law.

I received another call from Dr. Kayyali. Before she even spoke, I told her that I in fact knew a Carlos and explained, in a completely businesslike and journalistic tone, the tenor of our relationship.

"Carlos is there?" she said. Only she didn't put a question at the end of it. So maybe she was just saying, "Carlos is there." In either case, she told me that this was surprising and that the University of What It Is would send someone right away to see why their faculty member had never made it home.

I said, "He never mentioned a university to me."

And she said, "Do we ever dare to speak of higher education to the ones we love?" which is a valid point. Education is such a scary and forbidden subject that you would be a fool to mention it out loud. I forgive Carlos for this lapse. Or I will as soon as I can get him on the phone. Hey, Carlos. Call me.

In the meantime, I'll let you know what happens when the folks from the University of What It Is come by.

And now the community calendar.

On Monday, the Baristas of Night Vale are inviting everyone in town to come to the Barista District for the annual Barista Cultural Fair, where they will be performing traditional Barista dances like the Twice Dip and the Mustache Snort, and serving traditional Barista foods like lemon poppyseed scones. There will be a showing of Barista-themed movies like *Jaws* and *Jaws 2*, and Norah Jones will make an appearance via a photo of her tacked up on a wall so you can say, "Oh look, that's Norah Jones," while pointing at the photo.

Tuesday is a day for trying to find what you've lost. Tear through your house, dress in clothes you haven't worn in years, reenact situations from your childhood and try to get them to turn out differently. You will get it all back. You will finally have lost nothing. It's all possible and it's all healthy.

Wednesday is a secret that has been badly kept.

Thursday is a day of remembrance and memorial dedicated to all the people who will happen to die on that Thursday. The City Council would like us all to take a moment and think about the many, many people who will just happen to die within that particular frame of time, for unrelated reasons and adding up to no coherent picture of human existence. Please find the time within your life to mourn those who will, by complete chance, be gone. Unless you turn out to be one of those people. In which case, hey, you're off the hook on all this tedious grief stuff.

Friday is a plan that has been poorly thought-through.

Saturday is absolutely nothing you should be worried about, say hulking, buzzing figures hiding in all of our attics, in a statement that they issued today, thus revealing to us for the first time their existence.

Sunday is a lie that has been foolishly believed.

This has been the community calendar.

Jackie Fierro, who runs the only pawnshop in town (which for some reason is named Lucinda's Pawn Shop), announced today that she is having a sale on ideas about time.

"People keep coming by and pawning their ideas about time," Jackie told a friend of hers in confidence, never knowing that it was going to end up on the radio. "And, like, I don't want to turn them down because it looks like they need the money, but, dude, how many ideas about time am I supposed to keep? None of these ideas make any sense anyway."

So if you're looking for a gently used idea about time, or perhaps if you pawned your own idea about time and now are able to retrieve it, then get on down to Lucinda's Pawn Shop and talk to Jackie. Don't know where her pawnshop is? Don't worry. When you need it, then, *then* you will know.

And now, corrections.

In a previous broadcast, we swung a baseball bat wildly around the studio, knocking our microphone onto the ground until all it could pick up was the stomping of our feet as we systematically destroyed all of our possessions in a misguided attempt to make the world better and ourselves more happy.

After that, we mistakenly referred to Trish Hidge as the Assistant Deputy to the Mayor when she is in fact the Deputy Assistant to the Mayor. We deeply regret this error.

This has been corrections.

Still haven't heard from Carlos. The representatives from the University of What It Is arrived. They are besuited and behatted and be-a-number-of-other-things-besides. They move in a group of three, led by Dr. Kayyali herself, looking at everything and everyone they encounter with a critical eye and what looks like a sneer but could just be the natural set of their faces.

I rushed out to meet these people that could perhaps tell me something that I don't know about the love of my life, only to find that, flush with their recent victory over the carnival, Night Vale citizens had cornered the staff members from the University of What It Is, shouting and waving household items like sticks and police batons.

INTERLOPER they cried. INTERLOPER.

"No, no," I said. "Well, yes," I said, because they *were* interlopers, but good interlopers. If only there was a word that meant good interloper.

Dr. Kayyali did not seem afraid of the crowd. She considered the Night Vale residents before her and patted at the air in a placating motion. (And, by the way, did you know that the term for a "group of citizens" is a "mob"? The English language is so funny.)

The doctor's calm demeanor did not transfer to the mob around her. They howled and jeered, saying things like "Remember that carnival. Let's do that again!" and chanting popular slogans like "Uargghh OUTSIDERS!"

I, more than anyone, know that not all outsiders are bad. Most outsiders are. Uargghh outsiders. But some outsiders are great. The best. My favorite. And *these* outsiders know about *that* outsider.

"Listeners," I said to the mob, because the moment I begin speaking my relationship to them was one in which they were hearing me, I said, "Please, let us proceed with caution and empathy. We've never tried it before. Maybe it'll work."

But the mob was beyond hearing and they continued their advance. For the first time I looked out at the faces of my fellow citizens and saw them not as friends and companions, but as a dangerous combination of suppression and indoctrination. And so I did the only thing I could think to do in that moment.

"If you won't listen," I said, "then I will make you listen. I will make you all listen. To the weather."

**WEATHER: "Catfish" by Waxahatchee**

While the crowd was distracted by the sudden weather, I was able to flag down a passing Sheriff's Secret Police helicopter, which was conducting routine surveillance operations just overhead. I explained to the officers inside, all of whom were wearing loose-fitting gowns and Richard Nixon masks, that I was in need of a lift to the radio station for important community reasons. They did not respond, but they also did not do anything else, so I hustled the representatives from the University of What It Is onto the craft and we left the hostile mob listening docilely below us.

"Please tell me everything," was how I casually started the conversation with Dr. Kayyali.

She blinked.

"That would take a long time, and I feel like much of it would be things you already know," she said, continuing: "For instance, tying shoes, operating your own tongue, feeling insecure, and other things. You would know these already."

I clarified that I meant everything about Carlos and her university and this is what she said, as we hammered our way across the sky. She actually shouted it, to be heard over the rotors, so this is what she shouted.

She shouted that she is from the University of What It Is, and that they have been looking for some time for a faculty member named Carlos, who is a professor of science. He has been missing for decades and they were getting very worried. They had no choice but to hire a new professor of science, but it isn't going well, because the guy they hired is a new-media artist interested in collage as it intersects with social media and he isn't even sure what science is. They don't know why they hired that guy. It had somehow made sense when they did it.

She told me, in a quieter voice, once we had landed near the safety of the station and had decided that the Sheriff's Secret Police were not going to prevent us from leaving the helicopter, she told me that if this is how our town treats outsiders, then Carlos is in more danger than she thought.

I told her that Carlos wasn't treated that way, that he was well-loved by everyone and especially loved by someone and she said, sure, sure, but she didn't sound like she believed it, and then she said that there was much she needed to do but that they would make sure Carlos found his way to safety, and they were looking forward to him taking back over the one class they have on science because the new-media artist guy is really messing it up. She said she had to go, but gave me her card in case I ever wanted to get in touch with her. I imagine that I definitely will.

So there it is. So many questions. So many possible answers. And, like the title of that much beloved picture book classic: How many lies?

Listeners, I do not know everything about Carlos and he does not tell me everything. That is okay. We are not one person. How lonely that would be, a couple who has made themselves one so completely that they are once again alone. We are two people—separate, unique, and joined only where we choose to join.

I don't know what is his affiliation truly to the University of What It Is. Perhaps I will never know. But I can know about the taste of food he has made me, or the feeling of his hand in mine, or the absence of his hand not in mine. I can feel the distance between us, and I can know that that distance, viewed properly, is no distance at all.

But still, I think I'll keep Dr. Kayyali's card handy. Just in case I ever need her or what she knows. And that time may come. Certainly so many other times I never even thought possible have come before it.

Stay tuned next for a loss of words, an absence of silence, some noise, some noise, and then, perhaps, and then, perhaps, meaning.

Good night, Night Vale. Good night.

**PROVERB:** Language will evolve, irregardless of your attempt to literally lock it away in a secluded tower. Obvs.

# EPISODE 56: "HOMECOMING"

## OCTOBER 15, 2014

### GUEST VOICE: WIL WHEATON (EARL HARLAN)

DO YOU REMEMBER EPISODE 15 "STREET CLEANING DAY"? AT THE END of that story, we get a quick glance at some of Night Vale's citizens—their brief reactions to surviving the most horrifying day of the year.

There's one particular couple in that episode to look for: Wilson and Amber. In the dawn following the atrocity of street cleaning, Wilson asks Amber, a woman he barely knows, to marry him. She declines marriage, suggesting they start with dinner first.

Well, I love those two. I wanted to check back in with them forty-one episodes (almost two years) later. And here they are, after Night Vale's homecoming game is canceled, we hear the dejected crowd gathering together to tell stories.

It's only one sentence, and I imagine most people miss it, but here it is: "Wilson Levy and Amber Akinyi whispered the story of their vacation to Luftnarp last spring."

Look! They have last names! Also, a little over a year after Wilson's faux pas, they took a European vacation together. They apparently did go on that date after Street Cleaning Day. Wilson seems to have learned to pace himself, and I think they're falling in love.

That's all I ever want for two completely made up people who have almost zero backstory or personality.

I try to drop hints about their lives every so often into Night Vale. It's rare and usually brief. As of this writing, we're 135 episodes into the show, so I can tell you to look for updates on Wilson and Amber in Episodes 57, 103, and 130.

—Jeffrey Cranor

It is autumn, and nature is vanishing. It
is autumn, and nature is beautiful.

# WELCOME TO NIGHT VALE

It's that time of year again, listeners! This Friday night is Night Vale
High School's homecoming game! I'm not much of a sports fan, but
this is the one game I truly care about. All of the Night Vale High
alumni come together for it. Everyone: current students, former students, students long dead, future students who aren't born yet. It's
the one night we can see our loved ones who have been lost to time
and mortality. The dead alumni come out at halftime and we all get
to visit with them while the marching bands go spearhunting for
dinner.

I can't wait to see my late mother again this Friday night, especially after I found those old cassette tapes last fall. I have so many
questions. Important questions. And with Carlos out of town, I've
gotten kind of isolated, a little hermit-like lately. I need to get out.
This year's Homecoming means more to me than ever.

Plus, we're playing the Red Mesa High School Ant Carpenters,
who were dreadful last year. So, should be a fun night and a big win
for our team.

. . . team? It's a football TEAM, right? A baseball club, a soccer
unkindness, a hockey murder, a football team. Yes. That's it. Team.

And now a public service announcement from the Night Vale Seismological Society, who have released their schedule of upcoming municipally-planned earthquakes.

On Sunday, from 8:00 A.M. to 8:30 A.M. there will be a small series of minor tremors. It's likely you'll feel nothing, the seismologists say, as these quakes are just to test some new equipment.

At 3:00 P.M. on Tuesday, there will be an enormous earthquake, rating upwards of seven to eight on the Richter Scale, so wear long sleeves, or goggles, or gloves. Whatever it is you do to be safe during an earthquake. We're not entirely sure, the Night Vale Seismological Society said.

The following Saturday, be ready for anything. They're not sure what's going to happen. Maybe nothing. Probably nothing. Buuuuuuut, hopefully something really, really cool. They don't want to get your hopes up. So just be on the lookout, but no promises.

Oh man, fingers crossed, this could be super amazing, the Night Vale Seismological Society said.

This just in. There's news breaking of a possible scandal involving one of the Night Vale football players: senior running back Malik Herrera. According to an investigative report by Leann Hart of the *Night Vale Daily Journal*, Herrera doesn't actually exist. Like he's right there when you look at him, and he plays in a team of other players, so it would make more sense for him to be there than not, but Hart claims in her report that the all-district running back is, in fact, completely fabricated.

Anonymous sources say that Herrera is collectively imagined by the Night Vale High School fan base—a shared dream in the form of a boy who won the district rushing title the past two years and was freshman of the year three seasons ago. Red Mesa is threatening to cancel this Friday's game if Night Vale does not bench Herrera, citing district league rule 12, article 6 that states "All players must be real people. Don't not be a person, okay?" The rule continues:

"Because if you're not really real. . . . Man, I'm mad just thinking about it."

Night Vale High School head coach Nazr al-Mujaheed said they will not bench any player until a full investigation is performed, which can't happen until Tuesday, maybe. Monday at the earliest. Coach al-Mujaheed then concluded his statement by removing his goat-horned headpiece and comically large sunglasses, revealing tattoos of cat eyes on his eye lids.

"Cool!" the gathered reporters shouted.

Night Vale, if there's no game, there's no homecoming. If there's no homecoming, we will miss the one chance we have this year to see our lost loved ones. I will miss the chance to talk to my mother, to see many of my friends. To get out for once and not feel so lonely. We will not have our biggest night

of the year to come together as a community. I hope this scandal is not true, and, if it is, that it doesn't, you know, ruin anything.

Well, there is at least one old friend I'll get to see. Listeners, I'm so excited for this next segment. My old friend Earl Harlan is in studio today! Earl is the new sous chef at Night Vale's hottest restaurant, Tourniquet, and he's here to teach us a simple and delicious dessert recipe.

Welcome Earl!

**EARL:** It's good to see you again, Cecil. It's been a long time.
**CECIL:** Many of you listening may not know this, but Earl and I grew up together. We fell out of touch for a while, and then he was taken to another world during a Boy Scout ceremony, but I recently saw his name in the news releases about Tourniquet.
**EARL:** We were very close friends.
**CECIL:** We were, Earl. What happened after high school? I completely lost track of you.
**EARL:** Well, I turned nineteen, and I was nineteen for a long time. I don't even know how long. I was nineteen for longer than I care to admit. And then one day I was suddenly a grown-up. I had a kid and a house and a job.
**CECIL:** Some of us mature early. Some of us mature late. Sounds like you had plenty of youth left to live after high school and you just came to adulthood later.
**EARL:** Cecil, I meant that literally. I was literally nineteen for . . . I think it was decades, maybe a century or more. I don't know how long. Cecil, we graduated the same year, right?
**CECIL:** Of course we did. I remember our graduation party. We drank an entire case of warm orangemilk and told dirty jokes about the moon until we were frightened off by the sunrise.
**EARL:** What year was that? Cecil, what year did we graduate?

[*a very very long pause*]

**EARL:** You don't remember, do you Cecil?

**CECIL:** [*interrupting*] Tell us about your recipe, Earl!

**EARL:** Okay. Sure thing. Tiramisu is a popular dessert at many restaurants, especially at Tourniquet, but few people make it at home. Once they hear how easy it is, and how delicious Chef Mason's recipe is, they'll want to make it all the time. They'll want to never stop making tiramisu.

**CECIL:** Sounds good.

**EARL:** [*continuing over Cecil's last line*] *Never* stop making it. They'll lose their minds making it, Cecil.

**CECIL:** So what all do you have here. What will listeners need?

**EARL:** Everyone should have most of these ingredients already at home: a carafe of pre-made coffee, six eggs (go ahead and separate them into whites and yolks, but make sure to remove organs, teeth, and other debris), salt, two tablespoons of cocoa, one-third cup of sugar, two cups of mascarpone (which is a kind of fish), a package of gluten free ladyfinger cookies, two ounces of dark rum, and Chef Mason's special culinary touch: one and one-half cups of ground nutmeg.

**CECIL:** Oooh, I love nutmeg. It's been deveined, right?

**EARL:** Yes, you can buy deveined nutmeg at most supermarkets, but in case you're grinding it fresh at home, make sure to remove the thick vein running up the nutmeg's spine after you kill and clean the animal.

To start, just whisk the egg yolks and one-fourth cup of the sugar in one bowl and then work in the mascarpone. Then, in a separate bowl, you'll want to mix the egg whites, a pinch of salt, and the remaining sugar until firm. Like this.

[*There is the sound of heavy machinery and crunching, maybe the birds of prey noises too?*]

**CECIL:** That looks easy!

**EARL:** Mix that into the first bowl and add the coffee and the rum. Then dip the cookies into the mixture, lay them into a baking dish, cover with your ground nutmeg, and . . .

**CECIL:** Oh dear, Earl. I feel so silly saying this, but there's no oven here. I brought a professional chef to do a recipe on my show, and I don't even have a working kitchen.

**EARL:** Relax, Cecil. We wouldn't have time to completely cook a tiramisu on the air. It takes hours of slow baking in an earth oven. I already brought a finished tiramisu.

**CECIL:** Earl, how sweet of you. This looks delicious. I can't wait to share it with the staff.

**EARL:** Be careful. It is quite poisonous.

**CECIL:** Of course. Thanks for coming on the show. And congratulations on the huge success of Tourniquet. I hope to get a reservation there soon. Will you come on our show again with more tasty recipes? Maybe we can make this a regular cooking feature?

**EARL:** I'd love to, Cecil. I think we really have something here.

**CECIL:** Me, too.

And now a word from our sponsor.

Today's program is brought to you by Staples. Staples has the largest collection of office supplies anywhere. From printer toner to paperclips, Staples has everything you could possibly ever want to run your business. Just imagine it.

Imagine your office. A great mahogany desk with ornate leg carvings depicting old gods. A crisp new suit and high-backed chair made of a rare animal hide. Imagine a workforce that has all it needs to succeed. Imagine an open floor plan allowing you the freedom to see the stars, which geometrically describe the shapes of old gods. You wail to the stars. You howl your strategic plan to the stars. The old gods like your presentation.

You smell prey. [*whispered underneath: Smell the prey!*] Follow the bloodscent. Imagine the distant cries of your colleagues baying beneath moonlit pines, their teeth glistening with hunger. Imagine teamwork. Imagine a business running at its most efficient. Imagine a lone deer, trapped against a wild stream, a wounded leg, nowhere to run, surrounded. It will fight, but your business will fight harder. You have everything you need. Plus there's that refreshing stream, for a cold drink, when you are through with this gory work.

Staples. Worship Old Gods.

Terrible news, listeners. Just terrible news. Red Mesa High School has called off Friday night's game. There will be no homecoming. The campers and RVs that had started to fill up the Night Vale stadium parking lot have begun to file out.

Malik Herrera, the running back accused of a false existence, apologized for not being more transparent and for letting down his school and community. The Night Vale School Board forced the team's hand by suspending Herrera for his corporeal unreality, but it was too late. The game had already been forfeited. Our homecoming is no more.

I had so much I wanted to say to my mother. I imagine all of you had so much you wanted to say to your lost loved ones, to say to each other. I imagine all that could have been and all that is now lost. Our biggest community event of the year is gone, perhaps, because we imagined too much.

And to make things worse, a dangerous storm front is moving right now into Night Vale. You should seek shelter immediately from the eminent rain. And as a duty of public safety, I must take you now to the weather.

**WEATHER: "Understood" by Y.R Generation**

It's been five days, Night Vale, since that weather report began. It was a historically massive storm, and we needed the ongoing weather coverage. I hope you are all okay. I'm looking at some of you right now and you seem just fine. So, that's good news.

Sadly, the homecoming game remained canceled. League officials conducted an investigation into Malik Herrera's reality and determined he was indeed not real. They said he was tangible. They could feel a body when they touched him. They could hear a voice when they spoke with him. They could see a boy when they looked at him.

But Red Mesa coaching staff presented, as evidence, a photograph of the many galaxies of our universe and, after viewing this, league officials determined that Herrera was too immeasurably small to be considered real. Coach al-Mujaheed argued that it is unfair to discriminate against someone based on their reality. Just because someone does not exist does not mean they do not deserve equal rights, equal pursuit of happiness.

Even if al-Mujaheed and Herrera's appeal holds up in the league, it can't bring back the homecoming we did not get to have. We did not get to see our dead friends and relatives this year, Night Vale.

We had unanswered questions. We had unfulfilled hugs. We had unacknowledged I-miss-yous. We did not get to cry that night the way we wanted to cry that night, Night Vale, the way that perhaps we want to cry every night.

Even if there had been a game, the rain from the weekend was so monstrous and so intense that it would've been postponed anyway. There would have been no halftime in that deluge.

But. . . . in spite of all this, coach al-Mujaheed called a pep rally last Friday, in a gesture of support for Malik Herrera. This, as any time, is when we should join as a town, despite the game that never was.

Students and alumni—unfortunately only those still living— met that night in a rainy parking lot, in the well-lit shadow of an empty football stadium, and we told stories. Inez Cordova told me about her son who has started to walk. Teddy Williams told me he finally rolled a 450 in bowling. Wilson Levy and Amber Akinyi whispered the story of their vacation to Luftnarp last spring.

I told my friend Diane Crayton about Carlos and how I miss him but how proud I am of the great work he is doing. Diane introduced me to her son Josh, who is a monarch butterfly. Later when I saw him, he was a motorbike. He's a sweet kid, that Josh.

Everyone was sad, and everything was perfect. We stayed late into the night under the fluorescent corona of the bleachers, eating damp barbecue, wearing our orange ponchos, and telling those tales we wanted to tell to those loved ones who have left us, telling them instead to those who we currently or may eventually love. Tears were hardly noticeable on our rain-streaked cheeks by the time we said our good-byes.

"Good-bye," we all said.

"You too," we all replied.

"Let's stay in touch," we all added with wildly varying levels of intention.

Before getting into my car, I saw Malik Herrera, standing alone wearing a full football uniform—shoulder pads, knee spikes and all. I told him he'll be playing again soon. We're all on his side, even though he's just a figment of our collective unconscious. He said, "I don't even like football, sir." He said he likes painting and found poetry. I told him he could be an artist if he wanted. "Only if the town imagines that for me," he said. "Well, you're a real trooper," I told him. "Just a trooper," he said, "I'm not real. I gotta get to practice now, Mr. Palmer." Then he put on his helmet and jogged away.

"It's two A.M.!" I called out, but he had already vanished into the unrelenting storm.

"It sure is, sir," he called back faintly in my mind.

I fell asleep easily that night. I dreamed of sun, of being with Carlos again, of a lighthouse that was not a lighthouse, of a world that is not anything at all.

Perhaps a dream of things yet to come.

Stay tuned next for a radio program that only dogs can hear.

And as always, good night, Night Vale. Good night.

**PROVERB:** I've got more rhymes than the Bible's got Psalms. (One hundred fifty-one. I've got one hundred fifty-one rhymes.)

# EPISODE 57:
## "THE LIST"

### DECEMBER 1, 2014

ONE OF THE GREAT JOYS OF HAVING A SHOW WITH A FEW YEARS OF story to it, is that there are innumerable branching off points that you as a writer can return to and expand upon. Since we treated the continuity of Night Vale as sacrosanct, no matter how surreal it got, this allowed us to treat every one-liner as a possible seed for an ongoing story. This is really enjoyable as a writer, and it leads to me sometimes combing through old episodes, looking for little ideas that I can build into a larger story. In this case, I was looking through one of our first episodes, Episode 16: "The Phone Call," and I stumbled upon a little joke about a list that everyone would have to memorize for their own protection. I was interested in this promise of a future point in which they would need to know the list, and so decided that the future point would arrive in this episode.

The traffic report for this episode has an interesting origin. It comes almost word for word from a one-woman show that I wrote my wife for her birthday the first year we were dating. She was a performer and I got the show I wrote her placed in a festival at Theater for the New City in the East Village. The show was primarily about a period of extreme anxiety I was going through at the time, much of it related to death. My anxiety about death during that time would sometimes become so strong that I would simply stop functioning, and I wrote the one-woman show as a way of arguing myself out of the state I was in. This fragment takes as its starting point the fact that Franz Kafka died thinking his works would all be burned and so he had no way of imagining the impact he would have on the world. It is about the way that our lives scatter out into the world in unexpected ways, even after our consciousness is gone. I would later find a simpler and much shorter way of writing the same idea: Death is only the end if you assume the story is about you.

The ad for this episode follows a simple technique that can lead to a number of interesting outcomes. Take an existing phrase. Tweak its language a bit. And then follow the logic of the resulting phrase to whatever dark and strange place it takes you. What started as a simple twist on a phrase can become a little short story, a slice of a sad world where all the pets have left us. Where did they go?

—Joseph Fink

Breathe deep. Deeper than that. Get far below
sea level and breathe. Breathe in a cave.
Breathe in a deeper cave. Breathe deeper and
deeper until you can't find your way back.

# WELCOME TO NIGHT VALE

Some of you might remember, but most of you won't, that you were given a list. Nearly two years ago you were given a list and told to memorize it. Exactly. Keep it safe so that, someday, it would keep you safe. Well, listeners, the Sheriff's Secret Police would like me to inform you that the someday you've been waiting for is this day. This is the day in which you will need that list we gave you. Do you still have it? Do you remember it? Exactly? Are you safe? Are you safe?

Well, we will all find out soon enough. Good luck.

Harrison Kip, adjunct professor of archeology at Night Vale Community College, announced today that he has found something out in the desert. "Whoa," he explained to no one, a dot in a vast landscape of sand and wind. "Oh man," he continued, looking at the thing he found. He has declined so far to describe what he has found or offer any details or, for that matter, do anything but stare at whatever this thing he found was and continue saying things like "Wow," and "They're never going to believe this."

We reached out to Sarah Sultan, president of the community college, for additional information, but she would not provide any, saying only that Harrison is on a private dig funded by a small group of anonymous sponsors.

She said, "Although I have never met them in person, I have spoken to the sponsors by telephone and they have our best interests at heart. I'm sure of it." She added, "Plus they totally funded this dig thing, so what am I going to do, just start asking questions?"

A lone helicopter on a precautionary sweep of that expanse of the empty desert reported that Harrison is still kneeling over whatever it is he has found, explaining to himself in an unrecognizable language the incredible nature of whatever that thing is.

More on this, eventually, I guess, whatever.

The Greater Night Vale Medical Community, in conjunction with the mayor's office, announced the new city-wide campaign for Meatless Mondays. Each week, in recognition of the immense impact of meat on the environment and public health, Meatless Mondays will be the days we all set aside to try not to be made of meat. We will all sit quietly and attempt to will ourselves into a state of inorganic bliss, seeking to turn our feeble bodies into metal or silicon or stone. When we fail to do this, as is likely according to the most recently issued laws of physics, we will all engage in a group Denouncing Circle to try to understand whose betrayal is causing the continued failure of this important day.

And now a look at traffic.

We are eternal. We will not last.

Obviously you know that when you die, *the* matter that is *your* matter will just become "matter," no article attached. That matter will belong to any number of things. That matter is not you. That matter was never you.

We are eternal. We will not last.

But there is more to you than matter. When you die, you will not disappear until everyone who remembers you and whose actions are affected, however slightly, by your memory, until all of those people die and you are completely forgotten.

We are eternal. We will not last.

But even then you are not gone. Not until all the people who remember and are affected by those people who remembered and were affected by you are gone.

We will not last.

But even then you are not gone. Not until all the people who remember and are affected by those people who remembered and were affected by those people who and so on. And so on and on.

We are eternal.

You will persist, ever so faintly, ever so slightly, on into perpetuity, long after everything about you no longer matters.

Your life is so small, but, in the setting sun of this universe, its shadow is cast down through generation after generation, until it gets blurry, and hard to see, but still there, a breath of a wisp of a thread stretching out before you.

We are eternal, but we will not last.

There's a fender bender on Route 800 near exit 84B. Expect delays.

This has been traffic.

Update: We still aren't sure exactly when or how you will need that list today. You remember the list right? You were given a list some time ago. You should have memorized it. If you didn't, hmm. I mean, if you didn't, wellllllll. I mean, If you didn't, ermmmm. No one can make your destiny for you. Only you can make your destiny. Only you and the privileges you were born with and a whole lot of aimless, meaningless luck can make your destiny.

The Sheriff's Secret Police are going around town, checking in with everyone, and seeing if they have the list memorized. If you don't, they helpfully are shaking their heads and tsking and then saying "wow, you're in trouble," before leaving you to fend for yourself against whatever dangers this list would have protected you from.

More on this soon, as you desperately try to remember the list that was told to you, or even when it was told to you, and in what context. It is a very important list.

And now, a word from our sponsors.

An empty food bowl. An untouched water bowl. A silence in the house. A cage containing nothing. A feeling of unease that was once soothed by a joyous instinctual companionship.

We listen out our window and hear not a passing jangle. Not a "No" or a "Wait for me."

Nothing meows. Nothing does. Absolutely nothing meows.

The night is so quiet that our thoughts are a clatter keeping us awake. In the distance, a dog doesn't bark.

Petco: Where did the pets go?

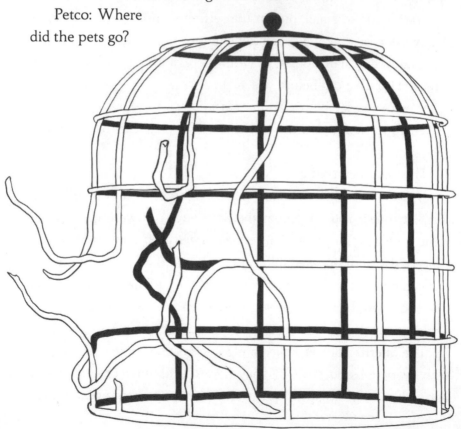

Old Woman Josie told me over a round of bowling down at the Desert Flower that construction on the new Old Opera House is continuing along well. They have already completed the initial arches, the outer floodbanks, and the primary stables.

"Yep," she said, holding her ball in preparation for her turn, "this town will soon have opera once again."

"But what is opera," everyone else in the league asked her. "Is it a kind of plant? Does it have rough, leathery skin?"

But she wouldn't say anything more, and just let go of the ball which was then carried by a creature named Erika—who definitely wasn't an angel—down the lane while Erika said "roll, roll, this is a ball rolling." And then Erika kicked over all the pins while saying "crash, bam, the ball just hit all these pins and knocked them all over. Wow, what a shot." Of course, none of us could legally acknowledge the existence of Erika, and so we had to let the strike stand uncontested.

And now an update on you.

Just now there was a man in a tan jacket, holding a deerskin suitcase, looking over your shoulder. You're sure of it. Only you don't quite remember it happening. It's blurry and distant, like a dream you had when you were little, and now as an adult you can't remember if it was a dream or something that actually happened to you.

But there was a man. There was a man, right? You grasp to recall but flail only at fragment and gap. He was looking over your shoulder with interest, a deerskin suitcase in his right hand. The suitcase was making a buzzing sound. Perhaps the man was, too? You don't remember.

None of this is real, you think. None of it happened. This is fiction. You are hearing a fictional story and this did not happen to you.

Still, you can't shake the feeling that it did happen to you. That just moments ago you turned and over your shoulder was a man in a tan jacket, holding a deerskin suitcase. He might still be there now.

You're afraid to check. Or maybe you already checked and now can't remember doing it. You turn to look. Nothing there. You turn back. Nothing there, you think with relief. Only now there is a question mark on it. Nothing there? Was there nothing there?

The man in the tan jacket spoke to you quite urgently about something. But what? He had a map. He was pointing at a place on the map. Now you don't even know what area of the world the map depicted, let alone where he was pointing.

This is all a made-up story, you tell yourself. You decide to feel entertained by the made-up story I just told to you. And yet. And yet. You can't shake the feeling, a feeling located just over your shoulder, that this made-up story might not be made up at all.

Oh, oh my. Listeners, the sun is gone. It is not covered by a cloud. It has left. And we know that the sun is generally pretty brave, and only leaves when something very frightening indeed is in the area. What could have frightened the sun away? Now is the time, I'm sure. Now is the time you need to know the list. Try to remember. Did you write it down perhaps? Scramble around in the junk drawer in the kitchen, among take out menus that are years out of date and fliers for health clubs that you never joined. Try to find where you wrote down that list.

But too late. There is a growl that comes from everywhere. Some sort of shape descends from the sunless clouds, and a voice, like through a loudspeaker, tells us that now is the time to recite the list. Or else. This is it. If you don't know, then you don't know.

I know. At least that. I know. Did Carlos know? Thank the mysterious lights in the sky he wasn't here. Who knows if his brain—so packed with science—would have let a few stray bits of language slip from his memory?

Listeners, those left to listen, I take you now, reciting the list, reciting for your very lives, to the weather.

Hazelnut. Mystify. Cuttlefish. Lark. Lurk. Rob—

**WEATHER:** "Upside Down World" by Paisley Rae

Beat. Beat Beat. Beat. Bea——— . . . oh. Oh, I am still here. I am looking at my fingers. I am examining my limbs. I am placing one hand on my chest, like in the Chanted Blood Oaths we were forced to swear to the flag each morning as children, and I feel the circulation of air and fluid through my body, the simple machine of liquid dynamics and electrical impulse that sustains, through some ridiculous coincidence of physical law, the sentience through which I am speaking to you.

Everything seems to be in order. In that I am nervous and uncertain and feel an emptiness sometimes which can never be filled, which maybe shouldn't be filled, and a sadness sometimes which wells up regardless of context or reason. So: everything perfectly in order. I'm fine.

We are, as a community, stepping out into the street. We are gathering in open places. I too am going. I too am stepping out into the street and gathering in open places. Here we all are in Mission Grove Park, and me among you speaking into this microphone, which, as always, I am uncertain is even connected to anything. But I don't care either way, because I know I am connected to all of you now.

I have felt disconnected lately. My being has been split between the here and the now, and the there and the now. My relationship with Carlos currently exists within the idea of distance, within the concept of space, rather than in any specific place. And there have been moments where I have doubted my fellow citizens, or have felt perhaps even threatened by them. But that is not the case now in this moment, here in this park.

Diane Crayton is with her son Josh, who this morning is a meadowlark. I feel only love for them.

Jackie Fierro, from the pawnshop, is showing Frances Donaldson of the Antiques Mall a cool knife that someone pawned by running in, shouting HIDE THIS, and running out. There is nothing not to trust and adore about this moment between fellow humans.

A cluster of hooded figures lurks along the corner of the park, pointing at various people, seeming to leer and laugh at the oblivious citizens. I am terrified of the hooded figures, but also comforted by their menace. I think they are even pointing now at me, whispering, and I have never felt more at home.

Janice, my young niece Janice, is here, joined with the rest of us in the park, along with her family, whom I don't like to talk about much, but whom I tolerate in all the requisite familial ways. Janice is with her friends Edmund and Megan and Patrice. She is waving to me. I am waving back. I am so glad she remembered the list. I am glad we all did.

There doesn't seem to be a single person missing. I counted, and every single resident of Night Vale is in the park and doing fine.

We heave our shoulders to express release. We sigh to show others we are relieved. We all breathe once in unison, accidentally.

"Wilson," says one of us to another. "How are things going, Wilson?"

"Oh, you know," says the other, although he does not know. "How are things with you, Amber?"

"Oh, good," she says, and she is right, things are good.

And they both take the hand of the person they love, and Amber smiles at Wilson and Wilson smiles at Amber and everyone smiles at everyone and at everything and no one is okay, exactly, but we're outside and we're smiling and that is a kind of perfection of its own.

Oh! A Sheriff's Secret Police representative arrives in the usual way, by rappelling from the sky and crashing into the middle of our happy huddle in a cloud of tear gas and flashing lights. As several people choke and disperse, the representative shouts to us that today was only a drill, that no one was in danger, that this was not actually the day we needed to know the list, although that day may someday come, is already coming, is imminent in the most general meaning of the word imminent, and that we are safe but that we are also in grave danger. "We are both at once and are thus free to fully enjoy our lives," a representative shouts into a bullhorn from somewhere behind a line of armored vans.

So there you are, listeners, all of you who have escaped the tear gas to listen to these words. We were safe all along. And we will stay safe until that time, sooner or later, but definitely always on its way, when we are not safe once again.

Stay tuned next for a surprised man shuffling papers frantically and saying "uh" into a mic he did not expect to be on.

Good night, Night Vale. Good night.

**PROVERB:** Beware of Greeks bearing gifts. Also beware of gifts of Greek bears. Gifted and bare Greeks are totally okay.

# EPISODE 58:
# "MONOLITH"

## DECEMBER 15, 2014

I LOVE SILENCE. OR RATHER, THE THEATRICAL DEVICE OF SILENCE. AC-tual, real-life silence is kind of upsetting. I don't like to be upset except when I'm engaging in art consumption and have agreed ahead of time to be upset as long as it is presented in an artistic way.

Silence in theater can be even more upsetting than real life silence. It usually indicates something has gone wrong: an actor went up on their lines, a technical failure, someone missed an entrance, etcetera.

But if you do it right, silence can be really rewarding. My first year in the Neo-Futurists, I wrote a short play called [*unusually long pause*]. Here's that play:

**EEVIN HARTSOUGH:** Hey, how's it going?
**JEFFREY CRANOR:** Fine. Just fine. [*brief pause*] You?
**E:** Great.
**J:** That's good.

[*short pause*]

**J:** This weather. Can you believe it?

**E:** Yeah, tell me about it. Whoo!

[*pause*]

**E:** How about all those sports?

**J:** Yeah! I'm having fun cheering for my favorite teams. How's that television drama you follow?

**E:** It's really great. I enjoy following the characters and gossiping about the actors, you know?

**J:** Sure. Yeah. No kidding.

[*longer pause*]

**J:** For the past twenty years, I've grown very perplexed about my relationship with my dad. We don't dislike each other. In fact, we get along okay. But now that he's in his 60s, I think he's feeling guilty about not being present when I was growing up, and the extra attention I receive from him these days seems forced. And I worry. I worry that maybe I'm fated to be a similarly distant and reluctant parent. Someday. If I ever have kids.

[*unusually long pause*]

**E:** Good to hear it!

**J:** Good seein' you.

**E:** You, too. Take care.

**J:** Don't do anything I wouldn't do.

That last unusually long pause was about forty-five to sixty seconds. And what was interesting about that was the audience response. About one second in, they realized the awkward pause and laughed at the simple gag. Then the laughter died down. About ten to fifteen seconds followed and there would be tittering again rising to full laughter and the process would repeat again, slightly more slowly but slightly louder too.

This was in 2007. I had only been writing material like this for a few months, so I had no idea this would happen like that. I loved it.

We use silence on occasion in Night Vale. This episode has one such example. (I encourage you to bookmark this page and go download and listen to Episode 58 just to hear how long that silence can actually feel.) I hope you laugh. I mean you're probably alone in a room, so laughing's kind of creepy to do by yourself, but you have my permission this one time.

—Jeffrey Cranor

If it looks like a duck and it quacks like a duck, you
should not be so quick to jump to conclusions.

## WELCOME TO NIGHT VALE

Listeners, someone built a monolith in front of City Hall overnight.
Last night there was no fifteen-foot tall, two-foot thick rectangle made
of blue slate towering over the faded grass and weakened tulip garden
in front of City Hall. But now there is. A monolith with indifferent
geometry and a long, sharp shadow cast by the low morning sun.

It is an ominous construction channeling ancient powers and
long-dead gods. Perhaps it is even connected to our primordial
extraterrestrial ancestry. And now, just a few days before Christmas,
this looming, dark stone shows up mysteriously in the night, casting
scornful shadows across both our dreams and our primitive understanding of the world.

It's super festive, and I love it!

Whoever put that thing up, good job. It must weigh twenty tons.
Don't know how you did it, but way to get us all into the holiday
spirit!

I talked to Carlos the other night, listeners. He's still trapped in
the—

Not trapped. I told him I'd stop saying he's *trapped* in the desert
otherworld. He's doing work there. He said after a few months of

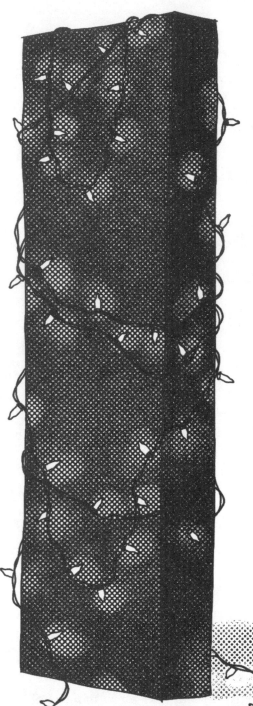

feeling helpless, he's made some friends—like the giant soldiers Doug and Alicia—and even gotten a lot of research done. He doesn't feel *trapped* at all.

I told him that he was locked in that alternate desert against his will and has been unable to return. So that seems to me like a pretty strong definition of trapped.

He said he used to feel that way, but now he no longer feels threatened by the rumbling beneath the sand or the strange armies that move about the beige wastescape, none of them fighting, only wandering. He feels like this desert—the most scientifically interesting place in the otherworld—is where he needs to be for now.

He quoted that old adage: "When God closes a door, God opens a window. Then God cracks a few knuckles. Then God kicks a pinecone up the sidewalk.

God also chews a whole bunch of gum. God recently quit smoking and is really fidgety." Carlos used that classic saying to point out that this desert is a great opportunity for his career as a scientist, and I respect that.

I asked if he found an old oak door with only one side that could possibly bring him back to Night Vale.

He said he hadn't, but then he asked, "Cecil, if I find that doorway, would you maybe come here again? Just for a visit. I want you to meet Alicia. Alicia has a bichon frise the size of a Prius and is really into astronomy. They also showed me some planets and comets they really like. Also the constellations change every night here. There are new shapes of mythic heros in the sky every night.

"I'd love you to come visit," Carlos told me.

"We'll see. It does sound nicer than I remember," I said.

"Neat," he said.

I'd love to be near Carlos again. We've had a great time talking nearly every night, but it's hard to know how much meeting eyes or touching hands means until it's gone. Plus, I could use a vacation. Other than that brief escape through that same desert otherworld this spring, I don't think I've been out of Night Vale, since . . . wow . . . Luftnarp? Svitz? Time flies, comma, is weird.

Oh, big news!

This Wednesday afternoon is the opening ceremony of the revitalized Old Town Drawbridge. Because of massive setbacks two years ago, and a complete lack of a body of water that would even necessitate a drawbridge, the opening was delayed by fourteen years, including a budget increase of over twenty million dollars. So technically we're still twelve years away from completion, but the City Council thought we might as well have the opening ceremony now.

"We've already burned through the twenty million dollars," the city council announced in unison via conference call from a cruise ship. The council were all wearing matching sunglasses and floppy hats and drinking a pastel liquid through long curly straws out of one large pineapple.

The opening ceremony will be held in a collective shared day-dream Wednesday afternoon. So make sure you're doing something that is unchallenging both physically and mentally on Wednesday so you can drift off into this fun community dream-event.

We're starting to get complaints about the new monolith that appeared overnight in front of City Hall. The monolith has begun to hover. I mean not by much. Don't freak out over a hovering mono-lith. It's like two or three inches, not a full foot or more.

The complaints, though, are not about the hovering. They're about the placement of the monolith. Our town (and country for that matter) was based on the separation of ancient long-dead reli-gions and state.

Juanita Jefferson, head of the community organization Night Vale or Nothing, announced her group's protest against a prominent symbol of old gods (and possibly our primordial extra-terrestrial or-igins) being displayed on government property.

The City Council retorted by slurping their cocktail loudly from the still-active Skype connection on a nearby Acer laptop that no one knew how to turn off.

Jefferson added, "Treeeeeeeees. They are us," and then bit into a small metal pipe wrapped in a hot dog bun. While she chewed, we could still hear her speaking clearly. "Treeeees," she said, her closed mouth moving in slow, undulating, cast-iron crunches.

Several others have come to Jefferson's side in this issue claim-ing that while they still fervently worship old gods—many show-ing off blood-stained shoes and sharp rocks wrapped in strips of flesh—they do not believe it is the government's place to express these beliefs so publicly.

"Slurrrrrrrrrrrrrrrrrrrrrrp," came the City Council's reply from the computer.

More on this controversy as it grows out of hand.

But first a word from our sponsor.

Today's show is brought to you by silent self-reflection. Are you aware of what's inside of you? No, not soft meats and deadly micro-organisms. More than that. What makes you *you*? How are you able to acknowledge that you are even a thing, separate from the rest of the universe?

Do you find yourself casting about in the white noise of the living world, your eardrums clogged with the filth of existence?

We here at Night Vale Community Radio recommend silent self-reflection. Give it a try. Here's some silence. During the silence, reflect on yourself. Reflect on your life, your being. Close your eyes and just reflect. Let in no sights, no sounds, and reflect.

Ready? Here goes.

[*thirty seconds of silence*]

Did you reflect? That was a long silence, right? Do you know how long that silence was?

It was two weeks! You've been unconscious for two full weeks. You've been pronounced legally dead. Your family misses you, but you're finally free to be the living ghost you've always dreamed of being. Congratulations. Enjoy a life free of legal consequence!

And now an update on the monolith.

Some protesters have shown up at City Hall carrying signs against the monolith. The signs read "NO MONOLITHS ON CITY PROPERTY" and then a slash through that phrase, which is confusing, because that seems like a double negative, but when you look closely, there's also a line through the NO part, so it's a triple negative which reduces down to a single negative.

There are other signs that are just painted solid colors, so it looks like the monolith has lost the support of the abstract expressionist community as well.

Fortunately, the Sheriff's Secret Police have already gently kettled the protesters into a fenced-in section of a distant parking lot where no one can see or hear their protests, thus keeping public order and still allowing for freedom of speech. A win-win.

Counterprotesters have also arrived in support of the monolith, demonstrating their distaste for people against the monolith. They are holding signs that have a picture of a monolith, or maybe it's the letter I or L or the number one. It's hard to say what with sans-serif fonts being all the rage these days.

Police have placed the counterprotesters into a pen next to the original protesters and covered both pens with an opaque and soundproof velvet drape.

We're getting word that the monolith is vibrating and loudly humming. Also it's glowing. But I don't know. I can't feel or see that, so not really my problem now is it?

Let's have a look at sports.

The Night Vale High School Scorpions had a rough 2014 season. It was capped off by a scandal involving junior running back Malik Herrera. The Scorpions had to forfeit all wins in which Herrera played, because he violated district rules by never truly existing.

One of the team's best defenders, senior safety Jessica Lexington, was sidelined most of the season with spinal parasites she got in late September after refusing to yield on a highway off-ramp.

Additionally, sophomore quarterback Henry Lexington, Jessica's younger brother, struggled in his first season as a starter. By year-end he showed some improvement as coach Nazr al-Mujaheed worked with Lexington on holding the ball with his own hands and throwing the ball with his own arms, not other people's, as he had been doing early in the season.

But on the bright side, it looks like former Scorpions quarterback Michael Sandero has gone on to great success after graduation. Many of you know Michael was recruited by a university called

Michigan. I'm not a big sports fan myself, so I have no idea what state the University of Michigan is located in, but apparently they have just completed an undefeated season with Michael as quarterback, and will compete in the college football playoffs against another school called Alabama (again, sounds like a private school; I've never heard that name before).

Michigan is favored to win the title this year, and Michael is a front-runner for the Heisman Trophy, given to college football's best player. His control over weather elements and powerful pyrokinesis skills proved invaluable to a previously struggling Michigan offense.

Good luck, Michael. Your hometown is cheering for you!

An update on the glowing and shaking monolith. The earth below it has split open, and the Secret Police have issued a statement saying they regret silencing the original protesters. They have since let the protesters out asking them to protest a little harder.

"Also protest closer to the monolith, okay?" the Secret Police shouted at the confused protesters whose eyes were still adjusting to the bright daylight after being in a dark pen all afternoon. "Try getting right up on the thing and protesting," the officers called from behind their cruisers.

The Secret Police also asked counterprotesters to try talking to the monolith. "You like it so much, why don't you marry it?" the Secret Police teased before adding "No seriously, go talk to that thing, okay? It's freaking us out."

But all protesters have scattered from the scene. The monolith is now shaking violently. I can hear it here in the station. I can feel it throughout my body. My skin is rattling. I can see the great, green glow. It is so bright, the cement walls of our station almost seem to be fading.

So as our physical being becomes either rent into atomic mist or subsumed by a sphere of cosmic energy, let me, in my final act as a tangible being, bring you today's weather.

**WEATHER:** "Anything I Want You To" by The Rizzos

Well the monolith split open. There was a deafening crack of shattered stone, a flash of blinding light, the stench and taste of sulfur as we felt rocky dust settling upon our cowardly, crouching backs.

In the hazy aftermath, we looked for the dead and found none. We looked for the wounded and found none. We looked for damaged streets and buildings and found . . . well, we found presents.

We found city streets strewn with gold-wrapped toys and parcels of fine chocolates. There were ornate bags filled with silk scarves and swirling gilded ribbons and glittery notes wishing every person in Night Vale seasons greetings, along with gift cards to popular stores like Target and the Ralphs and Hatred.

[*long pause, maybe a sigh*]

Look. I hate to rant. But given that Night Vale long ago abolished materialism, this seems like a cruel holiday prank. I'm glad no one was hurt, but this whole monolith thing was really annoying. It was not a deadly threat to our city or our lives, merely a time-wasting tribute to the worst qualities of the old gods. It took most of the afternoon to clean this mess up, but thankfully it's all been swept away and dumped into the landfill.

The City Council, upon hearing of the storm of holiday presents upon our town, swiftly and nobly returned from their tax-funded island vacation and offered their condolences for us having to witness this consumerist assault.

They reminded us that Santa is a CIA-created myth, and that the holidays shouldn't be about buying things or getting things or even giving things. Christmas, they chanted in unison, is about being a little less distrustful of neighbors. Of casting our eyes down more respectfully when we pass hooded figures or people wearing some kind of official-looking firearm. Christmas is about being at home with family, doors locked, everyone speaking clearly and within range of the hidden cameras.

At that moment a low-flying police helicopter passed over City Hall, its searchlight frantically flashing across the terrified face of every single citizen. It was truly a magical Christmas moment, and the whole crowd winced with holiday cheer.

One lone person asked "but isn't Christmas a religious holiday? Should the city really be promoting a religious holiday?"

The City Council quickly replied, "Not any religion that we're aware of," and the Secret Police kindly ushered that grumpy scrooge off to a less-public place.

Night Vale, sometimes we see something strange and different and our first reaction is to loathe and fear it. To bring rage and scorn against its very being. But that's not the Christmas spirit. This is the time of year we must learn to not shout down things we don't know or understand, but simply hide from them and later pretend they were never there at all.

And today we mostly did that. We mostly did good, Night Vale. Maybe it will be a merry Christmas for everyone. Maybe this is an auspicious start to the holidays.

Hey, that's the best part about the future: anything you want to be possible IS possible . . . as long as you don't think about it too hard.

Stay tuned next for the sound of something clawing its way out of your chest.

Good night, Night Vale. Good night.

**PROVERB:** It's not the size of the dog in the fight. It's the size of the *other* dog in the fight.

# EPISODE 59:
# "ANTIQUES"

## JANUARY 1, 2015

### GUEST VOICE: DYLAN MARRON (CARLOS)

I LIVE IN A REGION WITH A LOT OF ANTIQUE SHOPS. I DON'T KNOW FOR sure but based on driving around my area I would assume approximately 99 percent of my county's economy comes from New Yorkers buying antique clocks on weekend trips. Speaking of which, I once found a Chinese communist-themed clock in a local antique store. There are portraits of Mao, a second hand that is a fighter jet, and time is marked by a peasant waving a little red book. It's great.

Of course, in Night Vale antiques are some sort of dangerous wild animal. Other than that, I imagine antiquing works pretty much the same.

This episode features the slow growth of the plot of Chad and what he has done in the Shambling Orphan development. This started with the September Monologues, and the introduction of Chad. Chad, incidentally, came from the actor for the Faceless Old Woman, Mara Wilson, telling us that when performing her parts for the show, she often imagined she was whispering them into the ear of a frat-bro—type dude named Chad. "You've really disappointed me, Chad." So I decided to write her that monologue to Chad, and then that spun out into what would be the main plotline of the show well over a year later. This is the freedom of only two people writing a show: the storytelling can follow whims and interesting detours.

I didn't want this plotline to be too noticeable at first, and so I did my best to not have the same identifying details in a row when including it in the episodes but did include enough information that someone paying attention could start to connect the incidents. Can you find the others?

This episode might have the strangest intern death of any of the ones we did. I don't actually remember what all of them are, so there's probably something stranger somewhere in there, but "Bitten by an antique, and so turned into an antique himself" is a pretty interesting way to go. Most of us will just get cancer, you know?

The deaths of the interns was a running joke, one with many obvious antecedents. From *Spinal Tap* to *South Park* to *Harry Potter*, a job that is an invitation for immediate disaster to the long list of people who keep taking it is a classic. But like many others who use this joke, it started to get less interesting as we went on, and so as I write this, our most current intern has been in the position for almost two years and is still chugging away. Good old Intern Kareem. You finally broke the cycle. For now.

—Joseph Fink

It's not darkest before the dawn. It's actually darkest after all the stars have gone out. It's very dark then.

## WELCOME TO NIGHT VALE

We begin this new year with some troubling news.

Frances Donaldson, owner of the Antiques Mall, has reported that some of her antiques have escaped.

She said that when she fed them this morning they were all accounted for, but when she went back for the usual mid-afternoon watering, the fence had been cut, and over half of the antiques were missing.

"They didn't escape," she corrected reporters who were just trying to talk to her a bit about what had happened, were just doing their best to help her out, and so didn't need to have their heads bitten off for using a different word, but whatever. "They didn't escape," she said. "They were set free."

All surveillance cameras in the immediate vicinity (and this is not a particularly interesting or dangerous part of Night Vale, so there were only 344) had been disabled or moved to point away from the antiques' pen or had their tapes replaced with VHS cassettes full of *Matlock* episodes recorded and rerecorded over each other so that each tape showed ghosts of every Matlock at once, a single unified Matlock through the flicker and warp of video age.

The Secret Police warn citizens that antiques are wild animals and, while generally friendly, their behavior can be unpredictable. If you see an antique, do not approach it. Simply put your hands over your chest, scream "We're all about to be eaten," and run blindly away.

Although it's possible this may cause the antique to instinctually go into hunting behavior and chase you. "We didn't bother to check. Look, we were kind of busy. Was there something stopping you from doing this research?" the Sheriff's Secret Police concluded, before shaking their heads and melting back into the walls.

StrexCorp Synernists Inc., the company you might remember as our former unfriendly overlords (or you might not remember them if your memory has been altered or erased). Anyway, StrexCorp is, of course now owned by beings that are difficult to describe without using the illegal term *angels* but who are all named Erika.

As part of their continual process to turn the power of StrexCorp toward the betterment of

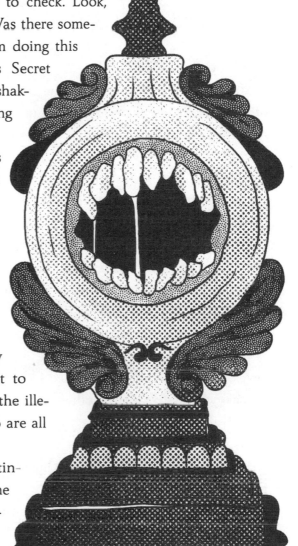

our world, the Erikas have started the process of releasing those people whose lives StrexCorp took possession of back during what could be termed its "bad boy days" or "dystopian capitalist hell days," whichever you prefer.

Among those released is Janice Rio, from down the street, last seen entering a condo, which you should definitely never do. Never go into a condo.

Also released, Lucy and Hannah Gutierrez, former owners of the former White Sand Ice Cream Shoppe, that's bankruptcy led to their lives being confiscated by Strex. They are looking well and fit, no worse for the wear than any ordinary person who is, say, imprisoned by the City Council in the abandoned mine shaft outside of town for voting incorrectly on municipal elections. We all experience extralegal, extended imprisonment at some point in our lives after all.

They pledged to restart their Ice Cream Shoppe and are currently running a Kickstarter to gather together the funds. In order to get better results, the Kickstarter is labeled as being for a blender you can plug an iPhone into to get real-time blending stats and earn blending points on the blending community. It is not actually for that though. It's for an Ice Cream Shoppe, and I don't know about you, but I can't wait to have another bite of that magical Gutierrez ice cream.

Chad Boenger, who lives in the Shambling Orphan housing development down by the haunted baseball diamond, said, "It is a sadness what we do to each other. It is a weeping and a gnashing of teeth."

I don't think this was in relation to StrexCorp, or Kickstarter, but he walked by and said that to me so I thought I'd throw it in. Thanks, Chad!

And now another edition of the Children's Fun Fact Science Corner.

Stick out your tongue. Farther. Farther. Is that really as far as you can get it? I bet you can get it a little farther than that. Wow, that's like three feet. Honestly I expected an inch or so. Now it's at five feet. How long is your tongue? How long is a tongue supposed to be? Can we get someone to check on that?

This is starting to freak me out a little, your endless tongue. This was supposed to be a fun and challenging exercise, but now I'm questioning everything about myself and my life. I'm shivering. Your tongue is reaching out the door, it's down the street, it's rolling out of town. Look how far your tongue stretches. You have not done well, young child, but you've certainly done something. You certainly have.

And somewhere the tip of your tongue is still rolling on, tasting a world that neither it nor you can see.

Say, are you related to . . . never mind. It doesn't matter.

Oh god, that tongue. That hideous, infinite tongue.

This has been the Children's Fun Fact Science Corner.

There are many reports coming in about the missing antiques. People have seen antique tracks, have heard creatures rooting around in their garbage, grazing on their lawns, loping through their backyards. It has been difficult to tell which direction the antiques are moving, because many of these reports contradict each other, and most are likely people mixing up the antiques with other similar-looking animals like owls or hyenas or bacteria.

Intern Maureen, who has, all told, been intern longer than anyone I can remember—well done, Maureen!—anyway, Maureen is back at school right now, so her friend Hector is taking over for a bit. Hi Hector, great to have you on.

Intern Hector is waving. He's saying hello. He doesn't have a mic so his hello doesn't exist for you. Nothing exists for you outside of my voice saying it does.

Anyway, Hector, can you do me a favor and go check out what's going on with the escaped antiques? Reports are muddled and we need someone on the ground, so to speak, in the ground, as they say, buried deep in the earth, as the saying goes, to understand what's really going on here.

Hector is nodding. Now that nod exists for you. Good-bye, Hector. Until we see you again, very soon and very well, I'm sure.

Now this: Imagine a man. This is a simple command leading to millions of conceivable scenarios. Imagine this man. Every possible physical form, location, and condition that a man can be in. Perhaps this man has been dead so long he is dust. Perhaps you are imagining dust and perhaps you are not wrong. Imagine a man. Imagine him. There is a buzzing lightbulb above him. He is standing on what could loosely be called the porch of what could loosely be called a tin shack. The lightbulb buzzes and buzzes. He looks up in irritation. You were wrong to imagine him as dust. Do you have him now? Do you know what he looks like? Imagine a man.

No, I'm sorry no. You were incorrect. And so the weekly Find The Man I'm Thinking Of contest will roll over to the next week. This is the 300th consecutive week without a winner, and the prize for next week will be 301 custom-made pencils that say I WON A THING. I hope someone wins soon. The giant box of pencils here is starting to get in the way of things.

Oh, guess who's in the studio with me. Well, not actually with me, but projecting himself into our physical plane. That's right, my favorite scientist and yours, but mostly mine, Carlos.

**CARLOS:** Hi, Cecil.
**CECIL:** Carlos, I know we just talked last night, but for the listeners, why don't you tell us what's new out in the desert otherworld you're tra——the desert otherworld you're spending some time in.
**CARLOS:** Well, I've been doing so much interesting research. I've learned the composition of the rocks, which are not of our world.

And the composition of the components of the rocks, which are of our world, strangely. And I'm trying to figure out how many stars there are. They are always changing size and position, but I do think there are a lot of stars.

**CECIL:** That sounds very scientific.

**CARLOS:** It is so scientific. The most scientific. I don't think I've ever been more scientific, and you know how much I love science.

**CECIL:** Yes, I am also very into science. But I miss, you know, touching. I miss this. Listeners, you can't see but I'm trying to hold his hand, and my hand is just going through him because he's not actually here.

**CARLOS:** I know. That's why I'm working on a way for you to visit. I think you'd like it here. It's super interesting and there's so much science. Plus people are way friendlier here. People in Night Vale can be a little . . .

**CECIL:** No, I know. I suppose it couldn't hurt to take a little visit, but I need to be back at my radio desk soon. It can be difficult to ask Station Management for time off work.

**CARLOS:** Great, I'll let you know when I figure out exactly how to get you here. I can't wait to see you in person again.

**CECIL:** Me neither.

**CARLOS:** Cannot wait. Cannot. It's going to be good.

**CECIL:** [*overlapping*] Oh, okay. Me neither. Well, thanks so much for this highly relevant report that had important information for everyone in town. Thanks, Carlos.

**CARLOS:** Bye, Cecil!

**CECIL:** Bad news, listeners. It seems that the antiques have gathered around City Hall and are behaving in threatening ways toward anyone trying to leave or enter. We are getting reports that while City Council has already safely evacuated using a rocket sled that they keep for this very purpose, Mayor Dana Cardinal is still trapped inside. The Sheriff's Secret Police are responding quickly by issuing press releases to explain why it's definitely not their job to deal with this situation because, frankly, it seems pretty dangerous and scary. They said that they have activated all available officers to work hard on deflecting responsibility away from them.

As the Sheriff's Secret Police slogan goes: "Not our job. Not our problem."

Oh no, I'm being told that the antiques have found a way into City Hall. The pack is entering the building. City Hall has been infiltrated by hungry antiques with no one left to protect our mayor. Who will protect Dana? Someone. Someone must. Will no one step forward? Will no one? Is anyone even listening to this? What kind of town are we? What kind of town are we?

Also, here's the weather.

**WEATHER:** "State of Mine" by Stöj Snak

*[very slightly out of breath]*

Well, listeners. Well, well. Listeners, it seems, it seems that all is well.

We don't know how, but our beloved mayor is safe once again. A person of unknown identity appeared on the scene, running into the City Hall and single-handedly defending the mayor's office against the pack of antiques.

This was foolish of that person. That person could have been killed or gravely wounded. Maybe they were. We don't know who the person is or where they went, and so their fate is as nonexistent as anything else I do not or cannot voice.

Mayor Cardinal gave a message of thanks, saying: "Whoever you are, thank you. I do not speak for the town, or for the city government. I speak for myself. As a person, as a human full of blood and worry, thank you for keeping me safe," she said.

Pamela Winchell, Director of Emergency Press Conferences, held an Emergency Press Conference in which she added to the mayor's statement by saying, "Clouds are the belt of the sky. Cinch them tighter. Make the clouds go tighter. Make the sky come closer." before hurling herself into the sky until she was just a dot in the upward distance.

So that seems to be another crisis averted, albeit in a sudden, and if I may be frank as a journalist, narratively unsatisfactory way. Perhaps we will never know who that unknown savior is or who the unknown liberator of the antiques was. Perhaps we will never know anything. We have certainly never known anything yet.

But wait. Intern Hector is returning. Hector, did you see who the unknown benefactor was? Do you have any information?

Oh no, Hector, he is . . . Hector he is holding up his arm. There is a tear in the skin, a deep and jagged oval. He has been bitten.

Oh, Hector. It was you. Wasn't it? I sent you to report and instead you involved yourself, and I thank you for doing so. Ordinarily that would be a violation of journalistic standards, which clearly say we should never help when we could merely watch, but Dana is a friend of mine. And so I thank you for ignoring our sacred rules just this once.

I'll be honest. I wouldn't have thought Hector was the type to do something like that, or even physically strong enough to fight off an entire pack of antiques. But people can surprise you. That is one of the things that people can do.

But Hector. That bite. You know what happens to someone who is bit by an antique. Hector is unable to speak, has been unable to speak since he arrived. Listeners, of course anyone bitten by an antique, becomes an antique themselves. Intern Hector, if only there was something I could do for you.

He is transforming. His body is elongating and lowering. His shoulders turn to haunches, his arms to wings, his feet to bladed multilegs. He is becoming an antique before my eyes, and I can do nothing for him. For this brave young person who saved my dear friend Dana.

He is out of sight now. I can hear only a click, a shuddering movement. He must have fully transformed into an antique. Hector? Hector? Is there any trace of your old self left? Or are you already hunting me? How good are the bolts on the studio door? He can't come in here, can he? I hear a rattle in the ceiling. There is a clear, viscous substance dripping onto my desk. I dare not look for its source.

Coming up next, hopefully, the sound of my successful escape from this room. Who just touched me? Hector? Hector?

Well, this is it, one way or another. Here I go, listeners. And here you go, off into radio silence, into places and times where my voice can no longer guide you.

Good night, Night Vale. Good night.

[*A clatter and running feet. A door slamming. Strange animal noises. Then off in the distance:*]

I made it. I'm fine. To the family and friends of Intern Hector—

**PROVERB:** If you want a picture of the future, imagine a person writing headlines about millennials forever.

# EPISODE 60:
## "WATER FAILURE"

### JANUARY 15, 2015

**GUEST VOICES: ERICA LIVINGTON (PHONE TREE), CHRISTOPHER LOAR (PHONE TREE), FLOR DE LIZ PEREZ (LACY)**

I THINK I WAS ASKED TO BE THE PHONE TREE IN A TEXT FROM JEFFREY. It didn't read exactly like that, "Will you be the phone tree?" But it also wasn't far from that. I said yes, obvs. Truth be told, it was a huge tether for me as I had a one-and-a-half-year-old son, had stepped away from art and theater in my pregnancy and had not really returned. Juggling a toddler is no joke and I had started a new career as a doula. So the ask of "Will you do this art stuff with us?" was so welcomed from these old friends that I had previously adored collaborating with.

The day of the recording I went to Meg and Joseph's place in Williamsburg, Brooklyn, stoked that it was by the Blue Stove and I'd have the excuse to get a slice of pie and a coffee from there. Meg and Joseph's place was so fun, as one might imagine, decorated with ease and eclectic eccentric joys, it's a very cozy place to set yourself down in. Once we were set up in the recording room and had had an appropriate amount of catching up talk and story swapping, I remember Joseph just saying, "Are you ready?" and I said "Yes." He hit record and I started reading the text. Once done he stopped the recording and was like, "Great." I was so confused. "Aren't you gonna give me notes or something?" "No, you nailed it." I couldn't handle the idea that I had just gotten it in the first take so against Joseph's desire I did two more takes. I know for sure he used the first one because he made a point to tell me this later. It was nice to hear. Now, here's the unexpected part of this tale, this lil' ole intro I'm writing . . . this was an important moment for me. It's a tiny thing but a story I've told before and will continue to tell. It's a moment of confidence in others. In trusting your friends. In trusting that art can be simple and easy and just fun. This is some of the truth that Jeffrey and Joseph have always taught me in little and huge ways. Night Vale and its creation is all about this. About taking what comes, trusting it and leaning into it. When I was later asked to do the voice of Alice in the podcast *Alice Isn't Dead* this story returned as guidance for recording that season. I went in believing that it could always be easy and fun, and that the first take isn't a throw away but in fact, frequently, the best one.

In the fictional world Joseph and Jeffrey have created, all conspiracy theories are real, the faucets are leaking yummy/scary smells, and who knows how many suns there are today, but in the real world they've created an artistic space for their friends to collaborate, an opportunity to put to good use the hundreds of logged hours on various phone trees, and a valuable world where you can just nail it in one take.

—Erica Livingston

**See some evil. Hear some evil. Speak some evil.**

# WELCOME TO NIGHT VALE

Sorry to start the show off with such a minor issue, but the water here at the station is not working. I was trying to make coffee. I got out the filters, grabbed some whole beans from the larder, finely ground them using a hammer and hateful thoughts, and placed them, one ground at a time, into the coffee machine, but when I went to fill the carafe, there was no water. I turned the faucet handle, and just heard a faint hiss. Forty-five minutes worth of coffee preparation for nothing.

This also means the toilets aren't working. Fortunately there's a huge ravine right next door to the station, so that's that taken care of.

Honestly, I probably shouldn't lead off my show with a personal complaint about how there's no water instead of an important news story like how there are suddenly two suns instead of one. But I can't help it. I just get all worked up about a lack of coffee. It's fine. I'll be fine.

But yeah, there are definitely two suns now and people are screaming in the streets. It's pretty apocalyptic out there with buildings being burned down and cars wrecking into fire hydrants and people running in all directions, mouths agape, clutching their heads. So stay inside and avoid thinking too hard about the capriciousness of our only home: the indifferent universe.

Let's have a look now at sports.

Former Night Vale High School quarterback Michael Sandero had a fantastic freshman season at the University of Michigan. He won the Heisman Trophy, and his team made it to the national championship game. Unfortunately, they lost in overtime to Michigan.

It was the first time in college football history that a team had to play against itself in the title game. Down by three points in overtime, Sandero threw a late interception, thus sealing his team's loss.

Sitting dejected on the bench, their heads hung low and shoulders sagging under the weight of regret, Sandero and his teammates could only watch as the other Sandero and his teammates celebrated their victory over themselves.

The winning Michigan team celebrated on the field until late into the night, everyone else having long since gone home and the lights turned out, until a flock of starlings covered their cheering, dancing bodies and carried them all into the sky.

Speaking through a Russian translator, the losing Sandero said, "I do not know where I am. Where is Michigan? I am so confused right now. Who are you? Who are you?" He was staring suspiciously at his own hands and crying.

Better luck next year, Michael. You can do it!

Many listeners have been wondering if I'll be taking time off of work to go visit Carlos in his desert otherworld. Well the answer is maybe.

I certainly would like to. I miss him so much, but first Carlos has to find the doorway between our worlds. Also, even trickier, I have to get vacation days approved by our station management, which is not easy.

I filled out the special form to request days off, which includes writing a 2,500-word description of what I will be doing with my time away from work. It had to be exactly 2,500 words, and I'm not sure if hyphenated words count as one or two.

Anyway, I submitted my form last Wednesday by going to Station Management's office door, genuflecting, and reciting the pledge of employee fealty, which is several minutes long. I was actually blocking the only path to the kitchen, so by the time I finished, there was a long line of co-workers waiting on me. All of them at some point have gone through this same emotionally devastating process when they wanted to visit a new nephew or go on a honeymoon or something. So they were understanding, but I chose to do this around noon, so they were also mostly hungry and frustrated.

Once I finished the pledge, I dropped the form into the drop box, which then glowed red and puffed out dark smoke. When I got back to my desk area, all of my belongings were gone and there was just an open pit, a hole that seemed to go on into eternity, and knowing management, it likely does. So the request was definitely received and we'll see what they come back with.

[*hissing sound from end of Episode 3*]

Oh dear. Station Management sounds upset. I don't know if it's because I'm talking about them on the air or if they're just now finding out that the toilets aren't working. Either way, let's move on.

Speaking of the water, all of the taps in our building are blowing a cool, dry air that smells of . . . toasted walnuts maybe? Or no. No, like French toast. Either way, it's pleasant. We've tried to turn off the faucets, but the handles just spin loosely and have seemingly no effect on the smell.

We tried calling the plumber but they just screamed something about there being four suns. FOUR SUNS, they howled into the phone before muttering for a while about nothing being as it seems, we've been duped by god, all is lost, blah blah something something

living nightmares. So I guess we're going to have to contact the water department directly about this issue.

Oh, also I should have mentioned earlier the two suns have now
doubled to four suns. There are now four suns in the sky. So that's
awful. But listen, better than no sun, right? Man, days with no sun
are just the worst.

You know what's not the worst? The sponsor of today's show.

Our program is brought to you today by Chevrolet and their
new line of all electric vehicles. These vehicles are made entirely

of electricity. You already own one. There's a Chevrolet inside your home's wiring this very moment . . . your microwave, your television. You will have to harness that power and learn to turn pure electricity into matter and then that matter into an operational vehicle and then figure out how to operate that vehicle. But it's all there. Right now. In your home.

In fact, since you already have the car, don't you think you should have paid for it? Don't you think you owe Chevrolet for the car you have? That's how the world works. There are no free cars, pal. Nope, please send $45,000 to Chevrolet right now. Or return the vehicle. You either pay the money or return the car. One or the other. That's only fair, right?

Chevrolet. We're trying to be reasonable here.

Local television station Channel 6 has come under fire recently for their decision to start broadcasting into viewer's homes whether viewers want to watch Channel 6 or not.

Many residents have written to their government representatives saying it must violate some law for a television news station to broadcast straight into people's homes without the residents even turning on their televisions. "It must be a violation of privacy laws, right?" these letters often read. Surely, the government must step in to stop this, the letters usually conclude.

We hear your concerns, but the government cannot stop this, the reply always says. The local television news station is controlled and managed by the government, and it is wonderful to be able to reach everyone in town at every point of the day with important news, the letter always continues.

Like, let's say there's a tornado—a rare event here in the desert, to be sure, but let's just say, the letter always supposes. How would you know how to protect yourself from such a danger if there were no government-controlled television station that could turn on in your home and shout terse, esoteric orders in a foreign language

(Let's say Russian! [It doesn't have to be Russian.]) as slow motion footage of salamanders running out of a rotting log plays? How would you know, the letter challenges. You wouldn't, the letter declares.

Maybe it's not an emergency, the letter concedes. Maybe we just have something really exciting to tell you. Maybe we got a new stand mixer and we want you to see it. Or maybe we're feeling sad and we just want to read you some poems we wrote. So, as you can see, the trustworthy local television news station must retain its powers, the letter always concludes. These powers help us care for you, citizen. The letter is always signed: Night Vale City Council. Those words are written in script dozens of times on top of itself, as if every member of the Council signed it in a single moment in a single space, without regard for physics or linear time.

Listeners, the unrelenting smell coming from the faucets is too much. Everyone in the office is salivating because of the delicious stench of French toast. It's impossible to work in this environment, and also because of the whole ravine thing. I'm calling the Water Department right now. This is ridiculous.

Plus we're all getting woozy and starting to lose our senses of sight, touch, and longing.

[*sound of dialing*]

[*Capital words/phrases marked with ** are separately recorded in a monotone voice. The rest is standard pseudo-chipper operator voice. Most of Cecil's lines in this passage are just kind of muttered to himself as he navigates the phone tree.*]

**RECORDED VOICE:** Hello! And welcome to the city of *NIGHT VALE*, Department of *WATER* Customer Service line.

Para continuar en español, oprima el uno.

Para continuar en español doble, oprima el uno dos veces.

[*voice effect here is echoed*]

To GIVE PRAISE TO THE MIGHTY GLOW CLOUD, press three
**CECIL:** All hail.
**RECORDED VOICE:** To continue in English, press four.
**CECIL:** There we go.
**RECORDED VOICE:** If you are Illuminati, pr——

[*beep of keypad 1*]

**RECORDED VOICE:** Thank you.

Do you have questions about or want to pay your bill? Press one.

Are you changing address? Press two.

Do you no longer believe in the existence of water? Press three.
**CECIL:** I do have my doubts.
**RECORDED VOICE:** Are you confused as to the difference between water and sugary sodas? Press four.

Do you like cabbage? Press five.

Would you like to report a problem with your service? Press six.

[*beep of keypad 6*]

**RECORDED VOICE:** If you are experiencing an emergency, please hang up and scream "Help! Police!" into any one of the many hidden monitoring devices in your home. If you're not sure where the hidden devices in your home are, try calling for help into a door knob, any large vases, a ceiling fan, any random microphone sticking out of your wall that you don't recognize, or an elderly pet.

If you undervalue your own life and the lives of others so much that you feel this could not possibly be an emergency, press the Not an Emergency Button.

[*squawking beep sound . . . maybe all phone keys pressed at once?*]

I'm sorry to hear you are having a problem with your service.

If you have low or no water pressure, press one.

**CECIL:** Hmmm.

**RECORDED VOICE:** If you have a leak, press two.

**CECIL:** No.

**RECORDED VOICE:** If you tried calling once before for emergency help only to find yourself serving a prison sentence for misuse of emergency services and now you are calling to argue semantics with a representative about our lack of definition of what constitutes an emergency, press three.

If your water has a strange color or odor, press four.

**CECIL:** That could be. . . .

**RECORDED VOICE:** If something that is clearly not water and smells like a tasty breakfast food is hissing out of your faucets and causing you to stand on your chair like there's a mouse in the room even though there's really no escape from what very well may be a poisonous gas of some sort and honestly you can't fathom why you jumped up onto this chair at all but it somehow makes you feel better, press five.

**CECIL:** That's it.

**RECORDED VOICE:** If you are afraid of knives—

[*beep of keypad 5*]

Please wait while we transfer you to a customer service representative.

**CECIL:** Oh dear. Oh . . . I can't wait much longer. I'm, I'm feeling light-headed. Please hurry. Please. Pleasss Hur—— [*thump*]

**RECORDED VOICE:** We are experiencing a heavier than usual call volume. Current wait time to speak to a service representative is *FOUR MINUTES*. Sadly, a lot can go wrong in *FOUR MINUTES*, but that's just how it is. Thank you for your *PATIENCE*. You know there are *SUPER VOLCANOES* set to explode any day now, right? Existence is so incomprehensibly *FRAGILE* and *CRUEL*.

Please continue to hold.

**[HOLD MUSIC: "Just Like My Heart" by Fault Lines]**

**LACY:** [*new voice*] Hello. This is Lacy with the Department of Water. Are you still on the line?

**CECIL:** [*slowly waking up*] Hello?

**LACY:** Thank you for contacting the Department of Water. I'm sorry about the interruption of your service.

**CECIL:** What is happening?

**LACY:** An intense period of multiple suns this afternoon affected our communications system. In the aftermath, it looks like our computers shut off your water and started releasing carbon monoxide into your pipes. That should only happen to customers who are more than sixty days behind on payments and your account appears to be fully paid, so we apologize for the error. Your water has been turned back on. Please open all windows to allow the punitive gases to dissipate.

**CECIL:** Why does it smell like French toast?

**LACY:** I bet you're wondering why our carbon monoxide smells like French toast. It's because French toast is pleasant and carbon monoxide is not. We here at the Department of Water think: Why not make unenjoyable things just a bit more enjoyable?

**CECIL:** That's very thoughtful.

**LACY:** It is very thoughtful. I'm very thoughtful. Is there anything else I can help you with today?

**CECIL:** No.

**LACY:** Then good-bye, Mr. Palmer.

**CECIL:** Thank you.

**LACY:** Actually. I'm sorry but I just have to say something. It's kind of unprofessional, I know, but I just wanted to say that I know who you are and thank you.

**CECIL:** Aww . . . Well, thank you. I love hearing from fans. Glad you like the radio show. Keep listening.

**LACY:** What? No. Not because you're on the radio. You're not the only one who cares about her, you know.

**CECIL:** I'm sorry. Her? I don't know what you're talking about.

**LACY:** Fine. Don't take a compliment. Not everyone's as thoughtful as me. Bye.

**CECIL:** Okay. Good-bye.

Listeners, I have brought you a subpar show today. I failed to report on the multiple suns that cluttered our sky and sent waves of destructive panic throughout our community because I was too consumed with my own personal issues.

I apologize for this. And for what it's worth, some vigilantes with hunting rifles shot the extra suns down, so we're back to having just one sun. Although the one remaining sun is currently setting in the north, so we'll see how that goes.

Our town is no longer consumed by weak and terrified humans rioting in the streets. Our town has returned to its normal state of weak and terrified humans huddling quietly at home.

I've been so preoccupied with not just the water outage, but also getting vacation time so I can see Carlos again, that I haven't been one hundred percent focused on my duties as your community radio host. For this I am sorry. I will try harder. I will report better. I will be the radio host you have counted on for, well, for however long it's been. How long has it been?

**LACY:** Time right?

**CECIL:** Oh, you're still on the line.

**LACY:** Yep. Thanks again.

**CECIL:** Thanks for what??

**LACY:** Ugh. Never mind. Jerk.

**CECIL:** Stay tuned next for time moving faster, faster than it seems, faster and faster until it disintegrates into stardust.

**LACY:** Oh, that actually sounds fun!

**CECIL:** Good night, Lacy. And good night, Night Vale. Good night.

**LACY:** Good night!

**PROVERB:** The reason we say "bless you" after someone sneezes is because we know they will die someday.

# EPISODE 61:
## "BRINY DEPTHS"

### FEBRUARY 1, 2015

### GUEST VOICE: WIL WHEATON (EARL HARLAN)

I KNOW I'VE SAID THIS IN AN INTRODUCTION IN ONE OF THESE VOLUMES before, but it is just an inescapable and constant part of my writing process: One of the most common forms of episode genesis for me comes not from an entire story springing into my head, but instead a single earworm phrase, a few words that sound so right to me that I can't let go until I'm able to find a story to fit that phrase in. As you might have guessed, this episode came entirely out of my brain deciding to latch onto the phrase BRINY DEPTHS.

The guest bit with Earl here is truly horrific, even though it only describes in accurate language a real thing that happens. This is part of our mission to make the weird feel normal and the mundane feel terrifying. I am not a vegetarian myself, although I limit my meat intake, but I think that if you are going to choose to eat animals, it's important to be able to face down what that process is in a clear-eyed way. Wil Wheaton's delivery of those lines really sold the entire bit, making everything he was saying sound like he was just in fact giving the recipe for some great pulled pork.

There is a good, old-fashioned, sound-effect joke in this episode.

This is a bit where the entire punchline is a series of sound effects taken from open source libraries on the internet. We used to do this pretty often and then kind of stopped because other kinds of jokes caught our attention, but it's a fun thing to do, both to write and to source and put together when it comes time to edit the episode. Maybe I'll do another sound effect joke soon.

There are often little inside jokes in Night Vale. References to experiences on our live tour or conversations the writers and performers have had over dinner. Mostly these are buried in story elements or into jokes that also have a broader reach, so that you would never notice them unless they were pointed out to you, which I will mostly not do.

But the word from our sponsors in this episode is an inside joke between my wife and I that is transplanted more or less intact and whole into the episode, which is why I brought her in to provide a voice for that moment. Like most inside jokes, there's not a great deal of explanation that can be made other than that we started reciting this ad exactly as it is here to each other occasionally. We found it very funny. Hopefully some listeners also enjoyed it.

Without giving it away, this episode's punch line is a bit of Night Vale absurdity that, like a lot of Night Vale absurdity, has some deeply unsettling implications if thought about for very long. How well do you know yourself? Is it possible that the purpose you are serving and the role you are playing are very different than the ones you think you are? How well, ultimately, is it possible to know oneself?

There's only one way to find out. BRINY DEPTHS.

—Joseph Fink

There's nothing under your bed. Nothing in your closet. Nothing waiting in the hall. You are surrounded by nothing. You cannot escape it.

# WELCOME TO NIGHT VALE

I have received several urgent Facebook messages and Twitter DMs from a vague yet menacing government agency, asking me to deliver the following message: BRINY DEPTHS. They said that there was nothing secret or important about the message, and it was certainly not related to any ongoing deep undercover operations that they can only communicate with using code words subtly buried in local radio broadcasts. It wasn't anything crazy like that. They just think it would be cool to hear me say BRINY DEPTHS. Do your deepest, smoothest voice, they said. Really sell it. Really give it your all. It would make us so happy. Please, it's our birthday. Oh, did we not mention? It's totally our birthday. All right, in your best voice, say it:

BRINY DEPTHS.

Well, there you go, vague yet menacing government agency. Happy birthday.

The Faceless Old Woman Who Secretly Lives in Your Home and Hiram McDaniels, who is literally a five-headed dragon, both former candidates for the mayoral role now filled by Dana Cardinal, were seen muttering together in a booth at the Moonlite All-Nite

Diner. Or Hiram was seen. No one has ever actually seen the Faceless Old Woman, but we all know that she is there.

When reached for comment by a nosy person sitting in the booth next to them, Hiram explained that they were just chatting, and were not involved in any sort of plans or schemes at all. He then held a conversation with himself about this matter, each head providing a different viewpoint in five different voices, the gist of which was that no, they were not planning anything.

"Definitely not," the Faceless Old Woman scratched with what seemed to be a long, jagged fingernail into the sole of my shoe this morning. "That's ludicrous," she suggested with a flickering shadow in the corner of my eye as I walked to work. "We would never," she whispered from behind me just now.

**CECIL:** Moving on, another installment of what I imagine is our listeners' favorite segment, "Cooking Stuff with Earl Harlan." As the name implies, we have my childhood friend and current sous-chef at Night Vale's hottest restaurant, Tourniquet, with us here in the studio. Earl?

**EARL:** That's me, yes.

**CECIL:** Well, Earl. Just a few weeks ago you showed us how to cook tiramisu, and that was delightful.

**EARL:** Please don't cook that recipe. It is extraordinarily poisonous.

**CECIL:** Haha, oh Earl, you're very funny.

**EARL:** It will kill you. It is actually poisonous. Don't cook that.

**CECIL:** So, tell our listeners, and me, of course, what you've been up to since we last spoke.

**EARL:** Mostly I've been working. Mostly living. I've been spending time with my son, trying to remember when I had a son. I've been trying to understand the flow of my life and how I don't remember going from being nineteen to the middle-aged adult I am now. I was nineteen for so long.

**CECIL:** Well, sure, that sounds fun. I'll tell you, lately, I've been getting into crosswords. Just can't stop doing them. Doesn't even feel like it's me doing them, like it's someone else compelling me to do them. Sometimes, I pick up a crossword I've never seen before only to find it's been completely filled in with my own handwriting. I'm glad we've both been up to such fun things.

**EARL:** Cecil, think. What year were you born?

**CECIL:** [*quickly, overlapping*] So what are we cooking up today, Earl?

**EARL:** Okay. Well. Today we are making pulled pork.

**CECIL:** Mmm, sounds yummy.

**EARL:** It is. And pulled pork could not be simpler to make. To start off with, you will need to kill a pig. You will need to find a living pig and kill that pig. You will probably need to hold down the pig. The pig will struggle. There will be blood and pain. Some of that pain will be physical. The pig will want to live, but you will need to make it die. That pig will need to die.

**CECIL:** Sure.

**EARL:** Then you will need to dismember the pig. The pig will be a whole being, but you will not be able to eat it like that, so you will need to take it apart. There will be knives and hacking. The skin will have to go. Peel back that skin and take the muscles and subcutaneous fat, which is the part you will consume. Leave the bones and skin behind to rot.

**CECIL:** Mmmm!

**EARL:** Then you just slow cook it with some vinegar, some sugar, and some chili. Put it on a bun and there you go. Pulled pork!

**CECIL:** Oh, I can't wait to try that. It seems so easy. I'll just use one of the pigs I have at home.

**EARL:** I'm sorry if I seem down at all, Cecil. I've been going through a lot.

**CECIL:** I understand. This has been a difficult time for me, too. Carlos is away and we talk regularly, but it's not the same as the physical presence of someone you love, you know?

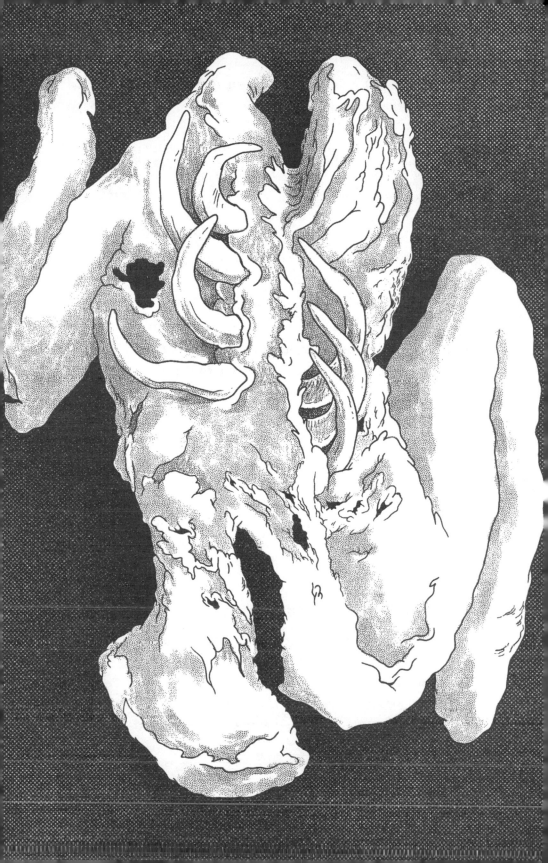

**EARL:** I know. But that's what we do when we have someone special enough to merit special effort. I'm proud of you for working through this.

**CECIL:** And I'm proud of you for dealing with how weird time is. And for raising a son, somehow. What's your son's name?

**EARL:** I . . . I wish I knew.

**CECIL:** Well it's been great catching up. We'll see you again soon, Earl!

I received another flurry of messages from a vague yet menacing government agency, saying that, well thanks for saying those words for us, that was great of you, but it looks like maybe it didn't work. "What didn't work?" they rhetorically asked. Not important, they replied to themselves. As we said, that was certainly not a code word for an undercover agent who apparently wasn't listening to the radio when they were supposed to be, which is by the way their only job and their duty and their life's mission to be listening to instructions from headquarters, so no biggie, but maybe just do something as simple as listen to the radio at the time we tell you to, anyway, none of that is important, the agency continued, and there is no particular reason we're asking you, but could you say BRINY DEPTHS again? It's for a friend's birthday. It's also our friend's birthday, we forgot to mention that. Please say it again.

So . . . okay. Here goes. BRINY DEPTHS. Happy birthday to your friend. I hope you enjoyed that but I really can't keep interrupting my broadcast with this stuff.

Little League Coach Betty Lucero is reporting that there are strange goings on near the haunted baseball diamond her team uses for practices and league games.

"No, no, I know it's haunted," she said. "I get that. You don't have to explain that to me. I'm saying that there is other weird stuff going on besides the usual ghosts."

She went on to describe anguished howls coming from a neighborhood nearby, and a red glow at night that made her skin feel loose and itchy when she looked directly at it. She also said that the baseball diamond has started to smell of rotten eggs, which is a detriment to her team's performance.

As we spoke, an apparition of a gray-skinned young woman in a tattered dress appeared hovering on the baseline between second and third. I may have yelped a little, maybe scrambled backwards a bit, but Coach Lucero laughed and said, "Oh that's just Lusia, our third-base coach. She died in 1843. Say hi, Lusia." The young woman flickered out of view then reappeared suddenly inches from my face, her pupil-less eyes staring directly into mine. I responded in a professional and calm manner, and Coach Lucero laughed for unrelated reasons, not anything to do with how I may have reacted, and said "That's our Lusia."

She then went on to say that she had a bad feeling about the weird goings on near the baseball field, and she probably said some other things but I was running away so I didn't hear her super well.

Listeners, this is exciting. I received mail today. I didn't think mail was still being delivered, not after what happened at the post office. But here it is, an envelope addressed to one Cecil Palmer in neat handwriting, with the address of the station right underneath. If you want to send us any mail, since apparently that is a thing which exists and is working now, our address is

[*the sound of waves crashing*]

[*a horn being blown*]

[*a crowd laughing*]

Night Vale, [*the sound of a paper shredder*].
Please do send stuff in, it's always nice to hear from fans.

But back to this envelope. Maybe this is silly but I waited to open it until I was on the air. It seemed more fun if we could find out together what was inside. I'm opening it now. Here we go.

It's . . . hm . . . it's a greeting card. It says THANKS SO MUCH on the front and it has a picture of a cat playing with a ball of yarn. Well, that's just the cutest, although I can't imagine why someone sent me this card. I'm opening it. Oh, a photo fell out, and—Dang it! It fell behind the desk. The inside of the card just has the words THANK YOU FOR WHAT YOU DID printed and then it's signed Erika over and over in multiple handwritings. Huh. Let me try to grab that photo. I'm going to have to crawl under the desk. While I do that, here's a word from our sponsors.

Today's broadcast is sponsored by Kobe beef.

**FEMALE VOICE:** Kobe beef!

**SINGING VOICES:** The beef that makes you fresh.

All right listeners, I [*grunt*] I got the photo, and it's . . . it's a photo of me. At City Hall. I'm fighting off a pack of antiques in front of the mayor's door. But that wasn't me. Intern Hector did that. Last month. He came back with that bite. I don't remember ever leaving my desk when the antiques attacked our mayor. What is this photo? It must be fake. It doesn't look fake. It must be fake. Right?

Why would I not remember saving the mayor?

More on this later, as I face my fragile self and try to understand my own reality.

Okay, now this is getting out of hand. The vague yet menacing government agency sent me a Snapchat and several anonymous asks on Tumblr saying that they were happy about me doing that whole broadcasting their secret code word thing before, but that the message didn't seem to be getting through. Or it's not a message. That was poor phrasing on their part. Sorry, they're just flustered talking to their favorite radio host. (Aww . . . ) They meant to say that they haven't had the best birthday ever yet. And neither has their friend. Plus, they forgot to mention, millions and millions of people have the same birthday as them. Think of how many people have their birthday today and all of them, the agency is sure, just want you to say that little thing again. Just once more. In your smoothest, deepest voice. They say that they've made it so our station is currently broadcasting on every single radio frequency, so no one could possibly miss these special birthday greetings, and it will finally be the best birthday ever.

This is the last time, Okay? I'm doing it just once more. Here I go, and really try to enjoy this, because I'm not doing it again: BRINY DEPTHS.

Whoa, what's going on? There's shouting coming from the break room. It sounds like a scuffle. There's also shouting coming from outside. A lot of shouting. A roar of voices, the stomping feet of a crowd. These birthday greetings were apparently very special. I need to go see what this commotion is about. I'll be back soon. In the meantime, those with birthdays and those who were never born, I take you to the weather.

**WEATHER:** "The Bends" by Doomtree

I'll tell you, that was quite a scene. I will tell you right now.

It seems that BRINY DEPTHS was in fact a code word (wish they had warned me about that) for an undercover agent in the field. Unfortunately, it seems that it was the code word for every secret agent in the field, the signal for all of them to do every nefarious action that they had been planted years ago to perform.

All over town, people we thought of as friends and family revealed themselves to be carefully planted agents. Adam Bair, weekday shift manager at the Ralphs, grabbed the discount soup display and carried it to an unmarked van that had been sitting in the parking lot as long as anyone could remember and then drove wildly away. Hundreds of bushes and trees leapt into action, revealing themselves to be suit- and sunglass-wearing agents in disguise, using clever costumes that fooled all of us for years, such as holding a handwritten sign that says "I AM A TREE." Larry Leroy, out on the edge of town, lit his refrigerator on fire, but he said that wasn't because of any secret agent stuff. He just wanted to do that. Someone had suggested it to him once, although he could not remember who.

In fact it seems that every single person in Night Vale was actually a secret agent waiting to be activated. We had all been implanted with the exact same code phrase, which is the kind of sloppy organization that is just what our government is coming to, or whatever. And such.

[*pause, sigh perhaps?*]

You know, look. Honestly, my heart isn't in this reporting. Blah, blah, everyone we've ever known is secretly an agent. Because here I am, listeners. Secretly a hero. Secret even from myself.

It was not Hector who saved Dana, but me. Me acting without memory or agency. What is happening to me? How do I not remember something so huge?

I need to talk to Carlos. Perhaps science can help me. Science so rarely applies to the real world, but once in a while it provides a nice metaphor or turn of phrase that makes you think about real things differently. I'm hoping Carlos can do that for me.

Now that everyone has been activated as a secret agent and did the one thing they were secretly supposed to do for years, everyone has just gone right back to doing what they had been doing before. Everything is back to normal, except that we all know we are all secretly undercover planted agents, here to spy on each other, and since we all know it, we are no longer secret agents. We are just ourselves, secretly.

Listen, I know it's confusing, but I didn't invent logic. Our extra-terrestrial ancestors did.

Stay tuned next for all the air being sucked out of the room you're in we're sorry we're so sorry but this is the only way.

Good night, Night Vale. Good night.

**PROVERB:** I let my haters be my motivators. Mostly they tell me I suck and then I get sad. This was a terrible idea.

# EPISODE 62:
# "HATCHETS"

## FEBRUARY 15, 2015

WHEN I FIRST STARTED WRITING THE CHARACTER OF LEANN HART, I was interested in the changing landscape of journalism. In the 1980s, television was destroying print. In the 1990s, cable television was. In the 2000s, it was blogs and free access to news online. In the early 2010s, social media accelerated this.

But listening back to older Night Vale episodes featuring Leann and the *Night Vale Daily Journal*, I can't help but notice that my satire seems pointed more at print media being somewhat at fault. Leann, the executive editor of the *Daily Journal*, takes a fairly defensive approach to the failure of her own paper.

Like most newspapers, the *Daily Journal* feels like something has been taken from them. That this new generation is draining the life force from her institution. But like a human body, a corporation can eventually die of old age. The body eventually shuts down. In humans, this is a genetic design. If an organism replicates more that it dissipates, it can overrun its host (see *cancer*; or in terms of humans on the Earth, see *climate change*).

The *Daily Journal*, like any being, wants to live, but rather than try to better its bodily health, just wants to blame the world around it. This is probably the same part of human nature that leads us to sneer at younger generations. We are so afraid of our own demise that we must attack those who will eventually erase what we built.

All of this is to say, it's hella fun to give Leann an arsenal of artisanal hatchets for her to keep her company viable. It's way less harmful to humanity than the news my family shares on Facebook.

—Jeffrey Cranor

Dare to dream. Do it. We dare you. Go
ahead . . . dream. It'll be fine. We promise.

## WELCOME TO NIGHT VALE

Leann Hart, Publishing Editor of the *Night Vale Daily Journal*, announced today that for a limited time the *Daily Journal* will print
actual newspapers again. No longer will subscribers have only the
Imagination Edition of the daily paper—a compulsory and automatic $60 monthly charge to imagine whatever news you want.
They will once again have the tyranny of a printed daily edition
where all of the stories are immovable declarations of recent history
told by a biased and underpaid third party.

"It's an exciting time to work in print journalism," Hart shouted
after a news blogger who was sprinting away from the hatchet-
wielding veteran of the printed word. Hart then hurled another
hatchet at the terrified representative of the *Daily Journal*'s digital
competition. She hit her target just behind the knee, felling him as
he made a sharp cry and a dull asphalt thud.

"Very exciting," Hart shouted. She added, "These printed versions of the daily paper are collector's items. We've deliberately inserted a bunch of errors into them, because true collectors know
that makes them worth a bunch more."

Listeners, I for one think a resurgence in the newspaper industry would be great. This could mean even more jobs here in Night Vale.

"This will create lots of new jobs for Night Vale," Hart will certainly have said by this time tomorrow. "Lots of real awesome jobs," I am sure she will have reiterated.

And now, a look at traffic.

There's an accident at the corner of Hollows Road and Great Hills Drive. It's a pretty bad accident. It is likely neither party saw an accident of this magnitude coming. Each driver stands, staring, dumbfounded at their two twisted cars, which look like one. One what? Not a car. A spiteful burning beast borne of mundane haste and arrogant industrial progress.

The two drivers cannot comprehend what to do. They are still mostly. Fidgeting sometimes. Thinking not at all. A neighbor who came out of her house upon hearing the hard smash of hard metal can't seem to process what is happening either. She's slowly leaning away as if wanting to leave, wanting to forget she ever witnessed this, but she cannot move. She cannot take that first step. Her eyes growing wide, wild, as her mouth opens slack at first and then slowly recoils into an unheard scream.

The two drivers feel the neighbor there, but they do not turn. They do not ask for help or aid. Too scared to move, they stand and gaze into the crumpled slits along the sides of the pressed cars— that damnable block of hot machinery and its black smoke swirls. And on the concrete there is glass and above the glass are arms and hair and drying blood. And the drivers stare at their own wretched bodies inside the mangled contraptions and they do not think about anything other than what they once were. They watch their bodies, hoping for a twitch, a breath, any kind of movement. Hoping for another chance in life.

So it's pretty backed up pretty bad near the Best Buy. Choose some alternate routes today.

This has been traffic.

You know me, listeners. I'm a pretty straight-and-narrow radio professional. I'm all about objectivity and impartiality. But it's time for a Cecil Palmer editorial.

Given the growing prevalence of the internet—not just on computers, but also phones and watches and owls and certain trees—our private information is just out there, waiting to be taken and exploited by the wrong kinds of people.

Of course, it's vitally important that vague yet menacing government agencies have access to our personal data, like income, dream journals, phone logs, embarrassing thoughts, and slash-fiction archives. Also the police and the World Government. And the mayor. And the faceless old woman who secretly lives in all of our homes.

Yes, those people should all have access to our private data.

But now there are things called scripts and algorithms that can just scan our e-mails and our purchase history and all those photos of cats wearing baseball mitts we like to share with each other. And these scripts and algorithms are sometimes called bots. And these bots are large cyborgs that break into our homes and look through our stuff and then feed these secrets to corporations and then these corporations make more bots and soon we will have to fight bot armies. But with what? Knives and guns are completely internet-based now. They will turn against us in that war.

We are not safe from the impending Bot Wars. So stop having personal data is what I'm trying to say. No more e-mails. No more job histories, Night Vale. No more cat pictures or erotic fan fic or text messages.

I know this is difficult. On the one hand, we enjoy having personal information like careers and friends and hobbies. On the other hand, we're talking about war. And on the third, eleven-fingered hand, nothing is to say bots wouldn't be benevolent leaders. But I do not wish to find this out.

I'm sure the naysayers will tell me that I'm overreacting, which I

am. But it's my opinion, okay. You don't get to tell me who's overreacting. You're underreacting, I'll say. I'll totally say that. I'll say that
to their face.

What—? What's that?

Oh. Okay.

Listeners, Intern Maureen just handed me a note explaining that
the City Council has just declared all information totally public, and
that since no information is private anymore, the giant corporations
and their bots cannot harm us by mining private data. The City will
keep all of our information safely out in the open and available to
anyone wearing sunglasses and a sidearm.

Thanks, Maureen.

Moments ago, the Sheriff's Secret Police held a secret press
conference reminding us all that murder is illegal. Also attempted
murder. "Like, let's say you try to kill a person but you don't actually succeed," a Secret Police spokesperson whispered from behind a
concrete pillar in the underground garage of the disused East Night
Vale Mall, "then that's still illegal. Even if you didn't kill that person."

"But what if you just *think* about killing a person but don't *actually* do it?" came one question from the batch of reporters who were
also whispering and hiding.

"Well, that's not illegal then," the spokesperson whispered in
reply.

"But I have it all planned out and everything," the reporter continued. "I just haven't done it yet. Is that illegal?"

"Well, that's just mean and kind of weird," said the Secret Police
spokesperson before walking out into the open, and saying "Leann,
is that you?"

"Um. No. . . ." came a comically deep voice that was obviously
fake. "Not me at all. I'm just an old bagel wrapper someone left on
the ground. I'm inanimate garbage."

"Leann, we know it's you," said the spokesperson. "Stop attack-

ing bloggers with hatchets. We found a dozen more wounded bloggers in Mission Grove Park this morning. They all had hatchets in
their backs and were very upset. It's not nice, Leann. It's also illegal,
okay?"

"I'm a bagel wrapper, you jerk," Hart replied, still whispering and
hiding.

And now a word from our sponsor.

You are thirsty. Of course you are. We are all metaphorically
thirsty for better things. But you are literally thirsty. Literally thirsty
for anything.

You can feel your dry lips, swollen and sticking together, their
crusted, gray edges adorning the pink pain beneath. You lick your
lips, feeling better for a moment but actually worsening the problem.

It's hot right? Pretty hot and dry, actually. Are those flies? Yes
those are flies. Are those birds? Vultures? Yes. Actual vultures. In
your home. "How did these soaring scavengers get in my home?"
you think.

Perhaps you could use some cool, pure, natural, and refreshing
Fiji Water. Yes, Fiji Water sounds so nice, doesn't it? But Fiji Water
is not who is sponsoring this show. Fiji Water doesn't even know
about this show. Who *is* sponsoring this show? We cannot tell you.
We're not allowed.

Fiji Water is completely unaware of you, too. So sorry.

This will not end quickly.

So very, very sorry.

This has been a word from our sponsor.

This afternoon Night Vale High School and the armed militia
that make up our Committee for Civic Pride are holding a ticker
tape parade for local sports hero Michael Sandero, who became the
first Night Vale High athlete to play in a college football national
title game.

Unfortunately, Sandero's team, the University of Michigan

Wolverines, lost to copies of themselves in the title game. But Sandero did win the Heisman Trophy for the nation's best college football player and did his hometown proud.

Intern Maureen, who I sent to report on the parade, is texting
me that there's a problem. I'm getting word that Leann Hart has
interrupted the festivities with an announcement.

According to Maureen's flurry of texts, Hart is claiming that
Michigan did not play itself for the title. As proof of her claim, Hart
passed out copies of a news article from *The Michigan Daily* from
January 13 stating that at the end of the season, Michigan lost more
games than they won and that their quarterback's name is Devin
Gardner, not Michael Sandero.

On the front page of that issue of *The Daily* is a headline strongly
indicating that people at the University of Michigan can remember
most things correctly. "PRETTY MUCH NO MAJOR MEMORY
PROBLEMS HERE," the headline reads.

She also claims that a school called Ohio State won the national
title over a school called Oregon.

Maureen confirmed that while Ohio is, in fact, a U.S. State,
Michigan and Oregon are neither states nor cities anyone seems to
have heard of before. We are still trying to figure out their languages
of origin.

Maureen is texting me that Hart is now shouting "Blogger!" over
and over. Maureen is texting me that Hart is hurling hatchets now.
Maureen is texting me that everyone looks pretty scared. Maureen
just texted me "I'm hit!"

Let me respond real quick.

[*saying slowly while texting back*] Is that slang for something,
Maureen?

She texted back, "I'm hit. She got me. I'm bleeding."

I don't understand young people and their weird text-speak
at all. Who even knows what she's trying to say. Well. Whatever.

While I text Maureen back with a quick grammar lesson, let me take you to the weather.

### WEATHER: "Anarchy Date" by Queer Rocket

Listeners, I have just learned that Maureen was struck with a hatchet thrown by Leann Hart. So then . . . . To the family of Intern Maureen. She was a good intern, a valiant intern, brave right up until the end. Sadly she is with us no more. She will be missed.

For the hatchet attack on Maureen, as well as several other attacks at today's parade and more than five dozen similar hatchet-based assaults in the past several weeks, the Sheriff's Secret Police arrested Leann Hart.

"We told you it was illegal to kill people, Leann," the Sheriff himself said from his hoveroffice in the clouds, "and also to *try* to kill people."

"But they were news bloggers," Hart replied. "I can't stay in business and create jobs if news bloggers are putting me out of business and destroying those jobs."

And the Sheriff agreed, saying it's the Secret Police's job to protect business interests as well as citizen interests. The City Council also agreed. So did the vague yet menacing government agency, nodding quietly from inside their long black sedans with tinted windows while snapping photos of everything they saw.

The Mayor did not agree. Mayor Dana Cardinal went against the City Council and said that she, for one, did not think people or businesses should be allowed to use physical violence against their competition or anyone for that matter. The City Council bristled, and then they all squawked and flew away.

It is unclear whether or not news bloggers agree, as many of them have gone silent on this issue, replacing their investigative reports and think pieces with pictures of cats wearing baseball gloves and top-rated recipes for invisible pie.

The Sheriff then announced that all charges against Hart would be dropped, except for the assault on Intern Maureen. Maureen, after all, was not a news blogger, but a radio intern who posed no direct threat to Hart's newspaper, the Sheriff said. And I agreed.

The Sheriff then played the entirety of Domenico Galli's *Sonata Quinta* on his gold cello.

"But she looked like a blogger," Hart insisted. "She was typing into her phone. All those bloggers do that. Bloggers love typing on phones."

"But she worked in radio, Leann," the Sheriff said, as he ended a series of lilting high notes with a single discordant bass tone. He closed his eyes and shook his head. "I'm sorry but that is attempted murder. You have to go to jail now."

"Oh! But I didn't attempt to kill her. You said murder and attempted murder were illegal. Murder wasn't my intent," Leann said.

"Then what was your intent?" the Sheriff asked.

"Oh, just throwing a hatchet at her. Nothing more. Nothing less," Hart said. "I meant nothing by it," she added, brushing her hands together and then holding them out, empty and clean.

Her open palms signified case closed, and the Sheriff, held to the higher law of gestures, had no choice but to acquiesce.

So Hart was set free, turned back into the world to print more news. To keep the industry alive.

Before she left she paused and said, "I think something's wrong in Michigan." (And listeners, that's how she said it. I don't know why. It's very clear how it's actually pronounced if you see it written out.)

And she held up her copy of *The Michigan Daily* from January 13 with an article that said "Michigan, Sandero Lose Close One to Themselves." And the front page of *The Michigan Daily* now showed a bold headline "WE HAVE FORGOTTEN SO MANY THINGS" and then several blank columns with no story, merely pictures of normal things like shoes and birds and ghosts, all captioned with a series of frantic question marks.

"I guess I was wrong earlier. I dunno. Weird, right?" Hart said with a shrug.

"That is crazy weird," the Sheriff agreed, finishing out the sonata before disappearing in a soft breeze.

"I agree," said a nearby news blogger, who was coughing up blood and clutching tightly to the hatchet lodged in her abdomen. "I can't wait to blog about it," the blogger said through gritted teeth.

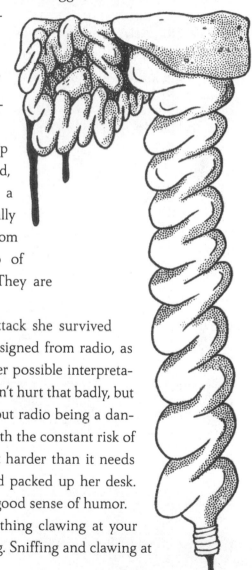

Leann tightened her grip on the hatchet in her left hand, raising it slightly. There was a tense pause that was eventually broken by a light smirk from Leann Hart. Then the two of them laughed and laughed. They are both still laughing now.

Because of the hatchet attack she survived today, Intern Maureen has resigned from radio, as I clearly and without any other possible interpretation explained earlier. She wasn't hurt that badly, but Maureen went on and on about radio being a dangerous job and totally not worth the constant risk of death. I told her she makes it harder than it needs to be. She rolled her eyes and packed up her desk. I miss her already. She had a good sense of humor.

Stay tuned next for something clawing at your window. It will also be sniffing. Sniffing and clawing at your window. Occasionally it will wail. Occasionally you will hear nothing. So, to recap: sniffing and clawing at your window over and over, with the occasional piercing wail, and then long silences. All that next!

And as always, good night, Night Vale. Good night.

**PROVERB:** Ask your doctor just who he thinks he is. Say it just like that. Say, "Who do you think you are?" See if he starts crying. I know I would.

# EPISODE 63:
## "THERE IS NO PART 1: PART 2"

### MARCH 3, 2015

SOME NIGHT VALE EPISODES START BECAUSE I HAVE A PHRASE OR AN image and I go looking for a way to transplant that phrase or image into the heads of the listeners. Others start more like games that I want to play with either myself or the listeners. This episode is very much a game.

The concept is simple, but with a lot of possibility. It's the second part to an epic two-part episode, except we haven't heard the first part and we never will because it doesn't exist. I wanted to play with the common structures and clichés of two-part episodes in television, the big cliffhanger, the point where all hope is lost, and skip right to the part where we figure out how to win.

With a game episode, instead of a plot outline, I'll often instead just make a list of every possible use of the concept. Given the rules of the game, what plays are there for me to make? Then once I have that list, I use it to build out a story that will take us through as many of them as possible. So every part of this episode is designed to make use of the two-part structure and the feeling that we missed all the important bits already.

Along with the game, though, there were some larger pieces we needed to keep moving into place. And so the entire two-parter is centered around the continuing story of Lot 37 and Cecil's loss of control. The Lot 37 plot was started by a guest episode written by the brilliant author Glen David Gold. In it, Cecil is very confused to find that he is up for sale at the Sheriff's Secret Police auction. He rushes downtown to bid on himself, and in Glen's original script, is successful. I made a change, which was to make him unsuccessful, and the winning bidder unclear. This impulsive edit turned into a story that ended up taking almost two years to tell, and the ramifications of which are still being played out in town as I write this.

Much of the fun of inviting guest writers on is that they tend to throw in these narrative grenades, little ideas that we can either let end with their episode, or, as is often the case, instead decide to pick up and carve entire new stories with, stories that sometimes take center stage. This is the beauty of having a small writing team with no oversight. If a thing seems interesting, we can take it in any direction we want, even if it wasn't our original plan to do so.

This episode also marks the beginning of a wedge in Dana and Cecil's friendship. They were always so close, and their relationship was one of the hearts of the show, so it seemed important to us to explore and test it a bit. Because it seems that Dana is the most likely winner of Lot 37. But would she do that to Cecil? How well does Cecil really know her?

The answers to those would eventually come. But first I had a game to play. A game in which there was a Part Two, but no Part One.

—Joseph Fink

There is no part one. This is part two.

# WELCOME TO NIGHT VALE

Listeners, I won't waste your time recapping everything that happened in the earlier part of this broadcast. There were so many events of such tremendous impact and significance that they are surely locked forever in your memory.

So let us, a town with an imperiled mayor and a brutally injured Sheriff, a town under attack, a town in the middle of something that we are seeing through from start to finish, let us continue right where we left off.

Harrison Kip, Adjunct Professor of Archaeology at the Community College, announced once again that he is super sorry about accidentally raising the Sand Golem by whispering sweet nothings to that talisman he found out in the desert. The team of six wealthy sponsors who backed his project and who he has only ever spoken to by phone told him that this was what mysterious talismans liked.

"Talismans love to be flirted with in a sexy whisper," the anonymous sponsors had told him, although they never mentioned that doing so would cause a Sand Golem to rise and turn against the humans around it.

"My bad," Harrison said, gravely, continuing: "Most def my bad," before fleeing into the desert, receding from human form to distant

human form to dot to smudge to misplaced pixel on the horizon line to memory to vague recollection to an idea just out of reach to something I knew long ago but now cannot grasp enough to feel its absence.

The Sand Golem along with thousands of angora rabbits, which were released from the Night Vale Petting Zoo by unknown, malicious parties, have reached the upper floors of City Hall and are attacking anything that moves or doesn't move or just exists anywhere on the spectrum of motion with its huge sand fists and their soft, harmless fur.

Director of Emergency Press Conferences, Pamela Winchell, held a nonemergency press conference, explaining that the situation seemed too urgent to distract everyone with the usual emergency press conference. She read a statement written by Mayor Dana Cardinal indicating that the mayor has given up on her previously announced plan to barricade the door and then found her subsequently announced plan to hide was ruined when she released the statement announcing it, and so now she is announcing her current plan, which is to fight. To fight and to win.

Listeners, I would gladly help the mayor, but as I've been regularly expressing throughout the morning's tragedies and this afternoon's attack, I have conflicted feelings here. Yes, Mayor Dana is a dear friend, and one of the citizens of this town I trust the most. But, but, the last time I helped her it was done without my will. Not against my will. Without. I was used as a puppet to save a good friend, and good friend though she is, it is not a feeling I wish to experience again.

I'll tell you what I think it is: I believe the culprit is whoever bought Lot 37 from the Sheriff's Secret Police Auction last year. Lot 37: one radio host, one Cecil Palmer, one me. I believe whoever owns that lot has manipulated me into the role of hero, like an action figure limp in the sticky hands of a child.

I do not wish to be manipulated again except in that way that anyone who lives in an all-seeing authoritarian state is constantly manipulated for their own health and well-being.

Such is the wish of all people. To only be manipulated in ways that are good for them.

But all to say, maybe someone else can help Dana this time.

More and more on this soon, as there has been much and much before.

Construction work is already commencing at the bowling alley after the shocking incident we reported on earlier today. (I know I'LL never look at one of those ball-return machines the same way again.)

Teddy Williams said the space should again be available for bowling by Wednesday at the latest, that league night is set to continue as scheduled, and that he's had enough, just enough, there's only so much one person, you know, that one person can take, and that limit was reached several months ago and he's just been coasting, you know, coasting, trying, doing his best, and now this? Now this! Right? Now this. He doesn't know what next. What now. He doesn't know what he's going to do. Probably not this anymore, he doesn't think. How old do you have to be to retire? How old is he? He doesn't know the answer to those questions. But he'll find out. And then he'll know, you know, he'll know. And again, league night is continuing as scheduled.

Which, whew. Wouldn't be a good week for me without league night.

And now another word from our sponsors.

You already know who we are. We introduced ourselves earlier. Let's not waste time reiterating the benefits of our product, how little it costs, how easy it is to get, how unwise it would be not to buy it, and where exactly we took your loved ones.

Instead let's concentrate on the legally required disclaimers. We forgot to do those and our lawyer got really mad about it. Have you ever seen a mad lawyer? Their ears stand straight up and they won't stop barking at you. It's terrifying.

[*following sped up in post-production*]

So, we need to add that using our product could result in sterility, senility, hearing loss, vision loss, finger decomposition, major toe swelling, like a lot of toe swelling, that might not sound like a big deal but wait until you see how big your toes get, scratchiness of the throat, throat loss, heart palpitations, and minor night screaming.

Also when we said hearing loss, we meant you'll be able to hear loss. As plants age, as pets die, as marriages break apart or evolve or settle from a fluttering of hands to a loose intertwining of fingers, as children leave home to go wherever it is that children go after the age of ten, all of these common forms of loss, you will be able to hear. It will be deafening.

[*end sped up audio*]

Oh, we could go on all day about the ways our product will severely ruin you, physically and emotionally. But what are you going to do? Not buy it?

I think that you and your (for the moment) safe loved ones know that you will buy our product no matter what we say.

So, let's not waste any more time. Our lawyer has stopped barking. Buy our product.

This has been another word from our sponsors.

I'm sorry, listeners. There is a knocking on my studio window. It is a man in a tan jacket, holding a deerskin suitcase. It is difficult to describe his features as they escape my mind the moment my eyes leave his face.

He is waving, indicating that he would like to come in and speak to me, and presumably, to all of you.

Yes, come in.

[*door opens*]

[*a hum like ringing in the ears*]

. . . but how would we even get there? I've never heard of that place. I . . .

I don't remember what I was just saying. I think someone was just speaking to me and to all of you out there about something that seemed very important but . . . now. Now. I can't remember. You all heard him, too. Do you remember what he said?

Why am I sweaty?

I think I remember him offering me a note, or some piece of paper. I didn't take it. Maybe I should have taken it. I don't know.

Speaking of notes, I am being handed another one by Intern Hannah. Hopefully it is better than the note she handed me this morning during the earlier section of this broadcast. It was such an awful note. (I don't have to tell you, right?) So sad. Sad and awful. (You remember.) Also kind of funny, though. Just a pretty sad, awful, funny note, really.

But this note, it seems . . . oh no. No, no, no. It seems that once again, during this recent bit of missing time, brave radio host Cecil Palmer has stepped in and helped Mayor Cardinal fight off the Sand Golem and the angora rabbits.

Cecil, showing strength beyond his stature, held the Sand Golem down while Dana wiped away the writing on its forehead that gave it unnatural life, dispersing it to inanimate sand. And then we just kind of shooed the rabbits. They were just rabbits and even in great numbers were not threatening at all.

This left the mayor safe, with only a few bumps and bruises and a wrecked office covered with sand that probably will never be completely cleaned away. Certainly better than what happened to the Sheriff. That poor man.

I am being told that Mayor Cardinal indicated deep gratitude for my help. I am being told this because I do not remember this. Because, I am certain now, the owner of Lot 37, the owner of Cecil Palmer, once again used me only to protect Dana. That is . . . I'll have to think about what that is.

But first, a continuation of our previous Children's Fun Fact Science Corner.

Children, it's now time to go check on those glass vials we pre-pared earlier in the broadcast. If you mixed everything right and placed it in a warm, dry place like we told you to, you should be able to now observe the start of the tendrils. Don't get close to them. Those tendrils have a strong grip. One could call their grip unbreakable, or even poisonous. You might also hear buzzing. Do you hear buzzing? Listen closely. Science is all about observation. Write down what the buzzing sounds like in detail. Draw a graph to show the buzzing. What that buzzing is telling you is that the thing in the vial has marked you as its prey. You need to run. You should have started running the moment you heard the buzzing. I'm sorry, I should have said that before the rest of the stuff.

If you don't hear anything, then congratulations. You can move on to the second part of the experiment. Lay down plastic sheeting in the room and we'll be back to give you the full instructions later.

This has been Part 2 of the Children's Fun Fact Science Corner

This day started bad, and it does not appear to be getting better anytime soon.

I, however unwillingly and unconsciously, helped the mayor fight off her attackers, and yet even that act was not enough to end this ordeal.

Hiram McDaniels, literal five-headed dragon, and the Faceless

Old Woman Who Secretly Lives in Your Home, both former mayoral candidates, have taken City Hall once again captive. Hiram is
preventing anyone from entering the front door using his massive
body, fire breathing, and harsh language.

Mayor Cardinal has issued a statement through her mouth
shouting out of an upper-floor window that the Faceless Old
Woman is stalking her through City Hall. Dana can hear bare feet
skittering across the hallway ceiling, can sense the memory of motion in the air when she turns, can feel breath on her neck, dry and
cold, like breath never is.

"She has come for me," Dana shouted, mayorally. "I will not be
able to avoid her forever. I will not be able to do anything forever."

Hiram, in response to questions asked by a group of lightly
scorched Secret Police currently trying to tase and then arrest him,
admitted that he and the Faceless Old Woman have been conspiring
against the mayor for quite some time, convincing Pamela Winchell
to enter a disastrous retirement, staging a blatantly consumerist
Christmas display involving gift cards and an ancient monolith,
freeing the antiques from their pen, funding the dig that led Harrison Kip to find the Sand Golem's talisman, unsealing and freeing
the army of tiny people under Lane 5 of the Desert Flower Bowling
Alley and Arcade Fun Complex this morning, working to sabotage
the ultimately successful defense led by the Sheriff today against the
tiny army, from which the Sheriff miraculously emerged unscathed,
then causing the Saw Cyclone that swept through the Sheriff's office, not injuring him at all but really messing up his draperies, and
then finally sending the Sheriff an angry letter which resulted in the
serious paper cut he is currently recovering from.

And now, all of these measures unsuccessful in removing Dana
from power, Hiram and the Faceless Old Woman have been left
with no choice but to attack the Mayor directly.

"Try to stop us," said Hiram. "Just try."

I'D LIKE TO SEE YOU TRY, PUNY MORTALS roared another one of his heads, although not the one you'd think.

Well, certainly I won't try. I've had enough of this mayor-saving business. My job is to report. That is what I do: reporting. That is why they call me what they call me: a journalist.

Now, let me report and only report. We are taking you all to the weaaaaaaaaaaaaaa—[*turning into hypnotized drone*]

[*microphone drop; door slam*]

**WEATHER:** "Heel Turn 2" by The Mountain Goats

Here I am, listeners. Whoever I am. Here it is, the me that is whichever me I am.

You can guess what happened, I think. Once again, it was brave Cecil who saved the mayor, throwing his body between her and the wrath of the Faceless Old Woman and Hiram. It was not an easy fight, and not an easy fight for me to remember.

Here is what I know: Hiram McDaniels is no longer at City Hall. With my help, the Secret Police almost apprehended him, but our efforts, while just enough to prevent his continued siege, were just under what was needed to capture a literal five-headed dragon, and in the scuffle Hiram disappeared. He could be anywhere. Svitz. Lemuria. The secret lost pet city on the moon. Or even still in Night Vale. Even that.

Here is what else I know: The Faceless Old Woman Who Secretly Lives in All of Our Homes was unable to complete her malicious plans against our mayor, and is now secretly living in all of our homes still. She did not need to change anything in order to hide.

These two rebels, who are against the mayor rightfully chosen for us by forces we do not understand, will not rest quietly, I have no doubt of it. I know that there is more coming, as always. This is what I know.

Here is what I do not know: the owner of Lot 37. Who bought me at that auction and did nothing with their prize for so long only to now use me again and again with one purpose? To protect one person. Dana Cardinal. Mayor Cardinal. My friend.

Here is who I do not know but thought I did: Dana Cardinal. My friend. And, I am starting to fear, and I am starting to doubt, the owner of Lot 37. Could she be? Who else would be so invested in protecting her and only her?

Dana, is it you? Could it be? It couldn't. It couldn't. It couldn't. But still. But still.

Ah.

Stay tuned next for Part 3 and Part 4 and many more parts, each succeeding moment after the one before, and some you will hear and some you will not, and none of them will be true, exactly, but all of them will be an honest attempt at the most accurate fiction possible.

Good night, to our recuperating Sheriff.

Good night, to a mayor I once thought I knew.

Good night to Old Woman Josie and the rest of the bowling team. I'll see you at League Night.

And good night, Night Vale. Good night.


**PROVERB:** History is written by the victors, and then forgotten by the victors, and then the victors die too.

# EPISODE 64:
## "WE MUST GIVE PRAISE"

### MARCH 15, 2015

IN 2017, WE WROTE AND TOURED A LIVE SHOW CALLED "ALL HAIL," which was entirely about the Glow Cloud, who first appeared in Episode 2 of the podcast (more on that in a future volume of episodes).

From early on we knew that Night Vale characters needed to have strict continuity, which meant that they needed to grow and change. They needed to get older, even if (as is the case of Cecil Palmer, Jackie Fierro, Earl Harlan, and Lee Marvin) they can stay the same ages, for centuries sometimes.

This is true even in the case of the Glow Cloud, who controls minds and drops dead animals. This episode was sort of an early study of what eventually became "ALL HAIL." The Glow Cloud is a sort of demigod in Night Vale, but it also is president of the school board. It's a responsible and concerned member of its community, even if at times it abuses its power. Listen, we've all been assholes when it comes to accomplishing something we think is important. Let's not judge.

These evolutions of character sort of undermine the Lovecraftian horror of early Night Vale episodes, and I'm perfectly fine with that.

While Lovecraft's stories undeniably influence anyone who writes in or near the horror genre, his was never an approach we wanted to replicate or honor. Lovecraftian horror is fear of the unknown or the strange. He was a noted racist and xenophobe and used these failures of his own humanity to ham-handedly craft spooky stories that didn't build into a full narrative arc.

We like narrative arcs. There's a lot of fun in eldritch horror, but there's a lot of emotional reward in exploring the complexity of a stranger. Why not both?

—Jeffrey Cranor

Don't judge a book by its cover. Judge it
by the harmful messages it contains.

## WELCOME TO NIGHT VALE

The enormous glowing cloud that serves as president of the Night Vale School Board announced a five-year strategic plan for the school district. The plan, put together over the past year by the twelve-member board, lays out new curriculum goals, organizational restructuring, and a comprehensive outline for eternal penitence before the mighty glow cloud.

Everyone present at the press conference fell to their knees and praised the Glow Cloud, their eyes solid white, gray smoky wisps swirling from their chanting mouths, hands clapping loudly in unison, as miniature glowing colorful clouds swept about them.

"CHILDREN ARE OUR FUTURE," the Glow Cloud said. "WE MUST GIVE PRAISE, GIVE OUR LIVES, GIVE OUR ALL TO THE CHILD OF THE GLOWING CLOUD, TO THE SCION OF INCORPOREAL RULE. ALL HAIL. ALL HAIL. ALL HAIL."

The crowd chanted along in worship of the Glow Cloud's child, who is currently a freshman at Night Vale High School. The young cloud is an active member of both Show Choir and the Speechless Debate Team. Their education has long been an important part of the adult Glow Cloud's leadership in the education community.

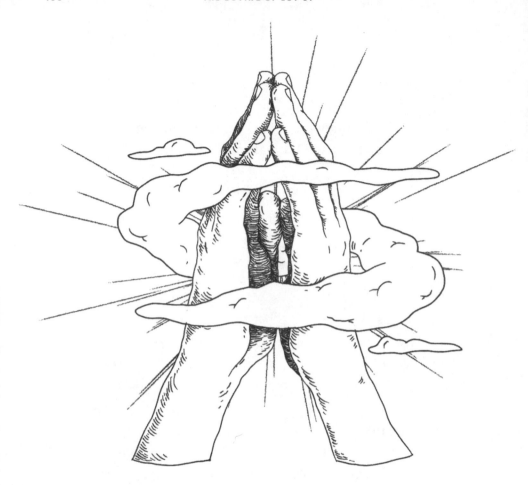

The Sheriff's Secret Police in conjunction with several vague yet menacing government agencies are calling on all citizens to be on the lookout for two fugitives. Both Hiram McDaniels and the Faceless Old Woman Who Secretly Lives in Your Home are wanted by authorities for their recent attempts to usurp mayoral control of Night Vale.

Hiram is described as literally a five-headed dragon. He is eighteen feet tall and his heads are colored blue, green, gold, gray, and purple. They each have their own personality, sentience, memory, and distinct markings and features. The grey head often feels blue and wears a green nose ring. The blue head considers logic the gold standard of intellect and has purple eyes. The gold head is actually more of a sable and will talk till he's blue in the face. The purple head has grown gray with paranoid fantasies and wears a gold neck chain that has a pendant with the word VIOLET written in green gemstones. And the green head is the real shouty one that wants to set everyone on fire all the time.

The Secret Police are also on the hunt for the Faceless Old Woman, whom they describe as an elderly female without a face, although no one has ever actually seen her, so we're all just guessing. But you'll know you're near her if you're at home, particularly if you're home alone and it's dark and you think you hear breathing and creaking steps in another room. Under no circumstances should you look. Don't look. You will not at all like what you see, the Secret Police said.

There is a reward for information leading to the arrest of either of these fugitives. That reward is a gift card to Pier One, a lifetime of gratitude, and a couple of handwritten coupons for things like "washing the dishes" or "a ten-minute backrub."

A couple of listeners have asked how my boyfriend, Carlos, is doing. He's still working on lots of interesting science projects in that desert otherworld. It's been almost a year since I last saw him in person. I miss him a lot.

I'm waiting to hear back from station management about getting vacation time so I can go visit him. It's nearly impossible to get approved for vacation, and even if you do, you never know when or how you will find out. At most businesses, you just file some simple paperwork or ask your direct supervisor, and after a few days, they have someone from Human Resources hide in the backseat of your car and when you're halfway home they grab your face from behind, covering your eyes with one hand and mouth with the other, and shout, "Your vacation has been approved! Congrats!" and then in your excitement you take them out for ice cream.

But not in community radio. You can wait weeks or months to hear back. In the meantime, though, I've been taking up watercolors again and I did something I've never done for anyone else I've ever been with. I painted a picture of Carlos. He's in profile, looking across his desert otherworld. He's wearing his Karl Lagerfeld-designed lab coat and there's a car-sized bichon frise atop a dune behind him.

It might be the best painting I've ever made. I had long given up this old hobby, and lately I've grown so, I don't know, out of touch, lost, disconnected, I just needed something to occupy my time.

Anyway, I hung it above my desk, near the window, and I tell you it really gets me through the days, seeing my pastel Carlos, in his brush-swept otherworld paradise.

Let's take a look now at the community calendar.

Thursday night, Dark Owl Records will be holding an open mic for anyone who promises not to play any music, perform any poetry or comedy, or produce any kind of art at all. Dark Owl owner Michelle Nguyen said she hopes to not have to listen to or see any more art for as long as she lives, which she is sure will be for a really long time. "It's taking forever, this life," Nguyen said, before inserting an AOL Free Internet for 30 Days disc into her antique CD player. "This is the only thing I can listen to anymore," Nguyen added.

Friday morning the Society for a Blood Space War will be traveling back in time and eliminating several future enemies before they gain training and grow powerful. According to the group's press kit, Friday is the official day of the event but since they'll be traveling back in time, it's kind of moot because they've already done it. It's just that they recently hired a new PR manager and he's being all like "you can't announce an event without a date." Anyway they'll have preemptively assassinated all future enemy leaders by Friday morning.

Well this certainly explains the people in space suits who broke into our break room here at the station last week and started a laser-knife battle with two folks from finance and our new intern Hannah Reff, who it turns out had some pretty sick laserknife fighting skills. The finance folks went down easy, but Hannah managed to fight two of her attackers off before the three remaining intruders grabbed her and jumped en sacrificial masse into the temporary black hole they had created near the coffee maker, thus ending Hannah's future reign of space terror.

To the family of Intern Hannah, she was a good intern, very focused and always a friendly presence here in the office. She was also a future warlord in the Blood Space War, but you couldn't have known that. Only Hannah could have. She will be missed.

Where was I? Oh, Saturday afternoon on the Great Lawn is the Ennui Fair, sponsored by the Last Bank of Night Vale. There will be some pouty clowns indifferent to simplistic balloon shapes of dogs. There will be local merchants and artisans standing hopelessly in small lots where they should be setting up booths to showcase their wares but can't bring themselves to do so because they've lost the thread, not just of the Fair but of their careers and lives. Organizers say they expect cold rain that day, so you should . . . and then their press release just trails off.

Sunday all day is the first annual Ultimate Frisbee Tournament, at the Softball and Field Hockey Grounds, which were discovered last fall by archeologists over near the Olive Garden in the Problematic Birds District. The archeologists determined this ancient site was built over four years ago by natives of this town who enjoyed outdoor activities like amateur softball and field hockey.

"Tuesday Afternoon" is a pretty decent classic rock song.

It has just been reported to me that the Night Vale PTA is upset about the strategic plan created by the Night Vale School Board.

Gordon Moreno, president of the PTA, issued a statement crit-
icizing the school board for not consulting parents and teachers
when crafting these changes.

Joined by treasurer Diane Crayton, whose son Josh is a ninth
grader at NVHS, and secretary Steve Carlsberg, whose stepdaughter
Janice is in second grade, Moreno said the School Board once again
showed its lack of care for parental input into the education and
development of its students.

"Parents' voices must be heard," Moreno shouted from atop
the statue of immortal film actor Lee Marvin. Sitting on Marvin's
shoulders, legs dangling like a denim-wrapped flesh scarf from the
bronze sculpture's muscular neck, Moreno called for more transparency in education planning.

Moreno then clenched his teeth and lips and eyes as he kicked
his legs back and forth in a groaning, full body tantrum.

Let's take a look at financial news.

Two-thousand, nine-hundred twenty-one is a number, which is
up from many other numbers. Definitely up, so you should get really
excited, or perhaps really upset, over this.

Also, the following words: prime, debt, capital, offering, and
portfolio. Write those down and learn what they mean. Do not remember anything that you learn, but seek the memory of what you
learned in dreams.

Here's another number: 9.8 billion. That's a very large number,
one of the largest numbers. Loosen your jaw and breathe in slowly
through your nose when you hear a number like that. Nine. Point.
Eight. Billion. That's billion . . . with TWO Ls. Billion. Wow.

This has been financial news.

John Peters, you know the farmer, called today to say he noticed that Frank Chen has returned to town. Some of you recall that
Frank went missing a while back, and a little over two years ago his

body was found by four kids who followed a railroad track. Chen's body was covered in extensive claw marks and burns most likely caused, according to the coroner's report, by a large dragon.

Anyway, John said he's seen Frank driving around town in his pickup truck doing some freelance construction work with a focus on carpentry and restoration, just like he always did when he was alive.

John said Frank looks good. "He's real tall now, and rotund," John said from atop a telephone pole, where he'd jimmied up a phone directly into the active lines. "Got a tail and a bunch of colorful heads now. Also he got one of them crossover toolboxes and a class-four adjustable hitch for his truck," John said, sounding impressed.

"Guess death isn't the end," John added. "We all have to live on in some way. Maybe it's in the legacy we leave, or the memories other people keep of us, or the feeling they have when they hear our names, or a stolen identity taken by someone still alive, or just actual, physical immortality. It's all a shame, whatever it is. Such a damn shame, everything is, I tell you."

And then there was a loud buzz and a staticky pop and a dial tone. And then a different voice said, "You can hang up the phone now, Cecil."

And I said, "Okay, Lacy, fine."

We've just received word that the school board has rejected the PTA's request for more transparency in long-term strategic planning.

The president of the school board and enormous glowing cloud cited School District Code 25.3B-2, which states "ALL HAIL. ALL HAIL THE MIGHTY GLOW CLOUD. YOU ARE WEAK. YOU ARE NOTHING. YOU MUST BOW DOWN AND GIVE PRAISE TO THE GLOW CLOUD," as well as Code 17.2A, which explicitly defines the powers of the school board president as

"OMNIPOTENT. OMNISCIENT. OBSTREPEROUS. INFINITE." That's exactly what it says. It even has that reverb effect when you read it.

PTA President Moreno, knowing he had very little leverage in his request for power of legislative review, decided to change his strategy into a request for forgiveness from the angry pulsing cloud.

Animals began falling from the sky, with heavy thumps and splats and splashes. The Great Lawn has grown dark with carcasses and shadows, as PTA officers run in search of cover. I've heard from my friend Diane Crayton that she huddled underneath the Lee Marvin statue, and that the lifelike bronze form of our nation's greatest living actor has done a tremendous job of blocking the various black bears and nurse sharks and ostriches falling so violently to earth.

The Glow Cloud has spread wide across the sky, blotting out important things like spy satellites and helicopters, as well as unimportant things like the moon and the illusions of mountains near the horizon.

From right here in the studio, I can see the darkness spreading. It looks like this is as good a time as any to take you to the wea——— [*THUMP*]

What was that? [*THUMP*] What the [*THUMP*] was that?

[*THUMPTHUMPTHUMPTHUMP. . . . growing rapidly more and more thumps of animals hitting the station*]

**WEATHER:** "True Trans Soul Rebel" by Against Me!

The school board and the PTA have reached a compromise. The PTA's earlier grievance that long-term curriculum and school district planning lacked transparency has been heard, and while the Glow Cloud and the school board could not offer complete openness and inclusion in all school district decisions for the PTA, they could offer to stop dropping dead animals on everyone if the PTA never mentioned transparency or questioned authority again.

PTA President Moreno agreed to these terms, panting, "Yes. Sure. Never again. Please just let us be. Please." He then breathlessly repeated all hail, all hail, all hail, as thick residue of some fallen beast dripped slowly off his swollen face and onto his torn shirt.

Diane Crayton, safe beneath the Lee Marvin statue, asked, "Perhaps a PTA liaison on the school board would be—"

But Moreno jumped in, "No. No liaison. We're just fine, Diane. We must give praise."

And Diane didn't say a word, but she said a lot. Moreno did not acknowledge the look in Diane's eyes.

Steve Carlsberg then added . . . I don't know. It doesn't matter. I'm sure he added something. Steve always does.

I hope you are all safe, dear listeners. I hope you are all okay. I know I am safe. Sadly, though, I am not okay.

The falling animal carcasses collapsed a small section of the outer wall around our radio station. No one was injured but it was the wall where my desk was. My new painting. I had spent so long on it. I mean. I can replace it but. It's just that—

It's just that it brought me such happiness. Such a reason to get up. Such little joys. Like it's not hard to find images of Carlos. We have science with its phones and screens and psychic projections and . . . But that picture. It was art. Creation. Destroyed.

I mean. I can paint another. I can.

I can just paint another. It'll be fine. Just an excuse to do some fun painting.

I'm glad we're all okay. Diane's okay. Even Steve. I'm glad he's okay, too.

I can just paint . . .

It's fine.

Yep. Everything's fine. Stay tuned next for the quiz show "Ask Me Another. But I'll Never Talk, You Fiend. I'll NEVER Talk." It's our most popular new program.

And as always, good night, Night Vale. Good night.

**PROVERB:** Don't bring a gun to a knife fight. Don't bring a knife to a knife fight either. Stop going to knife fights altogether. What's your deal with knife fights?

# EPISODE 65:
# "VOICE MAIL"

## APRIL 1, 2015

GUEST VOICES: DYLAN MARRON (CARLOS), KATE JONES (MICHELLE
NGUYEN), HAL LUBLIN (STEVE CARLSBERG), SYMPHONY SANDERS
(TAMIKA FLYNN), WIL WHEATON (EARL HARLAN), MOLLY QUINN (FEY),
MEG BASHWINER (DEB), MARA WILSON (FACELESS OLD WOMAN),
RETTA (OLD WOMAN JOSIE), JASIKA NICOLE (MAYOR DANA CARDINAL),
JACKSON PUBLICK (HIRAM MCDANIELS), ERICA LIVINGSTON (PHONE
TREE), CHRISTOPHER LOAR (PHONE TREE), KEVIN R. FREE (KEVIN)

I LIVE AN UNCONVENTIONAL LIFE. I HOLD EXTREME LIBERAL OPINIONS.
I make weird performance art late at night in moldy old theaters. I
travel the world talking into a new microphone every day. I wear
high-top Vans and a fake leather jacket. I have visible tattoos and
piercings. I hate rules. I hate authority. I hate The Man. I hate The
Man so much that I think that we should, in fact, stick it to him. But
I have a confession to make, I LOVE structure. That's right, I'm just
another damn square in dark-framed glasses. I love schedules: meal-
times, bedtimes, and rigidly enforced freetimes. My favorite thing to
be in the whole world is on time. Because what is structure anyway
but bones! And what is more punk than a skeleton? A skeleton with
a watch on its wrist bone.

I especially love structure when it comes to making art. For the most part, if you build a strong framework you can throw any damn thing at it and it will be great. Even better, borrow an existing framework. That's why I think this episode is genius. It is a great example of using an existing structure to do the heavy lifting of setting the tone and mood to the story. It uses the 1990s answering-machine trope to gift the audience with a private glimpse into the intimacy of Carlos and Cecil's long-distance relationship. Long-distance relationships are often carried out in phone calls, text messages, voice mails, telegraphs, carrier pigeons, and 1,000-mile stares out of rain-dappled windowpanes through longing eyes. So the choice to tell this story, in this way provides a very satisfying fit for rebellious lovers of structure like myself. Not to mention, it uses the structure of a chain of voice mail messages as a jungle gym for all of these fantastic voice actors to show off. This use of structure is brilliant in that it tells us something new about the story and something new about what voice mails can be. We should expect nothing less from the dudes who invented throat spiders.

My personal outgoing message is and has been since I got my own phone in 2000: "You have reached the voice mail of Meg Bash-winer. She encourages you to not spend your life waiting for the beep." This was cute and fun back when my phone was just for my friends to call me to talk about going to see *Rocky Horror* or smoking cigarettes behind the high school or whatever it was we talked about before texting and bitmoji existed. But now that my phone is officially for, like, important business shit, it is just strange. The only reason anyone calls me and leaves a voice mail nowadays is for work or doctor's appointments. I think callers find my voice mail jarring and this leads to shaky and confused voice mails from people who are trying to contact me in a professional manner. I suppose, they feel like they are forced into a choice between leaving me a message or finally taking the leap and going to blacksmith school, or however it is receptionists at gynecologists' offices would really like to be spending their lives. But I'm not going to change my outgoing message because, remember, I hate The Man. And challenges to the convention of voice mails are a part of sticking it to him. Another reason this episode rocks.

It was a true honor to get to perform one of the callers here. This episode feels a bit like a yearbook for the *Welcome to Night Vale* team in 2014–2015, with each guest actor getting to drop in and sign next to their photo. I am thrilled that Deb has her place in this episode. Deb is not a frequent player on the podcast itself, she is saved for the live shows. So I am always excited and nervous when I get asked to do some voice acting and not just the weekly cold read of credits and proverbs. Speaking of proverbs, the one for this episode is about the pack of feral cats that lived behind Joseph's and my old apartment. It says to stay tuned for updates. Here's the update: We have since moved. When we moved all of our patio furniture was covered in cat shit and hairballs. Those cats are probably dead now. Spay and neuter, friends, spay and neuter.

—Meg Bashwiner

**CECIL:** You have reached the voice mail of Cecil Gershwin Palmer. That might seem like an easy thing to do but think about how long you had to stay alive just to learn how a phone works and who I am. Congratulate yourself on that. Give yourself a vigorous pat on the back. And don't forget to leave a message after the heavily distorted sample of a man saying, "I JUST COULDN'T EAT ANOTHER BITE."

**HEAVILY DISTORTED SAMPLE OF A MAN:** I JUST COULDN'T EAT AN-OTHER BITE.

**CARLOS:** Hey, sweetie, it's Carlos. I know you're probably busy talking or not talking. Seems like you're always talking or not talking, you know?

I'll try again in a bit, but I just wanted to let you know what's up here. What's up? The sky. Ha ha. It's a funny joke but also scientifi-cally accurate. I only tell scientifically accurate jokes. I don't get how people can find inaccurate jokes funny.

Like: A horse walks into a bar and says, "I feel used. As a species even. I feel used." And the bartender is also a horse—this is the Horse District, where horses live when they're not being used by the humans—and the horse bartender says, "Don't I know it, buddy," and the first horse says, "I'm not your buddy" and then he says, "Man, I'm sorry. I'm sorry. That was awful of me. It's the anger."

So that's another example of a scientifically accurate joke.

Things are going really well here. With the help of Doug and Alicia and the other members of the masked army that live in this strange desert otherworld, we've been starting to build out an infrastructure. Of course, I had already set up a temporary lab, but now we've dug up the stones that were used in the old settlements up on the mountain and have been building important basics of life, like shelter, and roads, and Bloodstone Circles. It's starting to look downright homey around here, if you ignore the disquieting wasteland beyond. So it's just like the rest of the world, really.

There's lots of material to work with because, get this, we've been just finding stuff lately. Microwaves, toolboxes, old tennis balls. They look like they've been here awhile. I'm not sure how this stuff ended up here, but I'm going to find out.

Oh, that reminds me, I'm thinking of getting a tattoo with the definition of science straight out of Webster's dictionary. So it'll say: "I don't know, but I'm trying to find out, okay?" And then it'll have a skull and some roses. Maybe an anchor. To make it look old-timey.

I'm still working on how to get you here, but I will. How? I don't know, but I'm trying to find out, okay? Okay? Okay.

I love you. Talk again soon.

[*BEEP*]

**MICHELLE:** Hey, Cecil. Michelle from Dark Owl Records calling. The new . . . ugh . . . Woody Guthrie album is in for you. I can't believe you're still listening to that stuff. He hasn't been cool since his electropunk period. We're all listening to archival recordings of bees now. Come in for your stupid album and I'll show you the bee sounds while you're here. And maybe you can hang out for a while because I'm lonely and I need more human contact. Ugh, Woody Guthrie?

[*BEEP*]

*[Faintly in the background, we hear Lee Marvin's "Wand'rin' Star."]*

**STEVE:** Hey, Cecil. I know you said that I wasn't allowed to leave any voice mails on your phone and you marched around the room waving your arms and saying, "NO, STEVE CARLSBERG, NO VOICE MAILS" and then you tried to convince me that voice mails aren't real but you couldn't because I know what is what around here. I know what is what.

But anyway I just wanted to make a quick call to see if Janice could stay with you in a few months. Abby and I are looking at doing a nice little vacation, you know, just the two of us, somewhere romantic like the Warehouse District or the Sandwastes or Arby's. You of all people know how romantic a long weekend at Arby's can be. Which, listen, by the way, I meant it as just a nice gift when I printed up all those T-shirts of you and Carlos there looking up at the lights and you got all weird about it but I don't mind. Sorry I made you upset again.

Just get back to me about the Janice thing, or answer me on your radio show while ranting about me, either way is fine. Hope everything's going well with Carlos. Hope everything is just going. Hope everything goes. Hope it's gone. We all do.

Okie doke.

*[BEEP]*

**TAMIKA:** Cecil, Tamika Flynn here. I'm calling to let you know that me and the rest of the missing children are having a book drive. We're taking books and herding them out on the long trail, sleepless nights on our horses, books clear from our feet out to a horizon gone dusty with the dreary stomp of spine and page upon earth, the sad yelp of books taken in the night by coyotes or librarians. I don't know how long we'll be gone, but when my horse is neck deep in the Colorado and I'm watching the drowned carcass of some book that will never find a reader again float away on that relentless current, I'll think about you. Also it will probably be Thursday. We'll be back Thursday. We're not taking the books far. They can't walk and they're not even sentient, so this'll be a short one. Oh, gotta go. *Night Film* by Marisha Pessl is looking restless and I'm worried it'll start a stampede.

[*BEEP*]

**EARL:** Hi, it's me. Sure, I'd love to come back and do another segment of "Cooking Stuff with Earl Harlan." I have this great recipe for pumpkin pie. There's so much less blood splatter than you would think, but listen, I'm trying to schedule a little more time in my life for my son.

It's hard, for both of us, what with me having a full-time kitchen job plus going straight from being a childless teenager to a middle-aged man with an eleven-year-old. I mean, they have *Sesame Street* episodes about it that you can show your kid but even with PBS's help, trying to explain how weird time is, it's hard.

Time is unimaginably weird.

My son's name is Roger. I finally asked him. He told me. It was that easy and it wasn't easy at all.

I gotta get back to the kitchen. We have a lot of orders coming in, plus it's on fire. Cook with you soon, Cecil.

[*BEEP*]

**FEY:** Seventeen

Eighty-eight

[*DING*]

Forty-nine

Eighty-six

Eighty-one

Sixty-eight

[*singing*] Cause I am a champion and you're gonna hear me roar

[*sigh*]

Eighty-one

Eighty-three

[*DING*]

Four

[*BEEP*]

**CARLOS:** Hey, sorry to call again so soon. I know we talked about space and boundaries and all that, especially with this whole Lot 37 thing you're going through. Got to have time to think, and Ceec, I understand time to think, but I have made an important scientific discovery and you know the rules are different when an important scientific discovery is made. An important scientific discovery is grounds to interrupt anything.

I found people. Here in this desert otherworld. We—me and the members of the masked army—saw human shapes coming towards us. The masked army opted, as is their way, for something of a warlike response, but I convinced them that it was important to discover the facts before formulating a response, an idea to which Doug roared in a fearsome voice, "THAT MAKES TOTAL SENSE. LET'S GO CHAT WITH THEM AND SEE WHAT'S UP."

And here is, my sweet Cecil, what was up: These people were citizens of Night Vale. They had been lost from their home, as of today, for exactly two years, and they have apparently been wandering this desert since.

They are a tad traumatized by their years in a featureless wasteland, accompanied only by a distant rumble and a bright light that they felt primarily in the roots of their teeth, and so they haven't told me yet how they got here. But I have them resting in the hot yoga studio we recently built, so I hope to hear their story soon. And when I hear the story, you will, too. And then, I'm sure, everyone who listens to your show will, you old blabbermouth. It would upset me if it weren't just who you are. So much of each other would be annoying if they weren't also the essence of us.

Okay, more soon.

[*BEEP*]

**DEB:** Hello Cecil, it's Deb, the sentient patch of haze. I have some new ad copy I want to run by you. And then I want to disregard any petty human feelings you have about it. And then I want to run the ad on the air. Here goes, okay?

I drift above you. I see mostly the top of your heads. You are pitiful from that perspective. Your hair droops or falls out or hangs flat. I haze above you, sentiently. You slug below me, humanly.

Sentient patches of haze. We are the future. We are also the past. You aren't even the props. You are the backdrop.

So if you have any issues or questions at all about that ad, don't hesitate to not tell me. Hope you're having a great day. Okay, Cecil, bye-bye!

[*BEEP*]

**FACELESS OLD WOMAN:** Hello, Cecil, it's the Faceless Old Woman Who Secretly Lives in Your Home. I'm in your closet, listening to moths eat one of your suits. They make such a lovely crunch and tear.

I just wanted to reach out in regards to you protecting your former Intern Dana against Hiram and I's good work toward destroying her. You've foiled us more than once. I won't forget that, Cecil. I forget nothing. Unlike you, your brain a dusty surface so easily blown clean. My memory cakes on, it stains, it warps. My memory is erosion, it is on the very surface of the earth.

Do you feel my fingernails on your back? No. You don't. I could do so many things to you without you feeling it. Remember that, if you remember nothing else, which seems likely these days.

Tell Carlos I said, "Hi." I always liked him. And stay out of my way or I will destroy you just as these moths I caught outside and carried into your closet are destroying all of your clothing.

[*BEEP*]

**OLD WOMAN JOSIE:** Cecil, I'm here with Erika and Erika, just checking to see if we can get a ride to League Night later. My car's in the shop because I stopped believing in it, so if you can fit us all in there we'd appreciate it. Also I can't use my left hand lately, so it might be a little tricky but we're still going to win. We'll crush 'em, Cecil.

[*BEEP*]

**DANA:** Hi Cecil,

It's Mayo— It's Dana.

I hope you're doing okay. You seem kind of . . . I mean lately. Lately, you've been.

Isn't it weird how we talked more when I was trapped in that distant desert otherworld than now when we work a five-minute drive from each other? It's funny how life works. That word meant the opposite of its usual meaning. That's funny too, I guess.

I know you think I bought Lot 37. But you're wrong. I wasn't in Night Vale at the time. Yes, I projected myself into the auction that day, but I only bought some collectible spoons and a Lee Marvin—autographed baseball for my brother. That's all, though.

It's awful when you can see the reasoning for someone's feeling toward you while knowing wholly that they're wrong.

I wonder sometimes if my double could have done better. Or, if I am the double, whether the original me would have done better. Did I destroy my better half? Then maybe I was lucky that even half of me was better, once upon a time.

Cecil, I do my best with what I have. I don't have much. I hope we'll talk soon.

Night Vale needs me as much as it needs you. And when it comes down to it, I'll stand for that before anything else. It's my job.

Okay.

[*BEEP*]

[*weird alien sounds*]

[*BEEP*]

**CARLOS:** Hey, quick update, and then—poof—I'm gone again from your voice mail. I've put some of the junk we've found and some of the people we've found in my lab and I'm studying them using microscopes and vials of bubbling liquids and me making thoughtful expressions and saying *hmm*. So I'm really using all of the available scientific tools right now.

I feel like I'm on the verge of something big here. Something new. I'll call you soon. This is so exciting!

[*BEEP*]

**HIRAM-GOLD:** Well howdy, Cecil, uh, Frank Chen here.

**HIRAM-BLUE:** Yes, Frank Chen with 1000-percent certainty that is who I am.

**HIRAM-GOLD:** Right. So, Frank Chen, normal human with one voice. No other voices interrupting that main voice making me sound anything less than human.

**HIRAM-GREEN:** WHAT'S GOING ON? SOMEONE PUT THE PHONE NEAR MY EARS. I CAN'T HEAR.

**HIRAM-GREY:** Well, there's that busted.

**HIRAM-GOLD:** Just normal human Frank Chen playing a joke with funny voices, wanting to hear if the mayor told you any plans she might have. I'm curious because I'm a citizen and a voter.

**HIRAM-PURPLE:** This was a bad plan. I told you I didn't want any more to do with your foolish plans.

**HIRAM-GOLD:** Purple! Green! Blue! Grey! Come on, guys. We're in this together. And ugh. Just. All right. Frank Chen, average person of normal head amount saying good-bye. See you around, Cecil.

[*BEEP*]

**AUTOMATIC PHONE VOICE:** [*words with \*\* are performed by a separate voice, in a dry manner*] Hello this is your \*DAILY\* update from the automated \*WEATHER\* service. Here is the current \*WEATHER\*.

**WEATHER:** "Tag!" by Scarves

Thank you for using our automated \*WEATHER\* service. Have a \*NICE\* day.

[*BEEP*]

**CARLOS:** Cecil! Cecil! I did it. I understand. I hooked everything up to computers and I said *hmm* a lot and then I asked the people to talk about how they ended up in the desert and it turned out that they were all lured into the Dog Park during Poetry Week, and then the gates closed on them and they've been in this desert ever since.

And I thought about this. I thought about how Dana came in here with them on that same day. And about all of the stuff I found, which I think is junk that people got rid of by throwing them over the walls of the forbidden Dog Park. And I realized.

This is the Dog Park. This whole desert. The mountain. The light up on the mountain. We're in a vast, perhaps endless, and definitely endlessly forbidden Dog Park.

Which means . . . you can visit now. You just have to walk through that Dog Park gate and then, you know, walk a few more hundred miles after that to wherever we're at in this huge desert and then you'll be able to take that vacation here.

Call me as soon as you get this. Cecil! Oh honey-voiced honey! You'll be able to visit. Talk soon. Love you.

[*BEEP*]

**KEVIN:** Hey, friend. We haven't spoken in awhile. Not since all that . . . unpleasantness happened. I hope everything has been

super pleasant since then. Oh but hey. I've been working on something I'd like to show you. I think you'll be just jazzed about it. Get
back to me ASAP, okay?

Until next time, Cecil. Until next time.

**PROVERB:** Instead of a proverb today, I just have some important news about the stray cats that live outside my apartment. There is the usual one, named Bisquick, who is missing
one ear and is terrifying, but today I saw a second one, who is
fatter and less terrifying and who I have named The Baron. I
will keep you updated as events unfold.

# EPISODE 66:
## "WORMS . . ."

### APRIL 15, 2015

### GUEST VOICE: MARA WILSON (FACELESS OLD WOMAN)

SIMILAR TO EPISODE 64, AN EARLY STUDY FOR THE "ALL HAIL" LIVE show we would write two years later, Episode 66 is an early study for the second Night Vale novel, *It Devours!*, which was published in October 2017.

The moment we finished the first novel in late 2014, we started discussing the second novel. It didn't take long (like thirty minutes, really) to conclude that novel number two would be about the Smiling God. Exactly what about the Smiling God, we didn't know. Just that the Smiling God seemed like a cool thing to write a book about.

This is how all novels are written. Jane Austen was like, "You know what's a good name? Emma. I freaking love that name. I should write a book called 'Emma.' It'll be about . . . someone named Emma!" Octavia Butler famously had an entire yellow legal pad that was completely empty save for the phrase "Parables? Parables are p cool tbh" on the top page.

So with Carlos still living there, we spent some of 2015 exploring the desert otherworld and its relationship to Night Vale. This liminal space between universes and timelines seemed a great place to start building some of the basic elements around the Smiling God—creepy wormy things under the earth, rumblings, and giant holes.

This episode is not explicitly about the Smiling God. The worms, like cicadas in our actual world, kind of go through multi year cycles of proliferation. And unlike a lot of titular concepts in Night Vale episodes, they're not really the main conflict. They're a scary news story, yes, but it's all in Cecil's lack of attention to them, as he ponders how to go visit Carlos in a distant land.

—Jeffrey Cranor

*We all lie dreamily upon damp earth spotting clouds
shaped like animals we have yet to invent.*

## WELCOME TO NIGHT VALE

If you woke up today, you're probably already well aware of the worms. It's been about twelve years since the last round of worm-based terror in this town, but they're back. They're doing all of the usual worm things: flying around and dropping trees onto cars and houses, spitting venom at people, and eating stray cats and then leaving large, mewling pellets all about town.

Thousands of worms have managed to completely envelop the rec center annex, which is where today's "Continuing Education Course: Counter-Terrorism Techniques for Beginners" was taking place. Sadly, despite frequent pleas by many to classify worm attacks as terrorism, worms remain classified as a low-grade infestation and, thus, were not covered in today's Continuing Education coursework. This means more giant, squirming pellets to clean up.

[*sound of flipping pages*]

Yeah yeah. Worms. Great.

Hey, unrelated to anything. Just wondering, but have you ever asked yourself why the Dog Park is off limits? I mean, I know it's

a municipal park and all, but shouldn't citizens be able to use it? Seems kind of weird, right, that you can't just go to the Dog Park and hang out? Maybe even bring your dog? I don't know.

It's not like it contains any kind of vast desert otherworld where my boyfriend lives. It's, I'm sure, just a plain old Dog Park and not an alt-dimensional portal.

Maybe our mayor will try to open up the Dog Park for public use. Just temporarily, say for a few minutes. Maybe our mayor can help *me* out for once. That would certainly be a friendly and mayoral thing to do.

After years of applications for city approval, there is finally an official Night Vale Book Club, listeners. The Book Club, which is run by fourteen-year-old bibliophile and heroic vigilante Tamika Flynn, will feature weekly discussions of popular and classic fiction, as well as Q&A's with book experts about some of literature's most famous controversies, like last week's heated argument about whether or not Herman Melville really wrote all of the novels which bear his name, or just *Fight Club*.

The Book Club meets Tuesdays from 2:00 P.M. to 4:00 P.M. at Patty's Hardware & Discount Pastries. Members can candidly discuss the books without fear of most government repercussions while noshing on some delicious wheat and wheat-by-product—free pastries, sold at great discount to you. Patty's also specializes in hammers, crowbars, and anything heavy that fits in your hand and can be easily swung. "Shop at Patty's! They'll never suspect a thing!" Patty shouts in the looped recording playing from her perpetually squirming animatronic statue out front of her flagship store.

This week's book is Helen DeWitt's *The Last Samurai*. There is only one heavily charred edition of this novel left in the world, but Tamika assures us that she managed to "borrow" a copy from the Library's Forbidden Material collection. She did finger quotes around the word "borrow," while also shaking her head NO, and stomping "i am being totally facetious" in Morse code with her right leg. Then, an owl landed on her shoulder and winked.

Spring League Baseball tryouts are next Saturday afternoon at the haunted baseball diamond. Children new to organized baseball will be assigned teams automatically, based entirely on their personal dispositions. That way there's a whole team of courageous players; a whole team of clever players; one of conniving, selfish players; and one that takes all the rest of the players, just like the four Major League Baseball teams.

Tryouts are from 10:00 A.M. to 2:00 P.M. with volunteer coaches Betty Lucero and Lusia Tereshchenko.

The Night Vale Youth Baseball Association is asking parents to bring any extra baseballs to tryouts as coach Tereshchenko died over 150 years ago and is now a ghost and so has a hard time picking up ground balls during batting drills.

Getting an update on the worms. City Council has now elevated the warning scale from *worms* . . . , with a lowercase w followed by an ellipsis, to *Worms!!* with a capital W and two exclamation points. It has not yet reached all caps *WORMS*, but if something is not done, this could become a more destructive *Worms!!* outbreak than the famous *WORMS!* with all caps, one exclamation point, and underlined twice disaster of 1997.

You know, listeners, if the worms get near the Dog Park, perhaps the hooded figures who pace about behind the tall black fences would get distracted and then I could run in there and get to the desert other——I could just go check out the dogs catching tennis balls and have a nice relaxing afternoon in a local park. Or, actually, no, I'd make a break for the desert otherworld inside the Dog Park and go finally visit Carlos.

Or, you know, something.

And now a word from our sponsors.

Too much clutter in your home? Do you have excess furniture, old clothes, a couple of folding bikes you never ride anymore, jazz CDs that you no longer want because you finally realized how intellectually dangerous they can be? Perhaps you could put that stuff online for sale.

There's no reason to let old junk go to waste. How does that saying go? One person's trash is another person's leather body suit? It's true. I bet that couch of yours would look really good in, say, Denise Esposito's house.

In fact, it's there now. We went ahead and sold your couch to Denise. She's already come and picked it up while you were at work. Also we sold your TV to Sally Jansen, and your fridge to Mario Landis, and both of your cats to Pedro Reyna. We sold all your belongings and you didn't have to do a thing.

Craigslist. We sold your stuff while you were gone.

Due to today's worm attacks, the Sheriff's Secret Police are putting their search on hold for literal five-headed dragon Hiram McDaniels and the Faceless Old Woman Who Secretly Lives in Your Home. After the attempted coup at City Hall several weeks back, the Secret Police have been aggressively pursuing the two fugitives who have reportedly conspired many times to overthrow Mayor Dana Cardinal.

Mayor Cardinal has been imperiled several times in the last month only to be saved by someone controlling Night Vale Community Radio Host Cecil Palmer, who is still quite upset about being used against his will.

"If the mayor had just asked for my help, I would have happily come to her aid on my own," a frustrated Palmer said, just now, into this very microphone.

Palmer alleges that Mayor Cardinal purchased him last year in an auction and has been using him as her personal protector. The Mayor has denied these charges, but, like the Night Vale constitution says, denying that you are guilty is a major sign of guilt.

The Secret Police had previously warned against approaching either Hiram or the Faceless Old Woman, as they're both deadly. But the Secret Police have been so busy dealing with the worms today that they just can't deal with everything on their own.

"Maybe you could help us out a bit, ya think?" a Secret Police spokesperson said as worms gripped his legs tighter. "I'm sure you'll be fine. If you find either the eighteen-foot tall, five-headed dragon or the omnipresent, ethereal woman who you can't quite ever see, go ahead and bring them down. Thanks for doing that. Big help. Big help," the spokesperson said as the worm consumed, with one slimy gulp, the cutlass in his left hand.

The Secret Police added they received a tip from Night Vale human Frank Chen that he saw Hiram McDaniels flying far away to some other place and so, Chen said, Hiram is definitely not still in Night Vale.

"Hiram ain't coming around here anymore. I'm sure of it," Chen's long gold head stated.

"I WILL BURN YOUR FRAIL USELESS CORPSE, HUMAN," Chen's scaly green head added.

"Stop calling people humans. We are human. Remember?" Chen's blue head said.

"I—I mean—I am human, okay?" Chen's grey head said.

"Knock it off, you guys," Chen's purple head grumbled from behind the other heads.

Speaking of the Faceless Old Woman . . . she knows a lot about this town. I bet I could ask her how to get into the Dog Park, how to get into that desert otherworld. I should ask her, but I'm not sure I'll be able to find h———

**FACELESS OLD WOMAN:** Ask me what?

**CECIL:** Faceless Old Woman. You scared me.

**FOW:** I know. So, you want to go to the desert otherworld and visit your boyfriend?

**CECIL:** I—

**FOW:** You are upset that the mayor has been using you to protect her from those wonderful threats to her life and you're frustrated by this town, and you just want some time away to clear your head and so you don't have to always be saving the mayor from whatever great forces are trying to remove her from office.

**CECIL:** Well—

**FOW:** And by *great* I mean really incredible. Of course, who even knows who's been doing all of this to the mayor? I mean I know. I know everything. But all of these delightful rumors and lies about me. And Hiram! I mean how can people report such rumors? They're not totally untrue, I suppose. And how on earth could I even—

**CECIL:** Faceless Old Woman.

**FOW:** Yes. I'm sorry. I'm a bit distracted.

**CECIL:** You know how to get into the Dog Park?

**FOW:** I do. And I want to help you, because, well, I want you to be happy, Cecil. I will tell you how in a dream. You will be in a boat, which will sink, of course, and you will lose all of your teeth, and as you are trying to pick up your teeth, you will find an oil painting of a Victrola. You will then place the needle on the record and eat the entire painting. Your chest will open and dozens of red birds with gold ribbons in their talons will fly from you and the ribbons will lift your limp, open body, carrying you through the sea and dropping you onto a frantic eddy of pink fish near a pink reef. You must wake up immediately when you see the shadow of a young woman emerging from behind the coral. Do not look long at her.

When you awake, you will hear her whisper.

**CECIL:** And she will tell me how to get into the Dog Park.

**FOW:** I don't know what she will tell you.

**CECIL:** Faceless Old Woman, I—

**FOW:** I have to go. I have to get back to keep- ing a distant eye on whatever it is that Chad is doing in that cursed home of his.

You'll be fine.
Night Vale will be fine.
The mayor will be . . .
Take a nice long break, Cecil.
You've earned it.

    [*hum of station management*]

**CECIL:** Faceless Old Woman? Hello? She's gone I think.

    [*hum is getting very loud*]

Listeners, oh dear, I have made a bad mistake. I believe I have upset Station Management. I think my openly talking about the Dog Park has proved to be far too political a topic for this station's old-fashioned values that believe in not questioning local, world, or secret reptilian governments, nor their parks.

I have grown cavalier in my anxiousness to get out of town for a vacation, and this lack of care in my job perhaps will lead to my end. I do not like the color glowing around my studio door right now. I do not like the predatorial sniffing around the door's edge. I do not like that hum nor the heat of my skin nor the cold of my heart.

I cannot face them, listeners. I cannot. I just want a vacation. I just want to see Carlos, for a week. A day. A—

[*silence*]

An envelope. Oh no. The noise and the lights are gone. All that is left is a black envelope, upon which is a single silver glyph, lightly afire. I do not recognize the language nor even the alphabet, of this burning symbol. But I know in my mind exactly what this says. I wish I did not know. I must have courage. I must open this frightful news.

Before I do, let me say I am sorry to station management, and to the city of Night Vale. I have betrayed your trust with my careless speech. If spared, I promise to never speak ill nor question the Dog Park again. But for now, I will take myself to my punishment, and I will take you to the weather.

**WEATHER: "Little Black Star" by Hurray for the Riff Raff**

So guess what! The envelope wasn't about the Dog Park at all. I fell to my knees begging Station Management for forgiveness, but they silenced me immediately. They were simply letting me know that my vacation had finally been approved.

I was confused for a moment. I asked about the burning glyph on the outside of the envelope and what I thought it meant, which took some explaining, as I didn't know how to describe that particular horrifying experience in English. They laughed and said no, that glyph is just the ancient abbreviation for Human Resources. They're who approve the vacations around here.

Then they showed me the actual glyph that meant what I thought the other one meant, and I lost consciousness. I'm not sure for how long. When I woke I heard the whispered instructions from the woman in the coral. And then I heard laughter. Station Management was laughing.

And I laughed, too, and then they stopped laughing. Or growling. Perhaps it was growling they were doing. It's very difficult to say what that noise is they make. Ooooh, wow, I think it was growling. Now I'm super embarrassed about laughing.

Anyway, the worms have backed down, thanks to a flamethrower and fierce rhetoric by the City Council, resulting in some sick burns, both metaphorically and literally. The worms have left, sure to return for us again someday, as all of nature eventually will.

Friends, listeners, all of Night Vale. I love you very much, but I need time away to be with Carlos, yes, and also some time to myself. To reflect. Also I got a message from an old—colleague? acquaintance? nemesis?—who lives there as well. You know, I don't want to talk about it just yet.

Night Vale, we've had many great years together, and I won't be gone long, but I've also grown weary.

Weary of some friends who are less than friends. Weary of fights that need not be fought. Weary of not being myself some of the time, which is something I strongly prefer to be all of the time. Weary, sometimes, of Night Vale itself, I think.

I'll be back. Whenever. Refreshed. You'll know when. It'll be when you hear my voice again.

Stay tuned next for . . . I don't know. Anyway, time for vacation!

Good night, Night Vale.

[*sound of headphones coming off; maybe a mic bump*]

[*calling off mic; leaving the studio*]

GOOD NIGHT! Woo hoo!


**PROVERB:** When you wish upon a star, your dreams come true, but—because of distance— not for millions of years.

# EPISODE 67:
# "[BEST OF?]"

## MAY 1, 2015

### GUEST VOICE: JAMES URBANIAK (LEONARD BURTON)

I RECORDED MY LINES FOR THIS EPISODE ON APRIL 14, 2015, THE 150th anniversary of the assassination of Abraham Lincoln. (The episode's themes of the mystic chords of memory and Leonard Burton's own demise are purely coincidental.) My inspiration for Leonard's broadcast style was Harry Shearer's cadence on his public radio program "Le Show," the way he . . . [*pauses*] and then EMPHASIZES and then . . . [*pauses*] again. For all I know Mr. Shearer modeled his approach, consciously or not, on the old broadcaster Paul Harvey, who had a similar vocal attack. At any rate, Leonard Burton is part of a broadcast tradition.

I did two takes, occasionally stumbling on words like *outergalaxy warlords* and *sparklingly*. My understanding is Joseph and Jeffrey wrote the character with me in mind. I do enjoy wrapping sculpted phrases around my tongue and their writing has good mouthfeel. I recorded in L.A., edited out my mistakes and sent the file to New York.

The ease of podcast technology has spawned a revival of radio drama and a community of fans and creators. My own scripted podcast, *Getting On with James Urbaniak*, premiered in August 2012, two months after the *Welcome to Night Vale* pilot was posted. I was forty-eight at the time and podcast drama has become an essential and exhilarating new chapter in my creative life. It's a joy to be part of this community, making original work on our own terms (often in the comfort of our own homes) and putting it out there. As of this writing I'm planning a new series of *Getting On* episodes (with my writing partner, Brie Williams, who has also written for Night Vale). I can't imagine stopping at this point. I don't imagine the Night Vale team will either.

—James Urbaniak

**LEONARD BURTON:** The sun is actually cold.
It's cold and empty and all is lost.

# GREETINGS FROM NIGHT VALE

While your regular host, Cecil Palmer, is on vacation, we continue to bring you some of the highlights of his uncountable years here at Night Vale Community Radio, from lowly (but eager) intern filing reports from the field, to his tenure behind the desk at the greatest community radio station in America. Today I thought we'd start with a very special and rare clip: Cecil's first ever broadcast on our airwaves. Let's listen.

**TEENAGE CECIL:** Hi, it's Cecil! Oh boy! Or, oh, I'm sorry. Let me try that again and it'll be way more professional.

Hello listeners, Intern Cecil Palmer here, reporting live for host Leonard Burton. I'm way excited.

[*gathers self*]

I am standing in a vast stretch of desert in which no one has lived for hundreds of years. Neat right? But it's not even the neatest! Because some new folks have moved into the area recently. They look like they're from back east aways. This isn't their land, but they're going to set up here anyway. They're saying "this is ours," and pointing, ludicrously, at actual earth as though that were an ownable thing.

One of the arrivals, famous screen actor Lee Marvin, who just turned thirty today—oh hey, happy birthday, Mr. Marvin—said that they were immediately proceeding to found a town, a town they will call Night Vale, a home for themselves, complete with all the things a home needs: secrets, dread, omnipresent government, and areas that are forbidden. He then donned a soft meat crown as the other newcomers bowed to him.

And now, the community calendar.

Monday through Sunday, this will be a barren stretch of desert strewn with human debris shot out by a population explosion back east. These shiftless fellows will mope around and complain about the heat and lack of water. The shadows up on the hills will watch and watch but will come no closer. Squinting, the newcomers will see the shadows in the hills, and then they will squint further and further until their eyes are closed, and then they will hum until their minds are empty, and sit dreaming until their dreams are clean, and they will never look at the hills again. They will cease to believe in hills at all. Elevation will become a laughable thing. The sky, a starry stranger. The ground, a barren friend. The cliff dwellings are empty now, but their scattered children are manifest and filled with love and mirth and grief.

This has been the community calendar.

All right, back to you, Leonard . . . Mr. Burton, sir. Thanks for giving me this opportunity.

**LEONARD:** What fantastic old days those were. Everything old is wonderful. It is a shame anything had to change. I sure do dislike change. The sun has moved in the sky, and I distrust it completely.

Here's another early story Cecil reported as station intern. This was one of my favorites, a real turning point for our town and for

America and for the world, but also (quite unfortunately) for the outer-galaxy warlords who wish to prolong the senseless Blood Space War.

**EARLY-20s CECIL:** Intern Cecil here on the scene.

All I see is devastation. Devastation that once was mere existence. People and buildings reduced to holes in space and time, gaps both concrete and metaphorical, losses that would be overwhelming if everything didn't already proceed in a state of pre-loss, each thing defined in its existence by the nothing that will come after.

Devastation and ruins. Streamers and balloons.

So a happy big three-oh to immortal screen legend Lee Marvin, who is celebrating his special day by opening his Seventh Eye and incinerating onlookers by the wailing hundreds with his holy light. Happy birthday, Mr. Marvin!

And now the Children's Fun Fact Science Corner.

I recently took a fantastic trip to Europe. I don't have time right now, but one of these days I'll tell all of you listeners out there some of the funny stories from my European vacation. In the meantime, we're here about science, right? And from whom better to learn about science than a scientist, right? Well, on my trip I met a very smart, and very handsome scientist. His name is Guglielmo Marconi.

He showed me all sorts of things. All *sorts* of things. *All* sorts. But he also showed me a new device he's working on called, get this, *radio*. As unlikely as it seems, Marconi thinks that soon shows just like this will be carried by invisible waves right to your ears. He showed me the blueprints for his invention, full of strange words like "receiver" and "transmitter" and "community radio" and "three commercial-free hours of alternative music" that all are part of how this strange new mechanism will function.

Who knows, maybe one day I will see one of these "radios" for myself. Wow. Even the word sounds goofy.

This has been the Children's Fun Fact Science Corner.

**LEONARD:** Let's talk again about the good old days. Remember the 1930s (or the Sparklingly Clean 30s, as we once called them), when America was flush with cash and people literally could not, would not stop dancing with their hips and wearing sequined fringe? It was a great time to roll up hundred dollar bills and fill them with shredded up twenty dollar bills and smoke them like cigars. Just great. I truly wish for stasis.

**CECIL:** Intern . . . [*sigh*] . . . still Intern Cecil here. Big thanks, as always, to our host, Leonard Burton, in the booth, as he has been for what seems like a really long time. Not saying it is a long time. Who knows what a long time is, even? Not me. But it just seems that way. That's all.

It's New Year's Eve, 1934, and, here in Night Vale, as in towns all over this great country, we are celebrating with large swimming pools full of champagne. This is both fun and also practical, since we have way more champagne than we can drink or even safely store without the towering stacks of champagne crates threatening to tumble down onto our fragile bodies. So what better way of honoring the season than just dumping a ton of this stuff into a swimming pool and splashing around in it?

Turns out it's not great for swimming in, what with the alcohol content and acidity, but it's okay because we have pool floats made from compacted caviar.

Everyone is here and everyone is having a blast. Even little Josie Ortiz, young as she is, is getting in on the act, entertaining swimmers with simple magic tricks and minor prophecies. This is the best party Night Vale has had since last week's big blowout in honor of Lee Marvin's thirtieth birthday.

As I look out over the lush grassland and the verdant trees sagging with tropical fruit, an area that just a few years ago was flat empty desert forever, I feel the warmth inside, that American warmth that gives me great certainty. It will be this way from now to always. From now on, peace. From now on, prosperity. From now on, champagne swimming pools every New Year's. America is taking flight, and hardworking people are its wings.

Back to you, as always, Leonard. Always. I genuinely can't remember a time you didn't have that job.

**LEONARD:** Of course, just a few years later, the trees and grassland were gone, the second war had hit Europe, and all of Night Vale came together to make explosives and devices to launch explosives. Nothing shows the beautiful perfection of human community like intercontinental weaponized combat. It was a better time then.

This was also Cecil's first ever broadcast as the full-time host of this show.

**CECIL:** Cry havoc and let slip the hounds of war. Weep havoc. Squeeze grief like coal to diamonds until it slides, crystalline and compact, down your reddened cheeks, and let slip those ugly, useless hounds to do their ugly, useless work. *Welcome to Night Vale.*

Hello listeners. Here I am, as I thought I might never be, behind the studio microphone at Night Vale Community Radio. Yes, top news tonight is that our beloved Leonard Burton has retired in order to spend more time trying to understand what a family is, and so I will, from now forward, take over as the voice of our little community. This is a proud day for me, and a proud day, I'm sure, for my mother, who has been hiding from me for decades now but whose absence in many ways speaks to me more than words could.

With the big news out of the way, we go back to the usual day to day. There is, of course, a war in Europe and the Pacific and all around the world. We ourselves have been attacked. Or not *we*, Night Vale is still fine, but people who share our same broad category, somewhere, they've been attacked. And that will not stand.

Night Vale is, of course, very tricky to leave, so no one has actually joined the army or anything. But we are doing our part for America by buying war bonds, growing victory gardens, and chanting in Bloodstone Circles. Leading experts say that it is the indomitable American spirit, the fighting prowess of our soldiers in the field, and mostly chanting in Bloodstones Circles that will win this war.

Like those famous Rosie the Riveter posters all over town say: "Get chanting in Bloodstone Circles double-time, or me and the rest of riveters will come at you with rivet guns. You ever have someone come at you with a rivet gun? Well, bud, you don't want that, trust me."

Inspiring words in difficult times. But when the turbulent events of the past few years have you down, just remember your friend Cecil, behind the mic and talking you through it from this day forward.

**LEONARD:** Huh. While that clip was playing I found a few Fidelipac cartridges. They look pretty old. I don't remember pulling these for today's "Best Of" show. Let's see what this first one is. It's marked THE END? Question mark.

**CECIL:** Nulogorsk, our Russian sister city, is gone. The people of Nulogorsk, our friends, they are gone too. Since then the sky has been hot with death. So much fuel for so many rockets burning away at once, it makes the fall air seem a little warmer, even down here, not to mention that final sizzle at the end of each.

Blooms of death all over the world, hot and final. I speak to you for as long as I can, from a world ending. 1983. Our final year. I suppose as good a year as any.

Josie Ortiz, once young, now middle-aged, will never go on to be the old woman she could have become. Lee Marvin, famed screen actor, will die having just turned thirty, never to see another year pass.

And I will go too. Amidst a screaming of sirens that warn without helping, that make a show of protecting without protecting at all. I will never meet that someone. That someone who could have given my life depth and meaning, who could have been my other. I will only ever sit here, only *have* ever sat here, behind this microphone, until I am not ever, ever again.

Good night, from a world ending, Night Vale. Good—

*[static, radio tuning, fading in on a different Cecil]*

. . . looking to be a good year. At least as good as 1983 has been. Josie Ortiz would like me to remind everyone that this Thursday she is holding a benefit for the Old Opera House. It will be a lavish evening, with everything you would expect from a fancy night out, like a salad bar. Tickets are $100 and are not for sale to the likes of you.

In other news, Simone Rigadeau, professor of Earth Sciences at the Night Vale Community College, says that her reality has split, that she is experiencing another history happening now, a history in which all of this ends. She is shutting down the Earth Sciences program in order to devote herself fully to understanding what has happened to her shattered mind and this ended but yet also not-ended world. Well, best of luck in your new career, Simone!

**LEONARD:** Oh yes, those were glorious days. These days the world seems to never be ending for some and not others. The world is a worse place now than it ever was before, but far better than it ever will be again. The past is always better than the present, and the future is the worst of all.

This next cartridge is marked WEATHER. Let's see what's on it.

**WEATHER:** "When Can I Say that I Love You" by Kyle Fleming

**LEONARD:** And I have one last clip here. There's a piece of duct tape on the plastic casing upon which someone has written a thick, shaky NO. So let's play that.

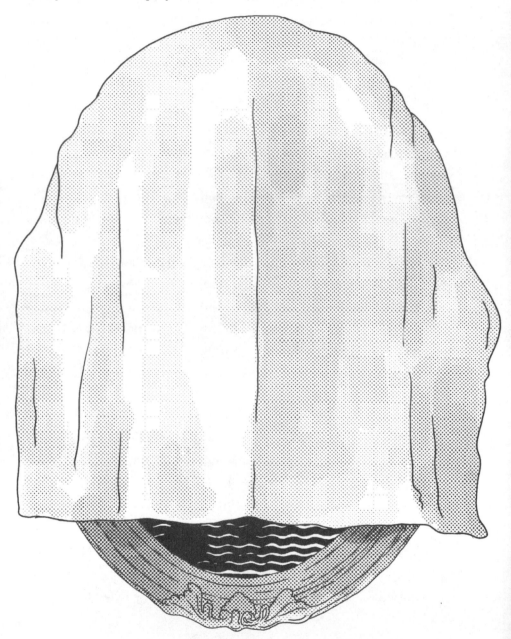

**CECIL:** Listeners, oh listeners. I come to you with sad news. I think you know the news. I think we all saw what happened. To the family and friends of former Night Vale Community Radio host Leonard Burton, I extend my deepest sympathies. Not that my sympathies will do you any good.

For what Leonard experienced is something that no human, no sentient being should ever have to experience. The blood, those stains on the broken asphalt. The skin, or I think that was skin. But then all those bits that were clearly not skin, of course. And then all the more blood, of course. And the wretched sound of the pulling. And the single, awful snap. We will all remember the sound of the snap forever. There is more. But I cannot. There is more. But I won't. And the fingernails, of course. Of course, the fingernails.

I mourn Leonard Burton with all my heart and my liver and kidneys. With the bones of my toes and with my belly button. I mourn him with my armpit and neck sweat. Every part of me. Every facet. The physical of me, I mourn him with these.

Leonard gave me my start. He took a chance on me. He gave me the life I have. And now he doesn't have life. It is an equation with a miswritten number. Nothing can be solved. It is an error.

The City Council warned that the mess left from Leonard Burton's death is likely to draw Street Cleaners and that we should all take shelter. Cover your mirrors. Shade your eyes. Stay indoors and mourn. Stay indoors and mourn.

Leonard's death and my barely contained grief have been brought to you today by Shasta Cola. Shasta Cola: Same great taste. Low, low price.

And now, moving forward as best we can, to political news. Of course the focus now is on the big debate about President Clinton: Who is he? What's a president? How did this strange news from the outside world reach our little desert hamlet?

For that let's bring in senior political analyst Lee Marvin, who, oh look what day it is, this is your thirtieth [*CLICK*]

**LEONARD:** I . . . Listeners. Have you ever forgotten where you put your keys? You were certain they were on the mantel. But they were not. Have you ever missed an appointment because you were sure it was on Wednesday at noon, not Tuesday at ten? Have you ever remembered a life you did not lead? Has a carefully collated series of words ever made you uncertain? Unconfident? Or un. Just un. Un as an adjective unto itself.

I do not remember that story at all. I do not like that story. That is a bad story.

It was a better day earlier, back when I hadn't heard that story. This present, this now, is no good. No good at all.

Stay tuned next for less of the best and more of the same. It's been a pleasure to fill in this week, in my old job, Night Vale. Cecil will be back soon. Until then, this has been Leonard Burton.

And as always, See ya, Night Vale. See ya.

**PROVERB:** "I'm all business," I say, peeling off my skin strip by strip, showing you what oozes out. "Business to my core."

# EPISODE 68:
## "FACELESS OLD WOMEN"

### MAY 15, 2015

### GUEST VOICE: DYLAN MARRON (CARLOS)

THERE IS NO QUESTION THAT I GREW UP IN A HAUNTED HOUSE.

I'm not even sure there is such a thing. I'm agnostic about ghosts and spirits, but there was something unusual going on there. Appliances turned on in the middle of the night, things moved from one place to another when no one was there, certain rooms were always much colder than others. It always felt like someone, or something, was there with us. Not a malevolent spirit, but one that followed its own rules, ones we would never understand.

I was a fearful child, often afraid, always anxious. But I was never scared of whatever seemed to be haunting us. If anything, it was a point of pride. We never played house when my friends came over, we played *creepy house* and I'd brag about our "ghost." Mostly, I felt safe at home, protected. It was what was outside that scared me.

Some cities have lush green trees or rolling hills or the ocean. Desert cities have the sky. It seems limitless, and endlessly beautiful . . . at first. But then comes the overwhelming smallness and the creeping realization that there's nowhere to hide. The valley suburb of Los Angeles where I grew up wasn't *quite* the desert, but we had the same overwhelming, expansive sky, and looking at it could be too much for me. The constant sunlight felt intrusive, even cruel.

Maybe this is why I first connected so strongly with *Welcome to Night Vale*. No one had ever put the creeping horror I could feel into words before. I had read stories about the horrors lurking in New England fog, or the spirits haunting Victorian houses in New Orleans, but where had the Desert Noir been all my life? There was so much about it that rang true to me, and still does.

Playing the Faceless Old Woman in *Night Vale* has been an honor. I've had the privilege to perform her in shows in lush green cities, cities with rolling hills, cities by the ocean. And of course, in the desert. In some places, she's a beloved character (her fan base seems to be particularly strong in Canada) and in some places she's feared. It's true that the Faceless Old Woman operates in ways that we can't understand. She seems impulsive, impassive, but what she does makes sense to *her*. She might haunt us, but I don't know if she's anything to be afraid of.

Perhaps that's too easy for me to say, though: I'm used to being haunted. And now I get to be the one doing the haunting.

—Mara Wilson

Get the body you've always wanted. We know where it's buried and can lend you a shovel.

## WELCOME TO NIGHT VALE

Hello, listeners. I'm back from vacation, and I'm feeling great. I, of course, miss being with Carlos in that desert otherworld and miss having so much time to relax with my boyfriend, but as with any vacation, it always feels good to come home.

We had such a delightful time. Carlos and the masked army of nomadic giants that inhabit that place have managed to build a little paradise there. There's now a roller coaster and an ice cream parlor and a beach resort hotel and spa. Unfortunately, they don't have operators for the roller coaster, nor any milk for making ice cream, nor any water along the beach resort. So most of those things just sit empty, except for the roller coaster which is constantly running and filled with the same people who got on it over two months ago, unable to stop because no one knew how to build a brake system. There were terrified screams dopplering up and down the otherwise quiet nights. Those people are just having the time of the rest of their lives.

More on my trip later, but first some breaking news.

The Sheriff's Secret Police just announced that they have captured the Faceless Old Woman Who Secretly Lives in Your Home.

The Faceless Old Woman is one of two fugitives the Secret Police have been tracking for the past few months. She and literal five-headed dragon Hiram McDaniels are wanted in connection with a series of attacks on Mayor Dana Cardinal at City Hall.

A Secret Police spokesdeer made today's big announcement by writing it in dirt with its hoof. The announcement began a couple hours ago, but we're just now getting to the good stuff and reporters have grown impatient with the spokesdeer who can only scratch one or two words at a time and then has to erase them before continuing with the next words.

The press conference turned ugly as a couple of reporters shouted, "Speak English!" at the deer, but then a couple more shouted, "PA ROOSKI!" and the spokesdeer, looking relieved, began speaking in fluent Russian. Which flummoxed those reporters who only spoke English despite their adamant demands that others develop a mastery of multiple languages.

But the big news is that they captured a dangerous fugitive, which is so shocking, because to my knowledge no one has ever even seen the Faceless Old Woman Who Secretly Lives in Your Home because she lives there secretly. Of course, without a face, I imagine it would be simultaneously easy and difficult to identify her.

More on this story as it develops.

Okay, so back to our vacation. Carlos showed me the apartment he built using his scientific knowledge of physical materials and spatial relations. It was a cute little one bedroom on the side of a low, craggy mountain. (I could hardly believe it. A mountain, right?!) We took turns making each other breakfast whenever we thought it was morning. Carlos cooks a delicious vegan omelet using thick fillets of ginger root for the eggs and filling it with dried cranberries and capers. I'm not a great cook, but I make excellent coffee. I generally don't let Carlos make the coffee, because I have a specific way I like to make it using a coffee hammer and angry chanting.

I like my coffee like I like my nights: dark, endless, and impossible to sleep through.

After a week's staycation in Carlos's apartment, we went with the giant masked warrior Alicia on several hiking trails around the desert canyons. Carlos and Alicia showed me the brilliant array of flora that grows in that desert otherworld. While the desert around Night Vale is mostly red and brown dust, with a smattering of white and brown rocks, topped with gray and brown brush, the canyons of the desert otherworld were flush with rich brush of charcoal and tan, rocks the color of snow and leather, and dust that was striped in shades of sunset and mahogany.

And there were mysterious lights in the sky. Just like here in Night Vale. We could not understand the lights, but we understood our lack of understanding, which is all most understanding is.

Some mornings, Alicia and Doug and the other giant masked warriors would see other masked armies and they would head off to war, gone for days at a time, only to return bloodied and fewer in number. Carlos and I didn't mind, because it gave us more time to ourselves. More about our vacation later, but there's some news or something.

An update on today's arrest of the Faceless Old Woman. Several residents across Night Vale are reporting vandalism inside their homes. Old Town residents Christopher Brady and Stuart Robinson report their living room walls were covered in writing that reads: "YOU TALKED! I SEE YOU AND I CANNOT HATE YOU BUT I CANNOT FORGIVE YOU." The text seems to have been written with hand-smeared mayonnaise. Also all of the toes were cut out of their dress socks.

Said Robinson of the damage: "I think it's because I reported to the sheriff that the Faceless Old Woman Who Secretly Lives in Our Home was secretly living in our home. I regret this now."

Brady added: "I told you not to do that, Stuart!"

Robinson then replied, head in his hands: "I know, Chris. You were right. You're always right."

"You should have listened to Christopher," came a cold whisper over their shoulders.

Stay tuned here, as we bring you more news of today's arrest.

And now, it's time for another edition of my popular advice segment "Hey There, Cecil." Let's get to your questions.

"Hey there, Cecil. I date a lot of people but never for very long. I find that while I sometimes say, "I love you" to my girlfriend or boyfriend at the time, I don't think I have ever meant it. How do you know if you're in love?" Signed: Loveless in the Barista District

Hey there, Loveless. I think when you're truly in love you'll know it. But you have to be in the right place with yourself to find that love. As my mother used to tell me, "You can't learn to love others until you learn that others are fiction and that self is unreliable."

Next question. "Hey there, Cecil. My husband and I regularly host dinner parties for our neighbors and vice versa. When our neighbors come over to our house, they never take off their shoes. I personally don't have a problem with that, but my husband thinks it's rude. What's your take?" Signed: Unshod in Old Town

Hey there, Unshod. This is pretty clear-cut to me. It is customary when you enter a person's home that you must always remove your shoes. Then you must remove their shoes. You must hold that person down. Take their shoes. Get their shoes off. This is standard etiquette.

We've got time for one more question. "Hey there, Cecil. You know the tower? The one that casts no shadow? It also sounds like an untuned cello? Do you know the one? Smells like sulfur? Well, it's glowing now." Signed: Malevolent in Mission Grove Park

Hey there, Malevolent. You know as well as I do that tower was destroyed a century ago. Never write me again. [*whispered:*] Please write me again.

Old Woman Josie and her friends who are not angels, just a bunch of really tall people with wings named Erika whom we cannot bear to look directly at, said that the new Old Night Vale Opera House was coming along nicely. Although, I drove past the construction site the other day, and it's still a mostly empty lot. The only difference is that they changed the sign from "Josefina Contractors Inc." to "StrexCorp Operatics Ltd." Also there's a giant opera house there. But other than that it still looks nearly the same as when they broke ground months ago.

Opening night of the new Old Opera House will be June 15 and will feature the world premiere of an original opera by the famous actor and composer Lee Marvin, Night Vale's own immortal legend of stage and screen.

Still no word on what an opera is. I'm being told it's like a petting zoo, but with fewer starving wolves and more intermissions.

Breaking news from City Hall as the Sheriff's Secret Police say they have now arrested more than a dozen Faceless Old Women.

The spokesdeer, still speaking in Russian for the Russian-speaking press, while also writing English words in the dirt for the embittered English-speaking press, says that the Faceless Old Woman Who Secretly Lives in Your Home seems to be several bodies connected to a single sentience. She seems not to be omnipresent at all, merely multipresent. The Secret Police spokesdeer then laughed in Russian while writing "hee hee hee" in English in the dirt.

[*a voice whispering into Cecil's ear*]

Oh. Oh dear. That's simply not true. I—

Okay, now there's a very long insect crawling into my ear. It's all the way in my ear. I am not okay with this, Faceless Old Woman.

Faceless Old Woman?

[*silence*]

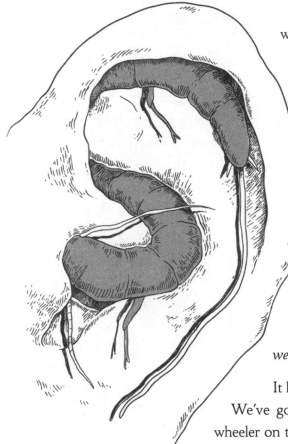

Gah! Listeners, hang on while I get this silverfish out of my ear canal.

*[off-mic: sound of ripping. then a great beast roaring. then maybe some loud hammer whacks or even gunshots? whimpering? silence.]*

Okay. Okay. So. Traffic.

*[voice is wavering. he can't hear himself very well in his headset]*

It looks pretty bad out there. We've got a jackknifed eighteen-wheeler on the shoulder of westbound Route 800 near exit 4 causing serious delays.

At the bus depot on Somerset, a fire hydrant was cracked open and now space and time have collap—

I'm sorry, listeners. Taking my headphones off. I'm having a hard time hearing myself. I think the Faceless Old Woman really did damage my ear.

Anyway, traffic's awful of course. Always is. Don't drive on Somerset, unless you want all of your matter collapsing into a singularity.

Really glad to be home! Great homecoming.

An update now on the multiple arrests of the Faceless Old Woman Who Secretly Lives in Your Home. Apparently they've managed to find fifteen more versions of her in homes all over town. But according to the spokesdeer, the Secret Police are running out of room in the jails. Also, even at the homes where they have arrested these Faceless Old Women, there are still reported cases of vandalism and whispers and suggested violence and sudden but inscrutable movements in the corners of vision.

In fact, these reports are happening even in homes where an arrest of the Faceless Old Woman had already been made.

Many city buildings, especially the Secret Police's Secret Police Station, hidden in a hovercloud have received quite a bit of damage: bird parts in filing cabinets, bullets replaced with worms, badges reading "ROTTED MEAT" instead of "SECRET POLICE."

Mayor Dana Cardinal has called on the police to temporarily cease their crackdown on the Faceless Old Woman. The mayor claims she's been terrorized by falling televisions and window-mounted A/C units as well as all of the carpet in her City Hall office being replaced by dark, heaving fur as if the floor were now the back of some terrible beast.

Listeners, I'm not falling for this bit again. Mayor Cardinal, once my friend, has abused my good nature too much. She bought me at an auction and has since been using me against my will to rescue her from danger. Well she's just going to have to figure it out on her own this time.

[*whispering voice again; then another silverfish in Cecil's ear*]

Uck gross! Stop it, Faceless Old Woman. Stop it! Weather! Let's go to the weather!

**WEATHER: "Matches" by Sifu Hotman**

Well I have cotton swabs in both ears now, listeners, and am more than a little bit irritated. But on with the news. The Secret Police just retracted their earlier reports that they had captured the Faceless Old Woman Who Secretly Lives in Your Home. They thought they had been arresting several corporeal forms of her across town, but in actuality they had just been arresting a bunch of faceless old women who *openly* live in their *own* homes. It seems in retrospect that the Faceless Old Woman Who Secretly Lives In Your Home still secretly lives in your home and has never stopped vandalizing your home in protest of these arrests of innocent women.

These Faceless Old Women are now filing a civil suit against the Sheriff's Secret Police for unfair profiling practices against elderly women who happen to have no faces, and the Sheriff just issued the following public apology: "Nonspecifically my bad," said the Sheriff from his hoveroffice in the clouds. "In general, real sorry about all kinds of things. We're cool now, right?" the Sheriff added before dissipating into tiny crystalline droplets, which fell gently, a silver movement to the hardened earth below.

Maybe I did speak too soon about being happy to be back home. While I was reporting the weather, I received this voicemail from Carlos:

**CARLOS:** Hi, babe. I heard you were apparently off saving the mayor again just now, sorry I missed you. So I wanted to ask. I was so afraid to ask while you were here because I didn't want to complicate our peaceful vacation with difficult choices, but here goes: Cecil, remember that building. The simple rectangular building with the tall point atop it, covered entirely in a tarp? You asked several times what that tarp was covering, and I said I didn't want to say. Yet. And you remember the familiar-seeming man wearing dark sunglasses with what looked like bloodstains on his shirt but I assured you was just barbecue sauce? Well he built that building under the tarp. Cecil, it's a radio station. Kevin built a radio station. He doesn't seem to be planning anything evil. In fact, he seems pretty relaxed and friendly these days. He built it for anyone who wants to broadcast or listen to broadcasts. And it got me thinking. And you don't have to decide now, and you don't even have to decide yes at all. But would you ever think about—Would you ever consider—oh this is tough to ask on voice mail. Just call me okay. Call me when you're off the air. I love you.

**CECIL:** Yes. Yes I would, Carlos. I think I really would. It was so serene there. So lovely. Okay. Private thoughts done. Let's turn my microphone back on now.

Well, listeners, I wonder what Carlos might be trying to ask me. I mean, it's probably nothing, and even if it was something, I don't think I would move away or anything—Move away? no one said anything about moving away. Who moves away? I have to stick around a bit anyway because my sister and brother-in-law are going out of town for a couple of weeks and need me to look after my niece, Janice. I don't want to disappoint Janice. I mean how could I disappoint Janice? By moving away? Why do you keep saying that? Who's moving away? Not me. So I'll be sure to stay very focused on being a good uncle and guardian. Plus, apparently the mayor needs me around to save her all the time. Hate to leave that behind.

Stay tuned next for the sound of folding cardboard and long strips of tape.

And to all of the Faceless Old Women, living secretly or living otherwise, fight the good fight. Just leave me out of it, okay? These cotton balls are already soaked.

And to everyone else. Good night, Night Vale. Good night.

**PROVERB: Don't be afraid of the dark. Be afraid of the terrible things that are hiding there and the terrible things they will do.**

# EPISODE 69:
# "FASHION WEEK"

## JUNE 1, 2015

NICE.

I worked for years at a prepaid debit card company whose offices were in midtown, right near the heart of New York City's fashion week. Once a year, there would be all sorts of events going on all around while I was just trying to find some falafel to eat for lunch so I could get back to a job I hated so much it would give me headaches if I made the mistake of thinking about the fact that I was still working there. But I just don't understand fashion. I'm sorry. I'm sure that there is a lot of complex and beautiful things going on there, but from my uneducated, Target-shopping eyes, it looks like tall, alien people wearing clown costumes. Maybe I do get it a bit. Tall, alien people wearing clown costumes is pretty entertaining.

This episode marks the return of a character whom I enjoy, but who has, according to my search of our script database, only actually shown up in four episodes, two of which were live shows. Still, I have a real soft spot for Janice Rio, from down the street. Mostly because her name is the epitome of a Night Vale naming convention that I enjoy, where people are identified by a recurring phrase.

John Peter, you know, the farmer. Larry Leroy, out on the edge of town. But Janice's is special, because it makes no sense at all. Down the street from where? From who? Why would she be identified by what she is down the street from? By divorcing the phrase from any possible useful purpose, her name becomes entirely about the words themselves. Which is a lot of the goal of Night Vale. Create images so weird they're impossible to concretely visualize and it becomes instead entirely about the words that are pointing toward the images.

Finally I want to talk about a part of this episode that is incredibly emotional for me, but that is easy to miss. The traffic in this section is actually a memorial to a person who was very important to podcasting. Harris Wittels was a comedian and TV writer, perhaps best known for being an executive producer of *Parks and Recreation* and co-creating *Master of None*. He was also a prolific podcaster, appearing on a number of shows and hosting a show called *Analyze Phish*, still one of my favorite podcasts of all time. In it, Harris, an avid Phish fan, tries to convince his skeptical friend Scott to like the band Phish. This is made difficult by the fact that Phish's music is, objectively, not very good, and so the gentle and friendly struggle between the two continues through episode after beautiful episode. I'm afraid of flying and when Night Vale blew up, I suddenly found myself in a job where I fly a lot. And so there were many airports where I, facing a panic attack, would pace around the airport listening to *Analyze Phish*. Harris talked me through these low moments in my life and, when he died of an overdose in 2015, it hit me harder than any other celebrity death in recent memory. Because he wasn't just a celebrity. He was a voice in my ear that had talked me through a lot of difficult times. It genuinely felt like losing a friend and I wanted to use my own podcast to say good-bye to him.

He was our tour guide through the cosmos. Sorry.

—Joseph Fink

———————

"I don't write the story of my life, I only live it."

When fans ask us, "What does Cecil look like?" we, the creators, say, "What do you think Cecil looks like? And that's the correct answer."

But while our fans usually create art of Cecil looking very dapper, in a vest and suspenders like a bespoke hipster bartender, whenever the podcast actually describes what Cecil is wearing, it's something completely bizarre—in this episode, it's "leather pants, and a Hawaiian shirt, and a baseball hat made of honeycomb."

My father gave me only one piece of masculine fashion advice ever, which was if you have to speak in front of a crowd and they're wearing jeans and a T-shirt, you should be wearing business casual. If they're wearing business casual, you should be wearing a suit. If they're wearing suits, you should be wearing a tuxedo. And I took that to heart. So when Night Vale first started performing these live shows that were more of an event than just a reading in a bookstore or coffee shop, I tried to dress the part of someone who deserved your attention for ninety minutes.

After the raw, emotional *Ghost Stories* tour, the script for *All Hail* seemed to have more room to play, in terms of physicality and audience interaction, and so an opportunity to experiment with the fashion thing arose. Side note: In the *Sandman* series, Dream of the Endless actually employs an entity called the Fashion Thing to make sure he is appropriately attired for whatever era he finds himself in. Leave it to Neil Gaiman to get right to the be-sequined heart of the thing.

I just happened to know an amazing, revolutionary designer, Bradley "BCALLA" Callahan who designs primarily for drag queens and, even though I am definitely NOT a drag queen and Bradley had never done traditional menswear, we started discussing collaboration for the "ALL HAIL" tour.

I invited him to come see a Night Vale live show at the Bell House to see what I did, then we met at a coffee shop in Bushwick to talk about our inspirations. I mentioned Rei Kawakubo's cutout collection for Comme Des Garçons and David Byrne's "big suit" from *Stop Making Sense,* while Bradley brought up maritime dazzle camouflage and the Grand Old Opry glamor of designer Nudie Cohn.

One of the moments that led me to fully embrace my Year of BCALLA was the tragic one-two-punch deaths of David Bowie and Prince. While doing an action as simple as talking, singing, playing an instrument, they were fully themselves on stage, but so much more than themselves and achieving iconoclast status.

It's simple: When given the opportunity to dress as a Batman villain with impunity, you dress like a Batman villain!

Acid-yellow checkered plaid suits, lined with black vinyl and silver zippers.

Tweed, suede, and leather fetish Western wear.

Sparkly blue vinyl tai-chi robes.

As someone who is not classically beautiful, but has a certain acquired taste je ne sais quoi, I have a love-hate relationship with fashion. I say most fashion is self-aggrandizing bullshit—what's "hip" or "in" or "everything." Will you be spared by the sphere or not? But style is something quite different. Style is personal. It is you, at your finest, your most comfortable and confident. And isn't knowing yourself worth so much more than being just another slave to the Fashion Thing?

—Cecil Baldwin

But don't you see? You never needed anything
else. The weird was within you the whole time.

## WELCOME TO NIGHT VALE

Hello, listeners. Later, News. Capital N. But forget about that. First,
news. Lowercase n.

It's Fashion Week in Night Vale, that exciting time of year in
which we all get to decide what is fashionable and what is not. To
use the charming colloquialism, we decide what is "in the sphere"
and what is "spared from the sphere." This is Night Vale's hippest
event, and everyone is there, because it is required by law. So everyone is there and scared and it is hip as heck.

Michelle Nguyen is the only one that doesn't look scared. This is
her favorite holiday and she is wearing a vintage summoning cloak
and a dogcatcher's cap and has two tiny neon signs attached to her
face indicating her eyes. She is the most fashionable person in town
and certain to be spared from the sphere.

Others are less lucky. Town clerk Veronica Rothschild is running
around saying, "Oh no, oh no" and adjusting her unfashionably dis-
tressed eyeglasses, casting glances backward at the sphere which is
moving implacably to devour the unhip and absorb the outdated.
Soon she will stumble and then the sphere will be upon her. It's like
that popular joke. Why did the hipster burn her mouth? Because

she survived the sphere and was able to eat her pizza before it was cool. And sure enough Michelle Nguyen, pizza in hand, is cackling madly, watching the chaos and listening intently to headphones that are plugged into nothing at all.

The Sheriff's Secret Police are seeking any leads or witnesses in the case of the disappearances at the housing development of the Shambling Orphan. Over the last several weeks, at least 12 people have vanished without a trace, except for our memories of their previous existence, which, according to a roving gang of pedantic philosophers who have been interrupting Secret Police press conferences, does in fact count as a trace.

"Memories are as real as any of our constructed experiences of the world," said one philosopher, without invitation, interrupting important information about the missing persons. "I bet you think reality is a thing," he continued, much to the delight of his fellow philosophers and not a single other person in attendance. The philosophers were last seen high fiving each other while drinking cheap but locally made canned beer.

The missing persons were last seen at home and on the street, about town, about their lives, just normally living, until suddenly and unaccountably, they no longer were seen anywhere at all. Residents of the Shambling Orphan and the nearby development, the Desert Pines, expressed mild concern over their strong fears about their abject terror.

More on this story as we grasp at narrative threads that can assuage our helplessness in the face of inexplicable tragedy.

Listeners, last weekend I had my niece Janice over while her parents were taking a romantic long weekend in the Kingdom of the Deros, deep within the Hollow Earth, which is of course easily accessed by ordering any item from the Arby's Market Fresh menu. It was really nice to get some time alone with Janice. She's getting older, you know, and is moving from a child, which is something of an abstract concept, to a person with adult ideas and thoughts and feelings, a human being who you can relate to and with, which is also an abstract concept.

We talked and watched movies. She let me put on *Cat Ballou* five times in a row because that was Carlos and I's movie-night thing and I had been missing that. We ate popcorn. I asked her about any girls or boys she might be interested in and she diverted me politely but awkwardly to other subjects. I let her. It's not for me to pry. That's the government's job, and if I'm ever curious I can look at the public registry of middle-school crushes, which is constantly being updated via mind-scanning satellite.

Janice gave me a feeling of family I rarely feel anymore. It was a good feeling. I hope I will be able to visit Janice regularly.

In an earlier program, we brought you this week's community calendar. However it appears there were a few errors in our reporting, and so we would like to offer some corrections to our previous calendar.

Monday, we said, was Free Hot Chocolate Day at the Moonlite All-Nite Diner. In actuality, Monday will be the day that a great craft crashes down from the heavens, and we all will surround the ominous bulk of it, still glowing hot and smoking from the impact, whispering and wondering, helpless to act.

Tuesday, we said was sign up day for the Night Vale Adult Kickball League in Mission Grove Park. We were right about an event taking place in the park, but it appears that this event will instead be a creature emerging from the craft, towering over us and, in a language we should not understand, and yet, and yet we *do* understand, demanding that we worship it.

Wednesday we described as being just a nice day to go outside and take a walk. Just a really nice day for it, we said. Just stretch those gams, we said. We said the word gams over and over, seemingly unable to say anything else. As it turns out, Wednesday is actually the day we will stage a brief but ultimately unsuccessful resistance against the horde of slimy, many-appendaged alien warriors pouring out from the landed craft.

Thursday we said would be the day that beings from another world fully defeat us and we will line the roads and avenues on our knees, heads bowed in recognition of our new masters, our new gods. Turns out we were 100-percent right on that one, so we didn't completely get the week's schedule wrong.

Friday we said would be the day that your Citizen Renewal Packets are due, you know, the reams and reams of paperwork probing every personal detail that you have to fill out in order to remain a citizen of Night Vale. Well, it's still the day to do that, but instead of turning it in to the City Council, who will at that point be locked in a hyperdimensional prison by the occupying extraterrestrials, you will instead turn it into the supervisor of your assigned HumanPod so that they can gauge how much energy can be extracted from your body.

Saturday we said was Caturday. We didn't mean anything by this, we just thought it would be funny. People didn't find it funny. They wrote and called the station, demanding an explanation. Janice Rio, from down the street, seemed especially disturbed. "WHAT DO YOU MEAN IT'S CATURDAY? WILL WE BE ATTACKED BY GIANT CATS? WILL THE GIANT CATS BUILD HUGE BLACK CUBES ALL OVER TOWN? WILL I BE FORCED TO ENTER A STRANGE BLACK CUBE THAT WILL ABSORB MY ESSENCE UNTIL THERE IS NOTHING LEFT OF ME? I AM ALLERGIC TO CATS!" Janice cried.

Well, no, Janice. And I'm sorry for causing a panic. Saturday will actually be the day the invading aliens start feeding on us, so don't worry. No cats that day. Caturday is just a fun word to say. Caturday!

And Sunday . . . well, we were right about Sunday, so there you go. Just as we said, Sunday will be the day that Tamika Flynn and the beings who claim to be angels team up to lead a dramatic attack against the occupying force with the help of every Night Vale citizen, driving away our new masters and reinstating our old masters, who are brutal and awful, but who at least are a brutal and awful we know and understand.

This has been corrections. Or . . . the community calendar. Community corrections. I don't know. This has been what it was.

Fashion Week continues, and the sphere is huge and pulsing. Everyone is screaming and running and looking just as fashionable as they ever have in their soon to be ended lives.

Director of Emergency Press Conferences Pamela Winchell is ostentatiously using decorated cigarette holders of ludicrous length, despite the fact that she does not actually smoke. She's not holding them delicately between her first two fingers but instead gripping hundreds of cigarette holders in her fist like a quiver of arrows.

"See how hip," she is saying, in a booming voice, levitating, quite fashionably, three feet off the ground. "See how absolutely of the time I am."

The sphere hums next to her for a moment, and then it rolls by leaving her be. So it seems like this year holding a quiver of cigarette holders is very "spared from the sphere" indeed. Good survival tip there.

Old Woman Josie, speaking from the headquarters of Strex Operatic Ltd., said that the new Old Night Vale Opera House is complete and that rehearsals are under full swing for opening night on June 15 of a brand new opera written, composed, directed by, and starring legendary screen actor Lee Marvin, who will also form the entirety of the cast and will be selling concessions during intermission. Josie said that Night Vale citizens should expect some of the usual disruptions resulting from rehearsal of any kind of live performance, namely stop-and-go traffic in a several-block radius around the theater, a wake of buzzards circling over the city, and a slight uptick in the number of patients at the emergency room.

So it sounds like this opera, whatever *opera* means and whatever it is, will be a blast.

And now traffic.

A man came and went. He was here before and now isn't. How briefly, the moment of *is* before the endless *was*. He was not a serious man, but then, this is not a serious life. We all heard him speak, did we not? We still do. He is speaking still even though he is not anything else at all. How comforting the continuation of communication past that point. He was our tour guide through the cosmos, he would say, and then apologize for saying it. He was not a serious man, but then, this is not a serious life. A man came and went. He was here before and now isn't.

We miss him.

This has been traffic.

The Faceless Old Woman Who Secretly Lives in Your Home made a public statement that she will not wait any longer. She will destroy Mayor Dana Cardinal once and for all, and claim the mayorship for herself. In her statement, which was stitched into the inside lining of my jacket this morning, she said, "You want opera? You want grand performance? On opening night, you will see a spectacle indeed. A spectacle indeed."

Meanwhile, still no word from Hiram McDaniels, the literal five-headed dragon and the Faceless Old Woman's previous partner in crime. According to local normal citizen Frank Chen, Hiram left town weeks ago and won't be seen around here again. Frank's other four heads agreed, except the purple head, which had a bag over it and was mumbling "Please don't include me in your foolish schemes ever again. If it were up to me, things would be very different. Things are different every time it is up to me."

The other heads hushed the head with the bag over it and reiterated that they are just a regular guy like you or me or anyone else who identifies as a regular guy with things like a pickup and pieces of denim clothing and enjoyment of certain types of music and being completely wingless, despite how powerless this must feel.

Oh, hear that? Listeners, the time has come. The sphere has arrived at the station. It hums, looming, it considers, humming, it looms. The sphere will decide whether this station and the souls within it are hip enough to be spared. I tell you now that I did not prepare for the sphere. It is not that I forgot. It is that I do not care and I am not afraid. I dunno. I wore leather pants and a Hawaiian shirt and a baseball hat made of honeycomb. I just wore the same thing I slept in last night. If I get ingested by a fashion-conscious sphere for wearing comfy casual clothes, then that'll just be what happened to me. I don't write the story of my life, I only live it. So while the sphere does whatever it will do next, I take you all, well all of you hip enough to still remain, to the weather.

**WEATHER: "Evelyn" by Kim Tillman and Silent Films**

Back from the weather. Still here. The sphere moved on, and is now out in the scrublands and sandwastes, deciding which cacti and cottontail rabbits are of the now and which must be assimilated into the pulsating dark innards of the sphere.

Of course, radio is always hip. Radio is timeless. Community radio exists outside of time and space and so is the most fashionable thing of all. Of course. We all know this.

So it's good that our station was spared and that I will continue doing radio for the foreseeable future. I'm not stopping radio broadcasting. I won't be doing it here, but I'll be continuing to do it.

Right, so.

I guess it's time then. At the start of all of this I promised News, capital N. Here is the News.

My next broadcast as host of Night Vale Community Radio will be my last in Night Vale. I am moving to the desert otherworld to spend more time with sweet, talented Carlos and the community he has built out there in that vast, sandy, alternate dimension. There is a radio station there, built by Kevin, who seems to have himself pretty under control, and his studio only has a little bit of blood, so I should be able to continue doing what I'm doing just fine. I won't be doing it in a way that you'll be able to hear. But that too, is just fine.

I've missed Carlos greatly, and I've also grown weary of a mayor that can't protect herself, of a town that fears outsiders, of a faceless old woman who secretly lives in my home and publicly wants to do me harm. And I think of a desert otherworld where it is always sunny, the mountains are real, there is a helpful masked army that can build anything, and your cell phone battery never dies even if reception is 4G at best.

There is the question: Is Night Vale worth it? Is Night Vale good? Is it a good town? Well.

I will, for the first time in my long life, live somewhere other than Night Vale. But as a poet once said, "No matter where you end up, you're still from your hometown."

I'll be back to visit from time to time of course. I need to see Janice and my old friend Josie, and many others besides. I am not gone. But I am going. I'm going to live somewhere I can feel good about, somewhere newer and better for me.

Stay tuned next, eventually, for me reporting on the opening of the opera house, and then not reporting on anything else here ever again.

Penultimately, good night, Night Vale. Good night.

**PROVERB:** Dress your dog for the job you want, not the job you have.

# EPISODE 70A:
## "TAKING OFF"

### JUNE 15, 2015

**GUEST VOICES: KEVIN R. FREE (KEVIN), DYLAN MARRON (CARLOS)**

FIRST CONFESSION . . .

I love Dylan Marron.

It's not much of a confession, because, um, who doesn't? It makes sense that I'd love him, because: a) he's a genius, and b) he's my friend. But this here episode, 70A, in which Carlos leaves Kevin and goes back to Cecil, made me so happy as we recorded it, because I recorded it with Dylan at Joseph's house. Dylan would practice the cute voice of Carlos before we recorded each section as I looked on adoringly; we made jokes about things (I can't remember which things, because we've made so many jokes about so many things); then we recorded the episode. At the end, Kevin's sadness was real—but it wasn't really, really real until I heard the episode. Because I don't see Dylan enough. I don't see anyone in the *Welcome to Night Vale* universe enough. And that's sad. So yeah, I love Dylan—and Jeffrey and Joseph and Meg—and I don't see any of them enough. Poor Kevin.

Second confession . . .

Kevin loves Carlos.

I imagined all kinds of things about Carlos and Kevin. Imagined how often they had sat in Carlos's kitchen and talked about the desert otherworld, about the giants who were building the world for them, about Cecil, glossing over questions about whether they were colonizers of the giants' land. I thought about how Kevin and Carlos probably cooked dinner together in the kitchen of Carlos's apartment every day for a year. The kitchen, from the description in the episode, seems to have an open floor plan, which was helpful for when Kevin and Carlos sang and danced every night for Doug and Alicia after dinner. Their favorite duet I think is the Streisand version of "Being at War with Each Other," which they always played from their phones because the melody is so difficult and because their phones never lost their charge in that place and because they both wanted Doug and Alicia to reach out to other giants in love and peace, in the same way that Carlos and Kevin had forged their relationship. Kevin was waiting waiting waiting for Carlos to love him like Carlos loved Cecil. That's not true. Kevin didn't wait. He proceeded in love because he assumed Carlos was too. Poor Kevin.

Final confession . . .

Kevin R. Free is not Kevin from Desert Bluffs.

Kevin R. Free loves pasta salad. The colder the better. No mayonnaise, please. Oil and vinegar and onions and tomatoes and black olives and feta cheese, red and green pepper and a little mustard. Stoneground. Salt (pink Himalayan, duh). Sesame oil or hoisin, just a dash of either, and red pepper flakes for heat. That Kevin from Desert Bluffs doesn't like it was a shock to me. Poor Kevin.

—Kevin R. Free

**KEVIN:** We all have to start somewhere. We all have to end somewhere too, but let's concentrate on the other thing. Welcome to . . . well . . . hrmm.

## WELCOME TO A DESERT OTHERWORLD.

We should come up with a better name for this place. Names are, after all, extremely important.

Hi, I'm your radio host, Kevin. I'm speaking to you from our brand new station, and this is our inaugural broadcast. I'm so excited to be back on the air. I'm not sure we have any listeners, yet, but we will. We will.

Later in the show we'll be talking to Doug and Alicia, leaders of the army of masked giants who roam this desert and who have been instrumental in building our new city. They've been so welcoming to us outsiders. Not all outsiders, though. They are, after all, a violent and territorial army, but some outsiders. People like me, and like my friend Carlos. He's a scientist. He's a beautiful man who does beautiful things. I have Carlos on the phone with us right now, with some breaking news. Carlos, tell everyone about the huge project you've been working on this past year.

**CARLOS:** Hi, Kevin. Thanks for having me on the show. First off, Doug and Alicia are here in my kitchen. Alicia built a refrigerator from some cactus pads, twine and three different kinds of birds, and now they're making a bunch of pasta salad for lunch this week. They'll save some for you, if you'd like.

**KEVIN:** How delightful! I'm totally disgusted by pasta salad. Can't stand the taste or the smell. In fact, to look at it causes me to heave. But thank you, that's so kind.

**CARLOS:** Right. So this new experiment—and I have to tell you, I'm really excited about it. You know how our cell phones always work in this desert otherworld even though there are no towers and how they never seem to run out of battery?

**KEVIN:** Yes, I love taking these facts for granted!

**CARLOS:** Well I'm on the verge of uncovering what's causing that. Here in my laboratory—which Doug and Alicia and one of the soldiers whose name is [*VOCAL FRY*] built for me!—I've been hard at work, pacing about in front of a row of conical flasks, beakers, and Y-tubes, furiously writing Greek letters and Arabic numbers, and I think later today I will make an enormous breakthrough.

**KEVIN:** What did you find out?

**CARLOS:** I can't say yet. I'm just waiting on my computer to finish calculating the—

**KEVIN:** Everything okay?

**CARLOS:** I don't know. Alicia and Doug look really agitated. They're jumping up and down by the window. The other giant soldiers are running into formation outside. I need to see what's wrong.

**KEVIN:** While Carlos checks on our favorite soldiers, let's get an update now on the roller coaster inhabitants. I'm referring to the roller coaster Doug and Alicia built for our new town months ago. It looks terribly fun. It has a tall first hill and a ninety-degree drop off that is almost six hundred feet, I am told, and then it goes into a series of loops and turns, and figure eights. Then some spirals where the riders go upside down several times per second. And then there's a sheet of flames that as you approach, it looks like you're about to go right through the fire, but at the last second, the track spirals again and you go through the fire upside down!

Anyway, it's an exciting-looking ride. I haven't been on it yet. That's because after they started it on its first trip, they haven't been able to stop it. They didn't invent brakes, so that's an issue. And even though they cut the power to the ride, it's still going with the same passengers caught in an interminable cycle of fun.

Oh, we have Carlos back on the line again. Carlos?

**CARLOS:** Doug and Alicia are gone. It turns out the commotion was over another army marching along the horizon. Doug and Alicia ran screaming around the house and though the kitchen, overturning my cutting board and grabbing their weapons. Alicia took my chef's knife and Doug made a makeshift slughorn out of one of my large funnels so that he could call their army to action.

**KEVIN:** Good for them. Protecting our community.

**CARLOS:** No, but, I was trying to explain that the other army was marching perpendicular to us. They were not marching toward us. This desert is filled with small armies always marching in different directions. We can't attack them all for no reason. And now my kitchen counter is demolished.

**KEVIN:** Oh, it'll grow back. So, I'm so excited to learn more about your research into the strange properties of this region. I think you once called this desert otherworld "the most scientifically interesting community in the U.S."

**CARLOS:** Well, no, my exact words were—

**KEVIN:** So when do you expect the results? Sounds like whatever you come up with could possibly be a monumental shift in how we perceive thermodynamic laws.

**CARLOS:** I'm at my lab right now, hunched over my computer waiting for it to complete its final report. Then comparing its results to my thousands of handwritten notes from the past year, I believe I can pinpoint the exact source of this desert's energy. It shouldn't be long. Please don't rush me.

**KEVIN:** Great. Let us know soon, though. While Carlos does that, perhaps I can tell you all a little bit about our new radio station—take you on an audio tour, if you will. We have a tall broadcast tower made of stones and adobe. Those zig-zaggy electrical bolts visibly shooting outward from the top of the tower? Those are actual radio waves!

Inside the building itself, we have a small broadcast booth with a couple of new mics. Some of the members of the masked army of giants helped me decorate my studio, too. It was so empty and bloodless before. It required a lot of lizards and rodents, but it's finally starting to feel like home.

I've got a producer's booth just off to my right. I can see my old intern Vanessa in there. Hi, Vanessa! We're a bit understaffed, so Vanessa has been having to act as my producer as well as head of sales and marketing and even answering phones. Good thing she has a doppelgänger to help out! Most people kill their double, but that's such a waste of a good opportunity. The more, the merrier, the more productive, I say.

Oh, and we're hiring right now. If you have experience in any of the following areas—ad sales, graphic design, office management, entomology, Fortran programming, falconry, or sports law—please send your resume to "Radio Station c/o Kevin." We have no postal service in the desert otherworld, nor any mailboxes, so it's important that you carefully reread *The Secret* by Rhonda Byrne in order to wish your resume into my office.

Sounds like Carlos is back on the line now. Did you get the results from your—

**CARLOS:** Doug and Alicia are back.

**KEVIN:** Oh, good. So wonderful to have dear friends around to be a part of your brilliant achievement.

**CARLOS:** They are in no condition to celebrate the great strides of scientific study right now. Most of the army returned from fighting but there are more than a dozen who did not. Alicia lost two fingers and Doug is bleeding quite badly because of a compound fracture in his forearm.

Everyone who returned is in treatable condition. I believe they'll be fine, but they're wounded and need lots of rest [off mic, as if shouting to people in the room] AND NO MORE FIGHTING FOR A LONG TIME. [back to phone] It's a mess over here.

**KEVIN:** Good thing they have such a good and helpful friend in you. So tell us about your study on the strange energy here in the desert.

**CARLOS:** I can't yet. The army came in so quickly, dropping their weapons everywhere along with some detached limbs that I don't even think belong to them. And all of my journals, which I had left out and open on my desk, have been rendered unusable. There are broken beakers and blood-soaked composition notebooks everywhere. I don't even know where to begin cleaning up all of this blood.

**KEVIN:** [slightly pleased sound]

**CARLOS:** I'm sorry did you say something?

**KEVIN:** Nope. I just like your story. Carry on.

**CARLOS:** [off mic] DOUG! DOUG! Come back. [on mic] Kevin, I have to go. Doug just constructed a makeshift splint out of rocks and snakes. He grabbed his axe and ran out the door. And there goes Alicia. [off mic] Stop going to war! You need rest! [on mic] Call you back, Kevin. They can't go on like this.

**KEVIN:** Listeners, I'm getting word of strong winds out of the east, stirring up dust devils and hurling plant debris and weak-willed animals through the air. This is a rare sunless day for our otherworld desert. While Carlos tries to get his notes unbloodied, let's have a closer look at the weather.

**WEATHER:** "Pyramid" by Jason Webley

Wow, that weather report was informative. I had no idea how dangerous a storm that was until I heard that report. To be a radio broadcaster who gets to tell stories about things that make us unhappy thrills me to my bones. Because by telling people about all that can make us unhappy, I prepare them to truly enjoy those happy moments when they come.

Once, my hometown of Desert Bluffs had a deadly outbreak of throat spiders. Hundreds were diagnosed with this usually treatable disease, but it was a particularly virulent strain and many people died or were left without voices and lower jaws when it was all over. Almost a day wouldn't go by where you didn't hear a fit of strenuous coughing punctuated by a muffled pop, only to turn around and see a cascade of tiny spiders pouring over the craggy ledge that used to be a person's lower teeth.

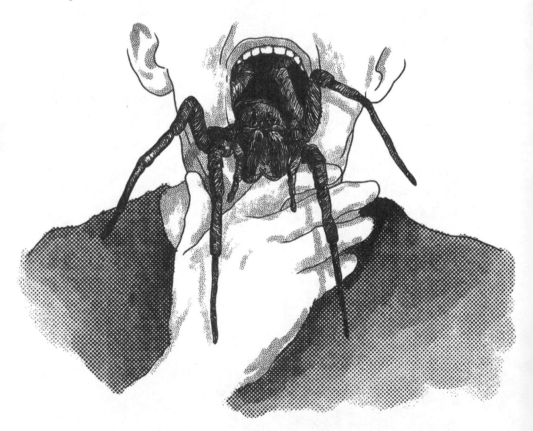

Each day I got to report these upsetting stories, but the best part about it was when Desert Bluffs residents eventually stopped losing part of their faces to throat spiders and we all rejoiced in our newly healthy and happy lives. As the saying goes: It's always dawn.

Oh, and speaking of sunshine, Carlos just arrived here, live in the studio with me. Carlos, did you go out in this weather? You're covered in dust and those look like friction burns in the shape of lab goggles on your face. Are you okay? Did Doug and Alicia make it back?

**CARLOS:** Not yet . . . They . . . What's this all over your studio? Is that barbecue sauce?

**KEVIN:** Oh that? That's just blood. And some old bones and loose teeth and beaks and things. I finally decorated. Thanks for noticing. And I just noticed you have a piece of paper in your hand. That must be your final report! Look at how we both notice things about each other! I love that!

**CARLOS:** I . . . I . . . Well . . .

**KEVIN:** You sound sad, which is great news because it means you'll be happy again eventually. It's a tough day, what with all the weather and the wars and the blood. But your boyfriend will soon be moving from Night Vale to come live here with you.

**CARLOS:** Well, about that. . . .

**KEVIN:** And. AND! You finally have the scientific results of your hard scientific work.

**CARLOS:** I don't. I don't have results, Kevin. When the army marched out again, I went back to trying to recover my notes. I had just gotten the lab desktops clean when Alicia's large dog bounded through the lab and out the front door, sending every glass tube and jar crashing onto the floor. When I bent over to see the damage, I saw my computer there too, on the tile, snapped nearly in half, a tuft of white fur covering the keyboard, singed slightly by the smoke streaking out of the broken monitor. I lost it all, Kevin. My entire year of study is gone.

**KEVIN:** What's the paper then? Did you at least learn some of your results?

**CARLOS:** This is nothing. It's just a letter I wrote to a . . . to a friend.

**KEVIN:** Oh, I love letters! Letters are so fun to receive!

**CARLOS:** Not this one. It's a sad letter. A letter about regrets. About mistakes. You know how sometimes you spend a lot of time with someone and you think that someone makes you happy, but then suddenly, one day, you realize maybe you weren't happy at all. Maybe you both would be better off doing what you love, in different places. Without each other. Maybe neither of you were as happy as either of you thought.

**KEVIN:** That is a sad-sounding letter. I don't understand or like that at all.

**CARLOS:** I have spent the last year all wrong.

**KEVIN:** I believe in you, Carlos. Don't let destruction, blood, and war hold you back. You're a brilliant scientist.

**CARLOS:** I realize I need to start everything over. Rededicate myself. I need to do it right this time. No more distractions. I can't spend another year like this one. So, it pains me to carry this letter, but I wrote it to set my boundaries.

**KEVIN:** So you know, there's no postal service here yet.

**CARLOS:** I know. That's why I'm hand-delivering it.

**KEVIN:** Remember, no one should ever be sad. Choose not to be sad, Carlos. In fact, choose to be happy. Perhaps your letter is the first step to choosing happiness, even while it makes someone else sad.

**CARLOS:** I understand. Listen. I should go. I'm headed to Night Vale one final time. I need to talk to Cecil about . . . well about some changes.

Thanks for everything, Kevin. You've been so kind to me in this difficult year.

**KEVIN:** Good-bye, Carlos. Well, it's a shame that our huge scientific breakthrough didn't quite happen today. As the old phrase goes, "The best laid plans of mice and men are completely different kinds of plans all together. Very different creatures, those two."

But it's not a total wash, our next show should feature spine-tingling adventure stories about today's desert battles.

We have so much to do, us. So much to explore and understand. So much to make here in our great desert otherworld. Say, we really do need a name for this place. Things without names don't really exist.

So, I'm going to call this . . . well . . . I'm going to call it Desert Bluffs. Desert Bluffs was the name of my hometown, and by naming it Desert Bluffs, this place becomes my new hometown. We are in my home. We are in Desert Bluffs, no matter where we are in space or time. What is a town but a name, right?

Until next time, new Desert—

Oh! It looks like Carlos left behind that letter he was supposed to hand deliver. I better not read it. No. better not.

Until next time, new Desert Bluffs, until next time.

[*sound of paper slowly opening; Kevin reads Carlos's letter explaining he's never returning to this desert otherworld, leaving Kevin alone; away from mic*]

Oh. Oh no. This is so sad. No. I don't like this. I am sad. No. No.

**PROVERB:** A rose by any other name is called something else.

# EPISODE 70B:
## "REVIEW"

### JUNE 15, 2015

IN 2015, I WAS STARTING TO WORK ON A NEW PODCAST IDEA THAT would eventually become *Within the Wires*. The first season of *Wires* is told entirely in the style of relaxation cassettes, which slowly unfold over the course of ten episodes to reveal a much deeper story about who you, the listener, are and what the narrator is really trying to get you to do. The second season was told as museum audio guides that slowly unravel the mystery of a missing artist.

I'm not sure what sent me down this way of thinking, but when writing this episode, I was really interested in couching a fictional story as something other than what it was about. Episode 70B is quite a bit more straightforward than *Within the Wires* in its narration and plot revelations.

But rather than have Cecil simply say, "Okay, gotta tell you a bunch of stuff that happened last night," I wanted to couch it as a review of the new opera at the recently re-opened opera house. Cecil's critique quickly goes sidewise because that's what happens anytime Cecil tries to deliver news.

Another thing to look for here: more mention of Lee Marvin and a reference to the confrontational theatrical stylings of the Italian Futurists, who often referred to their stage works, not as *plays* but as *battles*. They would do things like triple-sell seats or perform plays in whispered gibberish or fail to open the curtain more than a few inches, in order to cause audience confusion and incite some kind of anger. This is kind of cool sounding on the surface. Very avant garde! But let's remember also that they hated Jews and women and loved war ("the earth's hygiene").

They also wrote manifestos on how to eat pasta. (It involved sandpaper.) So let's pace ourselves on how cool they really were.

—Jeffrey Cranor

"I was terrified, yes, but like everyone, I'm *usually* terrified."

The year-three finale of *Welcome to Night Vale* is so vast in scope, it had to be split into two separate episodes, released simultaneously: While Episode 70A deals with Carlos and Kevin in Desert Bluffs (boo, Desert Bluffs), 70B is all about the intrigue going on back in Night Vale: murder, conspiracy, mistaken identity, mind control, mystic visions, reconciliation, family, and of course, love.

The backdrop for all this operatic *sturm und drang* is, appropriately, the gala premier of the new Old Opera House. All the usual suspects are in attendance, dressed to the nines, like a scene out of Martin Scorsese's *The Age of Innocence,* but of course opera in Night Vale is nothing like it is in our part of the world. (In a cool little theater-history Easter egg from the writers, the opera performance described in the episode is actually lifted from historical accounts of real plays performed by Marinetti and the Italian Futurists, the fascist avant-garde from the early twentieth century.)

In a previous episode ("Lot 37"), Cecil Palmer himself had been purchased at auction; the person who controls him, as well as their intentions for him, only now come to light, and Cecil finds himself being controlled as the instrument of some external design, like a character in someone else's drama. It's a sort of nightmare—or maybe it's the human condition, I'm not sure which.

And then comes the most Martin Scorsese moment in all of Night Vale: a long limo arrives to pick Cecil up after the carnage has ended, and in my mind, I picture it as the ultimate long-take Steadicam shot, the camera gliding past all the characters of Night Vale, everyone that Cecil loves and feels at home with. In the recording, you may notice this is the first time Cecil mentions Steve Carlsberg without sneering. This is a celebration of family and community, petty squabbles can wait for another time. And then, of course, there's the fate of our two star-crossed lovers (no spoilers!).

After a year of dramatic upheavals and frayed relationships, this episode achieves what all good season finales strive for: a satisfying resolution to stories known, and laying the seeds for stories yet to come.

—Cecil Baldwin

**CECIL:** If you love something set it free. If it doesn't come back, it probably died of sadness because it thought you loved it.

# WELCOME TO NIGHT VALE

It's difficult to say good-bye to your hometown. Difficult, indeed.

We'll get to all of that soon, but first, we bring you the item of, I'm sure, most interest to all of you: a review of last night's opera, the inaugural performance of the new Old Night Vale Opera House, a tribute to the building which once stood proudly in this town for decades before succumbing twenty years ago to an unchecked puppy infestation.

The new Old Opera House is luxurious and stylish. I had no idea what opera was until last night, so my expectations for the building were pretty low. I mean, I don't know what you think opera is. I was expecting something like fenced in yards full of filthy straw occupied by hundreds of heavily drugged wolves, but it turns out that opera houses look nothing like petting zoos. This place had a chandelier and velvet seats and lush red curtains and a snack bar and people wearing just the fanciest clothes you could imagine: tuxedos and ball gowns and balaclavas and shin guards.

Old Woman Josie and all of her tall, winged friends who go by the name Erika and who claim to be angels were there. They were the driving force behind the building of the new Old Opera House.

It was only fitting then that before the performance, Josie gave a toast from the stage. She toasted opera and Night Vale and all of the donors who made the opera house possible. Finally she toasted old friends, and when she did, she looked at me and grinned. I blushed and looked down at my shoes, which were tasteful sponge clogs that matched my tights perfectly.

Okay, so I'm sure you're asking the same question I've been asking for years: What even is opera? I don't have any training in opera, but I'll do my best to describe it.

Basically, opera is kind of like theater, but they don't raise the curtain all the way up, so you only can see feet shuffling about while you hear high-pitched wailing and combustion engines. This particular opera was called "Amara." It was composed and conducted and mostly performed by acting legend Lee Marvin. It was about a young girl who goes on some kind of . . . adventure?

It wasn't clear, because opera is super interactive and

entirely nonlinear. Sometimes people from the audience throw old fruit at the stage and then actors jump into the audience to wrestle these people. Audience members are encouraged to yell out things they think the performers should do and performers often vocalize their distaste for the audience. At one point in the first act I shouted, "Sing a song about old love and new horizons, about wanderlust and uncertainty!" and then a member of the chorus spat at me and moments later I felt someone handcuff me to my armrest. It was super fun.

They did raise the curtain all the way once, revealing a detailed set of a storm-tossed ocean, upon which a great ship lurched skyward atop a curling, monstrous wave. The details of the painting and the carpentry were flawless. I have never been in such awe of a stage set as I was then, but I think the stage manager recognized the error in allowing the audience to see this and quickly lowered the curtain to just a couple feet off the floor.

I didn't recognize most of the performers because they kept the curtain so low and the stage lights so dim, but I did note that Frank Chen was in the cast, looking every inch the normal human with, I can only assume, a normal number of heads.

At the start of the second act, I sensed a blurry motion in my periphery. I felt a cold touch on my chained hand.

"Nice handcuffs," a whisper said. "Looks like you won't be able to save your friend Dana tonight."

I was terrified, yes, but like everyone, I'm usually terrified. I also felt rage. Rage at the Faceless Old Woman whispering behind me. Had she handcuffed me so that I could not save my former intern, my former friend, my current mayor, Dana Cardinal from whatever evil deeds were coming her way?

I looked up at Mayor Cardinal in her loge box. She was staring straight at the stage, focused and stony. And despite all my anger at my old friend that she had presumably bought me at a Sheriff's Secret Police Auction last year and had been using me for the last several months against my will to protect herself against the five-headed dragon Hiram McDaniels and the Faceless Old Woman. Despite all of that, I looked at Dana's face hoping she would see me pleading for her safety. I want to trust and love my friend. And for that moment, I did. And I was sorry that the Faceless Old Woman had restrained me so that I could not help her, even if this time I had wanted to.

I followed the Mayor's gaze toward the stage. The house lights dimmed and the curtain split open. I saw normal human Frank Chen, center stage, each of his heads huffing and snarling, preparing for his aria. (As an aside, I am told this was to be opera's first ever quintet aria, but honestly, I don't know what either of those words even mean.)

Actually, only four of Frank's heads were snarling—the gold, grey, green, and blue ones—but his purple head was looking right at me and I felt something familiar but at the same time something that I didn't understand. My hand strained against its chain but there was nothing I could do.

As the orchestra, led by and comprised entirely of Lee Marvin and a slidewhistle, swelled and Frank Chen continued to belch fire and hiss, we all knew something was wrong. I mean it's possible that an aria is just a bunch of roars and flames. I'm no expert. But it didn't seem likely.

Frank Chen then tore off his bowtie, and in doing so revealed he was not five-foot-eight-inch, middle-aged human Frank Chen at all, but Hiram McDaniels, an eighteen-foot tall, five-headed dragon. Hiram leapt into the air above the orchestra seats. I heard a muffled scream from above. I looked to the mezzanine and saw Trish Hidge, Deputy Assistant to Mayor Cardinal, trying to quickly escort the mayor away, but it was too late.

I caught a brief glimpse of someone I had never seen before. Or had never seen in my waking life. She was standing just behind Trish and Mayor Cardinal. It was a woman I had once seen in a dream. In my dream she had been underwater, among coral, young and whispering and faceless. And now, in this world that is very likely not just a dream, I saw this same woman, and she was old and shouting and faceless.

Hiram flew up, past the chandelier, toward Dana in the mezzanine, all of his heads focused on their target, teeth bared and angry, except the purple head, which twisted away as though trying with just its neck to deflect the course of its body.

At that moment, I felt myself rising against my will. There I was, Lot number 37, being called into use once more. I looked up at Dana but she was not looking back at me at all. She was preparing to defend herself alone.

And then everything went black. I saw nothing. Felt nothing. I was nowhere. I heard a voice. It was whiny and panicked. It told me it was sorry to keep using me, that it had bought me at an auction two years back just in case. You never know what could happen. Nothing can be trusted

The voice told me it especially didn't trust the other heads it shares a body with, who are always scheming, always making new plans. Plus it was tired of having to commit violent crimes and constantly living life on the run. The voice just wanted to settle down. Maybe start a family. "Night Vale's such a nice town, don't you think?" the voice asked me.

And I asked, "Hiram? Is that you?"

And the voice said, "Not all of Hiram. Most people call me purple head, but I prefer Violet."

"Why me?" I asked.

Violet said, "One head couldn't work against four, I've known that a long time. I needed another body. Lot 37 was put up for sale and the other heads were distracted by Lot 38, a normal human disguise, so I bought you."

I was furious of course. I told Violet that I thought Dana had been doing this the whole time. I blamed her over and over. "I have lost a friend because of you, Violet," I said. "And do you have any idea what it's like to have you control me this way?"

"Yes," Violet said. "I only have control over my own body. This is my life all of the time, carried along against my will by the foolish plans of those closest to me, betrayed by my own limbs, by the beating of my own heart. But I am sorry. I really am."

"You need to fight your own fights," I said.

"I will, Cecil," Violet said. "I'm giving you back Lot 37. I transfer ownership back to you. You are yours once again. And whatever else happens tonight, I'm sorry."

"You should be," I said.

"But," Violet said, "Don't blame me for losing your friendship with Dana. You were the one who didn't trust her. That was you and only you."

Then his voice was gone.

I woke up, on the floor of the opera house, which was dark and empty. I was still handcuffed to a scorched armrest that had been completely burned off of the chair itself. Most seats and wall sconces had been heavily scorched and destroyed. I wasn't sure if it was Hiram who did that, or maybe that's just the standard aftermath of an opera.

I walked outside to the curb watching the rain in the streetlights. I saw the drops flickering in a puddle below. I do not like reflections that flicker. I thought of my mother for the first time in a long time. I missed her. And, same word, different meaning, I missed the opera, and the afterparty, too. And, same word, both meanings, I missed my friend Dana. I wished I could have saved her. She was gone and I had failed her. No one was around to help with the weight of my guilt or to unchain me from the armrest.

A huge storm was coming through, a rare weather event for the desert. Let's have a report on that night's weather now.

**WEATHER:** "Align" by Aby Wolf

The storm passed, and I began my walk home, my clothes soaked, my clogs now several sizes larger. The streets were quiet, and I took it all in, knowing these were my final days in Night Vale, certain I had made the right decision. Then I smelled the sandy earth, wet from the storm, and saw the buildings of what would soon no longer be my town, washed clean by the driven rain and I wavered in my certainty.

Lost in thought, I failed to hear the car tires on the slick concrete or see the headlights swinging my shadow across the sidewalk. I heard, "Cecil, get in," and, like any citizen of Night Vale when ordered to get into an ominous unmarked car, I obeyed without thinking. Inside the black stretch limo, impossibly large inside, were dozens of opera supporters and local celebrities. Old Woman Josie and her tall winged friends named Erika were there. Waiters passed around hors d'oeuvres and champagne. I hadn't missed the afterparty after all.

My sister, Abby, and her husband, Steve, and my niece Janice were there. Janice threw her arms around my waist and said, "Uncle Cecil, I loved the opera so, so much. Thanks for the tickets. I loved the part where the dragon flew out over the audience, like whoosh, and then it started fighting itself. The purple head started biting the other heads, and it was really funny. Then it flew away, out of the theater and there was a lot of fire. And I thought I saw an old lady with no face ran out, too, and the mayor was saved, and Mr. Lee Marvin sang a beautiful song about all the animals we can see using mirrors, and then it was over and everyone cheered. Opera is cool. Mom said you were moving away. Why are you moving away, Uncle

Cecil? Uncle Carlos says you don't have to move if you don't want to. Will you still come to my birthday party?"

Janice continued chattering but I was dizzy at the name she had just said. I interrupted her. "Carlos? Janice, did you say Carlos?"

"Duh, he's right over there, Uncle Cecil," she said.

I turned and I saw him, and he was already looking at me. And I started to say . . . and he started to say . . . and then we just hugged. So tightly. And in my ear, Carlos said, "Sorry I missed the opera. I had to let Kevin know I was returning home and staying there."

I jerked back my head and said, "Staying here?"

And Carlos said, "This is your home. You belong here."

Then he said, "This is also my home. I belong here."

"Carlos, anywhere we're together is home," I said. And I repeated it. And repeated it. And I said, "But Carlos, is Night Vale where we should live? Is Night Vale even worth living in?"

Carlos held my shoulder and said, "Night Vale is just a name, Cecil. Night Vale is just the name for an area where everyone you love lives," he said. "Don't worry about the name. Worry about the everyone," he said.

Over Carlos's shoulder, I saw Dana, my old intern and current mayor, in the crowd. She looked at me but did not smile. I struggled to meet her eyes, which were wary and gracious. Her deputy, Trish Hidge, circled behind me and removed the handcuffs from my wrist with a small key she had pulled from her jacket pocket.

"Sorry that we had to do that," Trish said. "But we wanted you to be safe, to not have your body willed by some other force into a fight you were very clear you wanted no part in. We had to physically hold you out of the way so that we could fight this fight on our own."

From across the impossibly large car, Dana winked and finally smiled. I mouthed, "I'm sorry," and she did not respond, but, still winking, a slow, strange wink, she receded into the crowd like a distant walker into mist.

At the end of the night, the car dropped Carlos and me back home and I don't think we slept the whole night, talking about our new old life together. All these memories and plans. We are back together in our home. And I am back with you, in my studio.

My final show as host of Night Vale Community Radio was to be a review of an opera. And that's still true, someday. But it won't be this opera. Carlos and I are staying in Night Vale for now. I will be back on the air with you again very soon, with more news, with more stories, with more operas.

I think Carlos is right. Night Vale isn't a single unified thing that can love or be loved. It's just the name slapped onto a set of borders and rules that some old bureaucrats wearing soft-meat crowns devised centuries ago. But they don't live here anymore. We do. I do, and I can make it worth it. I can't just leave it, I have to live it. Live it and make it better. For myself. For Carlos. For my friends. For Abby and Steve and Janice. For Old Woman Josie and all of the Erikas. For Dana.

And for you, listeners. We will together celebrate another homecoming game. We will together survive another street cleaning. We will together . . . well we will see.

I can't promise I'll never leave you. No one can promise that, but until that moment, let's keep working on this town, this collective idea. This Night Vale, whatever we want that name to mean. We can always start over if we have to, rededicate ourselves, do it right.

To start with, the Secret Police have once again jailed Hiram McDaniels for his numerous crimes against his fellow citizens, although in recognition of the violet head's valiant struggle against the other heads and his own contested body, they have put a small hole in the wall that Violet can stick through and be outside of the jail walls, since technically he is not under arrest.

Stay tuned next for happenstance, reconstructed into narrative and falsely interpreted as having significance.

And as always, good night, Night Vale, good night.

**PROVERB:** You say potato. I say potato. [*beat*] Potato. [*beat*] Potato. [*beat*] Potato. [*beat*] Potato. [*beat*] Potato. Yes. This is very good. Let's keep going. [*beat*] Potato. [*beat*] Potato. [*beat*] P———

# "THE LIBRARIAN"

## JANUARY 2015

### RECORDED ON JANUARY 16, 2015, AT THE
### SKIRBALL CENTER, NEW YORK, NY

**Cast**

Cecil Baldwin—CECIL PALMER

Andrew W. K.—INTERN ANDREW

Meg Bashwiner—DEB

Symphony Sanders—TAMIKA FLYNN

Kate Jones—MICHELLE NGUYEN

Dylan Marron—CARLOS

THIS WAS THE FIRST LIVE SHOW SCRIPT WRITTEN SPECIFICALLY TO TOUR. Jeffrey came up with the idea early on that it would be about a librarian escaping the library. As soon as he did that, I knew what I wanted the climax of the show to be. I've always admired the work of William Castle. Not his movies, which, if I'm honest, I've never seen. But the theatricality he brought to his presentation. He would park ambulances outside of movie theaters, advertising that they were for people who had heart attacks because the movie was too scary. He offered money back to anyone willing to stand for ten minutes in a "Coward's Corner" because the movie was too much for them. And, in his most famous stunt, he had a scene where the monster was released into a movie theater. A monster that could only be killed by screaming. And the movie theater had been rigged with buzzers in the seats. So people felt movement on their back as the narrator on the screen urged them to SCREAM, SCREAM FOR YOUR LIVES.

Brilliant.          .

So I inserted into our show outline the phrase "William Castle scene." I didn't know quite what it looked like, but I knew I wanted the librarian to get loose in the theater, and to play with the audience in some of the ways that Castle did.

This ended up giving us the blueprint for how Night Vale live shows work, which almost all involve audience participation in some way. We love to make the audience aware that they're a group of people experiencing an event together, rather than passive listeners just hearing an episode. This is the magic of theater. And we owe a lot to that master of doing whatever it takes to get a rise out of the crowd. This one's for you, William Castle.

—Joseph Fink


We become different people after every new experience. We are altered by the people we meet, the places we see, the new things we are excited to try, and those to which we are forced to adapt. In a normal life, this happens gradually but in the life of a touring performer, this happens at a breakneck pace. You are not the same person who packed your suitcase six cities ago and you are now, in fact, very angry with that person for packing like a jerk.

There is a special place in my heart for this live episode. "The Librarian" was our first real touring script. We had done a few one-off live shows but this script was our first real deal tour. I shudder when I think back to about how green I was, how unseasoned. My hands uncalloused from never having hauled a rolling suitcase around the world. My hair still unbroken from the many merciless teasings into a bouffant yet to come. My life void of wild stories from the salty road. This was the tour where the character of Deb was truly formed and where I began to find my feet as a warm up comic and, conveniently just in time, as an adult human.

There is a saying in the touring world: Your worst day on the road becomes your best story. At this point, five years into the game of learning things the hard way, I have some great stories. Stories about bombastically falling down stairs during a performance à la *Showgirls,* stories about backstage stalkers traveling five hundred miles to find out if Cecil Baldwin was a kid who died in the 80s (wtf?!? creepy), and stories about emergency surgery in foreign countries. I'm not going to share any of those here because I want to tell you instead about my best day on the road.

In the fall of 2014, we were touring "The Librarian" through the UK and Europe. This leg of the tour had been particularly tough. Europe is tough your first time through. Working in a country where you are not accustomed to the language, currency, and culture is exhausting. The travel schedule was not for the faint of heart, we were trying to do as many shows as possible to take advantage of our first oversees tour. We weren't sure we would ever be back. Most seriously, our tour manager had gotten very sick and needed to be hospitalized. We were all tense and drained. When we rolled into Copenhagen, we were pretty beat down. Joseph and I had about one hour between when we arrived at the hotel and when we needed to be at sound check. We were both hangry. We were both tired, but the hotel smelled like shit and was too depressing to be in for any longer than we had to. So we made our way to the train station to find some food. We aggressively and grumpily ate some fruit and a pastry. When we emerged from the train station and we saw it: the Tivoli Gardens, a wonderful and weird amusement park just steps from our tired feet.

We decided to go for it. We had forty minutes and a fist-full of Danish kroner. The park was beautiful with lots of local birds and enough charm to enliven our weary eyes that had seen nothing but airports, train stations, hospital rooms, and grimy backstages for weeks. It is fabled to have been an inspiration to Walt Disney when he was creating Disneyland. As we strolled through the park, all of the crap from the tour began to melt away. We rode the strange Danish roller coaster and then rode it again for good measure. To end our time in Tivoli, we rode the massively giant swings that showed us the whole city. We weren't tired or hungry or jet lagged or carsick or nervous. We were just us, floating over Denmark at 4:00 P.M. on a Tuesday in a weird little theme park, stealing this magical moment in the middle of our stressful workday. High up on those swings, we were the two luckiest kids in the world, who would come back to the ground markedly different than the people who had left it just minutes before.

—Meg Bashwiner

*If wishes were horses, those wishes would all run away,
shrieking and bucking, terrified of a great unseen evil.*

## WELCOME TO NIGHT VALE

Construction crews are on hand at the Night Vale Public Library today to begin the renovations that were approved last year by the City Council. Some of the improvements planned for the library are a new children's wing, something called a Knife Pit, an upgraded computer room with several empty desks and a loudspeaker that repeats "technology ruins lives," and, most importantly, thicker plexiglass to protect citizens from the librarians who were previously allowed to roam freely throughout the building.

City Council said renovations have been delayed for several months because it has been difficult to find construction crews willing to work in such dangerous proximity to librarians. But they finally found a very talented and brave crew to conduct this project: Colston Contractors, Inc. The City Council is asking that no one mention to any of the Colston workers that they're working near librarians. They think they're building an elaborate new Pinkberry.

The City Council added: "Hissssssssssssssssss." And then they released a bunch of badgers into City Hall much to the delight of the onlookers who thought that the badgers were kittens. The onlookers were quickly and painfully corrected in this matter.

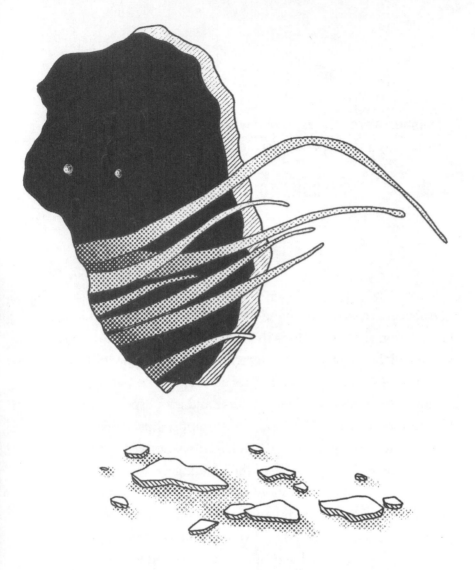

More on this story as it develops. But first today's horoscopes!

ARIES: You have much in common with a tree. A sadness that no one can see or understand. Communication only through silence and wind. Skin made of wood. The way you collect sustenance through roots buried in soil. You are very, very much like a tree. Almost impossible to tell the difference.

TAURUS: Today is the day you change everything. Oh, I'm sorry. Misspoke. Let me try that again. Today is the day that everything changes you. You will be completely unrecognizable. Yeah, there we go.

GEMINI: How scared are you of centipedes, Gemini? I mean, no reason. The stars are just asking. Like, are you super, super scared? Because like if you're really, really scared of them, then, well, I can't say exactly, but you're pretty brave right? Like you can handle a few centipedes? You can handle a bunch of centipedes, right, Gemini? I mean, no reason. Just asking.

CANCER: Today is an excellent day to demand a promotion, to approach the one you've been secretly thinking about for years, to try your hand at that new hobby you're considering. Unfortunately, it's a terrible day for getting a promotion, having that person say yes, or not injuring yourself badly on a power sander, but you should at least feel great about the attempt.

LEO: There's just a thick green smudge here and the word CRYPTOTOXICOLOGY. That's probably a good sign, maybe.

VIRGO: There's still some of you left? But how did you survive the Great Culling of Virgos that swept through . . . oh, I'm sorry. That's not until next week. I was really confused there. Yeah, today looks pretty good for you. Maybe use this nice day to get your affairs in order. Just a thought.

LIBRA: All your dreams will come true today. Or I mean, one of them will. You know that recurring dream where you are chased through a house that seems like your own but isn't quite, by a swarm of bees that you can't see even though you know they're there? Well, it's not that one. It's the other recurring dream. I'm so, so sorry.

SCORPIO: Your arms look weird, and your face is a natural irritant. Your personality leaves much to be desired, the principal desire be-ing your immediate absence. You disgust me, STEVE CARLSB———. I mean, Scorpios. Ugh. Gross. Scorpios.

SAGITTARIUS: Buy a tourniquet. The best money can buy.

CAPRICORN: Today's lucky number is imaginary. Coincidentally, so are you and your entire experience of the world.

AQUARIUS: Want to make money fast? I dunno. Rob someone. Commit fraud. There's lots of ways.

PISCES: You've won another brand new car! You stare bleakly at your home, filled with stacks upon stacks of new cars occupying every possible space at impossible angles. Today's brand new car is wheeled in, and as its bulk presses against you, taking the last bit of your home that had still been yours to live in, you feel tears hot upon your cheeks. Congratulations on your prize.

Listeners, I've just received word that there has been an accident at the library. The intricate papier-mâché and balsa wood scaffolding has collapsed.

The Sheriff's Secret Police have reported no serious injuries from the accident, but they say that one of the dense titanium and heavily electrified cages containing a librarian was damaged and that that cage is now empty.

Night Vale, this is terrible news. There is a librarian on the loose in our city, Night Vale, and there is no triple-thick armored wall or bloody animal carcass laying over a bamboo-covered pit of sharp sticks to protect us from this stalking oblivion.

Without the military-grade steel walls of the library to keep the librarians contained, Night Vale, we are helpless. We are doomed.

Watch your back, Night Vale.


**CECIL:** Oh, I almost forgot. We have a new intern. That's always fun. Let's have him introduce himself on air.

**INTERN:** Hi, I'm Intern Andrew. I'm super excited about being here. There was a way long waiting list when I signed up, and I had to wait, oh, three days before all the other interns had "left the station" and my name got to the top!

**CECIL:** Well, we're thrilled to have you here.

**INTERN:** I look forward to a long and healthy life in radio.

**CECIL:** Say, what do you know about librarians?

**INTERN:** Librarians . . . Oh no . . . Librarians . . . When I was young, my mother used to work in the coal mines, before they were converted into a holding pen for those who vote incorrectly in municipal elections. She went out each day, miner's helmet under her arm, pick slung over one shoulder, fencing sword tucked into her belt, and bloodied axe across her back. The usual miner's get up. She would descend into the dark with her fellow workers, seeking out coal or the tiny, valuable hearts of rare bats.

**CECIL:** Fantastic! So your job—

**INTERN:** My mother saw terrible things down there in the dark. Hazy, feathered things. Swarming, weeping things. Gawping, gasping things with claws and spokes and stingers and more claws. Day in and day out, this was her job. Mining coal, and fighting the denizens of the dark downwards for their hearts. When she came home, she'd be covered in coal dust and lymph.

But my mother was never afraid. Nothing fazed her. Except for the day I had to get a book from the library for a school science project. She insisted on going in ahead of me and clearing the way. But after a few minutes she came out, shaking, pale, her fencing sword bent, her axe broken in half. RUN she shouted RUN. Librarians are feared even by the fearless. I got a B on the project anyway.

**CECIL:** Well, good news! That was a well-told story. Also I need you to head down to the library and do some research on librarians.

**INTERN:** To the library?

**CECIL:** Yep! Good luck! Listeners, I can't wait to hear what Intern Andrew comes up with! On your way now. I can't wait.

We're getting reports from all over town about the escaped librarian. Liesl Schmid, who owns the auto body shop near Somerset and Gray, said she heard whispers. The whispers sounded as if they were coming from just next to her. "Where do you live Liesl?" "Do you like cars?" "How many cars will you fix before you die?" "What is your favorite color of paint?" "Do you know what I look like, Liesl?" "Would you like to?" "Would you like to?" The whispers echoed off the closed garage doors of the vast, empty workshop. Liesl said with each question, a halogen work light would fade to black, her auto body shop slowly darkening until the whispers were all she could see, and yes, somehow, she could see them. Until the final question: "Liesl, can I come live with you? I am all alone, Liesl," and the last light exploded. The room went black, and before she could even start the usual process of panic, Liesl felt—here she is, alone, in the dark—a small hand slide slowly into her own.

Liesl tried to pull away, but the childlike hand kept sliding further and further into her palm, and the childlike hand was thick, serpentine, enlarging continually and wrapping around her wrist and forearm as she felt the sharp pierce of what seemed like blades but were likely just the rigid caudal spine common on most librarians.

Liesl tried to scream but only gasped. She gasped, through a clenched throat and bared teeth, "Please, let me be. I have a family," and it was the possession of this family that saved her, as her business partner and sister, Heike, having just arrived, fired a blowtorch at the book-loving monster and it slitheringly scurried and scurriedly slithered away.

I've also received word from Green Market Board President Tristan Cortez that he cannot stop feeling his own heart beating. He feels it throughout his entire body. It feels like there is an enormous engine buried in the earth beneath him, shaking the foundations of the land, but it is not an enormous engine, it is a heart and it is actually so fragile and small.

There's something just on the other side of his front door, he said. It is breathing. He is also breathing. He cannot bring himself to look outside. He knows who it is, what it is. His heart is reacting as any heart would in the presence of a librarian. The rhythm of his own liquid life pulses through his tongue and lips, throbbing and impossible to ignore. He can feel it in his feet as he tries to stand still. He can feel it in his chest as he tries to yell over the din of his pulse, the boomboombooming of his heart and finally he manages one terrified shout into the cool morning air.

Tristan could not say for sure that it was a librarian on the other side of the door, but he did say that he could smell that familiar librarian odor of burnt coffee during a sinus infection. He also said that after the beast left, the day's mail had appeared on the porch so it could have just been a really spooky postal worker.

And now a word from our sponsors.

Today's show is brought to you by American Express. I have with me a representative from American Express in the studio, here to tell you all about this amazing card's many features. The representative is a slight haze in the air, and her name is Deb. Deb?

**DEB:** Thanks, Cecil. Hello listeners out there, I think I speak for all American Express employees and also for all sentient patches of haze when I say that I am just thrilled about the new American Express Obsidian Card.

**CECIL:** That sounds very exclusive. I'm still using the Amex I got in college. It's a post-it that says, "REAL AMERICAN EXPRESS CARD" and has a drawing of a thumbs-up. I trust this card completely, although admittedly I have yet to find a merchant that will accept it.

**DEB:** Well the new Obsidian Card will solve all of your problems. It is accepted worldwide, by any merchant that keeps their store dimly lit and lingers sadly all day on memories of lost loved ones. It's easy! If you hear crying, then your card is welcome!

And the benefits are better than ever. The Obsidian Card features full purchase protection, extended warranty on electronics, a deathless hunger that can never be sated by mere carnal appetite, and the quiet loss of one part of your body every month. We don't tell you which part. It's a surprise! It also gives you points for airlines. Or it points at the nearest airplane if put on a flat surface. I don't remember which.

**CECIL:** That really does sound great.

**DEB:** I don't care what it sounds like. It's already in your wallet now. It's in the wallet of all of your listeners. It has replaced the wallet of your listeners. Many objects in their home will now be replaced by the American Express Obsidian Card. Everything they touch will turn into a black, volcanic stone credit card. They will accidentally kill people, people they care about, and whose only crime was being touched by the cursed listener. American Express: Don't leave home.

**CECIL:** Wow, what a product and/or service. I try not to listen to or remember what anyone says to me. Taking in knowledge can be a super dangerous thing to do.

Speaking of danger, the librarian was seen near the Dog Park. The long-taloned creature with its many round, black eyes, and hairy, brown teeth was seen scaling the Dog Park fence. City Council has warned us many times that the Dog Park is off limits, that dogs are not allowed in the Dog Park, that people are not allowed in the Dog Park, that we may see hooded figures in the Dog Park. Well, witnesses said that as the librarian approached the Dog Park fence, the hooded figures ran away in all directions, cloaks fluttering in the wind of motion, revealing matching black and white Nike tennis shoes.

But before the librarian could enter the Dog Park, a small band of masked children showed up holding slingshots and well-worn copies of Chinua Achebe's critically acclaimed post-fatalist novel *No Longer at Ease*. By all accounts, this was the same group of fifth through eighth graders who bravely escaped last year's Summer Reading Program at the Night Vale Public Library. The leader of that escape, thirteen-year-old Tamika Flynn, was with the group of kids at the Dog Park trying to back the librarian down from the fence.

As a small boy blew a low, long tone from a conch shell, Tamika held aloft the severed head of the librarian she defeated last summer—still surprisingly well-preserved—as a gruesome warning for the librarian currently terrorizing the forbidden municipal park.

Witnesses said the librarian shrieked meekly and leapt from the fence, as the children chased after it shouting suggested additions to the library's fiction stock. "Maxine Hong Kingston," came one shout. "Larry McMurtry is a keystone of new Western literature," another yelled. "I have never read Elizabeth Barrett Browning. I hope you add her," came a final call as sling-shotted rocks plunked hard off the retreating librarian's exoskeleton.

Tamika then spoke. We have her actual speech, because we are all being recorded at all times by several different government organizations and amateur community spying clubs. Here now, is Tamika Flynn's statement.

**TAMIKA:** People of Night Vale. We are your children. We are your children who survived the librarians. We are your children who defeated StrexCorp. We are your children who learned the power of books.

The power of books is that they teach you how to destroy what is but should not be. The power of books is that they show you what it might be like to think as someone other than this person you are stuck being. The power of books is poisonous gases and spring traps.

Nothing is more powerful than a book. A larger book is slightly more powerful than a smaller book, because it can also be used to hit your enemies. Smaller paperbacks are terrible for that.

Take it from me, I have tried. *A Hero of Our Time* might be a classic of Russian literature but it is useless against the hide of a librarian, even when launched with a handmade book launcher.

This is why Vladimir Nabokov's famous translation added several thousand blank pages and a carbon steel, bullet-shaped dust jacket.

But your physical stature is unrelated to your strength. You are strong because you are many. You are strong because you are in this together. You are strong because of that weird rain that gave many of you double-quick hand combat reflexes and seventh eyes. You are strong because if enough people believe in their own power, even if armed only with mass-market paperbacks, they could bring down not just a librarian, but an entire corpocratic regime.

As for us, your army of missing children, we are not missing. We are found.

Here is our plan, Night Vale: We will give up. We will lay down our arms and quit fighting. We will close our eyes and sleep. Yes, that is what we will do once we have crushed every enemy in our path. Once we are victorious and bathed in blood, and placing stickers on reading levels far beyond our age, reading levels that are yet to be discovered, pizza reading rewards in quantities and kinds that are unimaginable for the unenlightened.

As Indira Gandhi once said, "You cannot shake hands with a mangled fist that has been chewed up by an unchained librarian." You are not alone. You were never alone. We will advance on the librarians together. Believe in us Night Vale. We will exist either way, but you might as well. You might as well.

**CECIL:** Unfortunately, witnesses were too shaken to see where the librarian disappeared to. Listeners, I urge you to follow Tamika's example of strength and courage. Be brave like Tamika, but do so indoors. Keep your homes locked and listen here for further instructions.

Let's have a look now at the community calendar:

This Thursday afternoon at the rec center is the Sheriff's Secret Police's semi-annual Gun Buyback Program. If you have an illegal or unregistered gun, bring it to the rec center, and the Secret Police will buy it from you, with full amnesty, no questions asked. A Secret Police representative said it'd be especially cool if you had fully automatic rifles and some grenades. Really cool, she repeated, eyes darting about, knuckles rhythmically cracking. Also, please don't tell anyone we're doing this. It's totally covert, she whispered.

**CECIL:** There's an event this Thursday night at Dark Owl Records. For more on that, we've got owner Michelle Nguyen on the phone. Michelle?

**MICHELLE:** Hi, Cecil.

**CECIL:** Welcome to our show, Michelle.

**MICHELLE:** Am I on a podcast?

**CECIL:** No. It's a radio show.

**MICHELLE:** Oh good. Podcasts are dead. I hate podcasts.

**CECIL:** Michelle, I got a press release saying you have a special event this Thursday at Dark Owl Records.

**MICHELLE:** I wish I hadn't sent that out. I didn't want anyone to know about it.

**CECIL:** It doesn't say what the event is. It just says "Dark Owl Records. This Thursday Night. You probably wouldn't understand and probably won't be invited."

**MICHELLE:** So this Thursday night, the Dark Owl staff and I are going to try to discover fire. It's a private event, and I've ordered them never to tell anybody what we find out, because if everyone knows how to make fire, then everyone will start talking about how to make fire. And then people will be making fire all the time, and suddenly making fire won't mean anything. We will no longer feel what it means to create flames. We will no longer cry under the glimmering orange lamp of nature's most cruel and useful force. If everyone loves making fire, then how can we truly know what it even means to feel heat or light a scented candle or fry an egg or take revenge on your own diary.

**CECIL:** Not to be a spoilsport here, Michelle, but fire was discovered a long time ago.

**MICHELLE:** I know that. Fire's been around for decades. Blah blah blah. History blah blah. I get it. But it is important that my staff and I discover it for ourselves. It's like Bono said moments before he died, "It's all been a lie and I wish I had been more aware."

**CECIL:** Well, it sounds like a cool event.

**MICHELLE:** Please don't ruin it with adjectives.

**CECIL:** It sounds like an event. Michelle, I don't know if you've heard the news today about the escaped librarians.

**MICHELLE:** I found out about the escaped librarian years ago from this underground magazine called *Fütür* (with two umlauts).

**CECIL:** I've never heard of *Fütür*.

**MICHELLE:** Of course you haven't. The only way to get a copy is to walk out to the middle of the Whispering Forest. The trees there will try to lure you into becoming one of them by complimenting your outfit and physical appearance, but I'm immune to positive feedback so I'm one of the only people who can walk through there. My friend Richard is a tree there now. He used to intern here. He wanted me to tell you, "Hi, and you have a nice voice." You have an okay voice, I guess.

Richard's the one who told me about the magazine. In order to read it you have to climb this one tree, this creepy cedar named Reg, who appreciates my hats way too much. At the top of Reg is a plastic magazine kiosk that's covered with band stickers and misspelled cuss words. *Fütür* magazine comes out weekly and it tells you news well before it happens, ensuring that I never have to have my parents or someone over thirty tell me something I didn't already know. So, yes, I knew about the librarians well before anyone else.

**CECIL:** So what happens? Did *Fütür* explain how we were able to save our town? Or if? IF we were able to save our town?

**MICHELLE:** Probably. I don't remember. It wasn't very interesting. There was a review of an Amanda Palmer album that comes out in eight years. I read that instead. Anyway, I'm covered in spiders. So know that.

**CECIL:** Oh my gosh. I'm sorry. Please. Go call an exterminator right now.

**MICHELLE:** No! The spiders are my outfit, Cecil. I'm not going to kill them.

**CECIL:** Okay. Well, thank you Michelle. Listeners, this Thursday night at Dark Owl Records, Michelle and her staff will try to discover fire.

**MICHELLE:** Please stop knowing this.

**CECIL:** Do you have any special approaches or techniques you're going to use to discover fire for yourself?

**MICHELLE:** We're going to use simple elements, like cigarette lighters and gasoline. I gotta go, my hat is crawling down my back.

**CECIL:** Okay, then.

Friday night all lanes of Route 800 will be shut down in both directions as work crews stand in the middle of the empty dark highway repeating *Bloody Mary* three times just to settle this thing once and for all.

Saturday afternoon on the Great Lawn near City Hall is the annual Children's Fair. There will be face-painting booths, street food, balloon animals, real animals, hungry animals, feral wild animals that fear no human. Children and adults are prohibited from attending until they get these animals under control.

Sunday morning the Night Vale Junior League will be opening the one-hundred-year time capsule that was buried there by disgruntled Subway employees all the way back in 1914. It's very exciting to see what kinds of bread and cold cut slices they buried in that cardboard box for an entire century. We're sure to learn a lot. And then forget it, only to have it resurface subtly couched in horrifying Jungian dream imagery for the rest of our lives. This is how time works.

Monday would like for you to leave it alone. It's not its fault that you are emotionally unprepared for your own professional lives.

How are you doing right now, dear listener? Are you afraid? I would like to tell you that I am not afraid. I would like to be strong in the face of imminent death, Night Vale. I am the voice of a community, and I must be neutral, impassive, simply reporting the news.

I'd like to feel something resembling confidence, but I am feeling something resembling petrified terror. I am very similar to a scared person.

The City Council announced that . . . oh dear listeners . . . I do not know how to tell you this. The City Council announced that ALL of the librarians have escaped.

Night Vale, we do not yet know how many librarians there are or what exactly they are capable of. We were already too scared to read or even think about good literature, but now even our book-free personal space will be invaded by these monsters. Like the great American writer Mark Twain once said, "Reading is hardly worth all the bloodshed. This is why all of my novels are wadded up candy store receipts that I leave on park benches. They should never be put in libraries, even after I die in the next few minutes at the hands of this drunk minotaur standing in my parlor right now."

Mark Twain was wise enough to know that libraries are a bad idea. Listeners, I'm calling my boyfriend, Carlos, to see what he thinks. He's a scientist, and so he might have some idea about how to handle these unholy beasts.

[*phone ringing*]

**CARLOS:** Hello.
**CECIL:** Carlos. Hey, it's me. I'm calling you from the show.
**CARLOS:** Oh hey, I was listening earlier but I got distracted with work. I'm standing in front of a row of beakers full of different-colored liquids, intermittently rubbing my chin and writing down long, complex equations. There's a giant computer next to me, too, with several blinking buttons. So I missed most of your show, but I

heard there's a new wing at the library opening. That's exciting.

**CECIL:** No. No. Carlos, it's not exciting. Well, yes, technically, yes, it's exciting. But horrible excitement. There are escaped librarians on the loose. We are in great danger. Carlos, have you not boarded up the doors?

**CARLOS:** No, it's such a nice day today. I've got the windows open and everything. Why would we need to be afraid of librarians? Librarians are helpful and kind. I mean, I don't want to generalize about all librarians. There are certainly some mean librarians, just as there are some mean people, just as there are helpful and kind librarians and people. They are no different than any of us.

I myself have never actually seen a librarian. Since I am a scientist, and not a writer or editor, I have never actually had to read a book and thus have never been inside a library. But I had friends in college that were literature or journalism majors, and they told me that librarians did things like help recommend good books and find important information related to their interests. And nearly all of my friends that have visited a library are still alive. Well, a little over half, anyway. I don't see what the panic is about.

**CECIL:** Carlos, listen to yourself. That is insane.

**CARLOS:** Perhaps. As the great mathematician Albert Einstein once said, "The definition of insanity is available inside this cave. Come inside this cave. Please enter the cave and the definition will be told to you. It's so nice in this cave."

**CECIL:** True. But please, for my sake, lock the doors and turn out the lights. Do not let the librarians know that you are home. Do not answer the door for any reason, Carlos. I don't know what I would do without you.

**CARLOS:** Okay. I will. I need a break from all these experiments anyway. I'll try doing some quiet mental science in the dark. I'll see you tonight.

**CECIL:** I love you. Be safe.

**CARLOS:** I love you, too. And I'll be fine. I am a scientist. A scientist is always fine.

**CECIL:** Well, I certainly feel better having talked to Carlos even though I have learned absolutely nothing new about librarians. Night Vale, all I can tell you is to board up your doors and windows. Turn out the lights and do not answer the door for any reason. We do not know how long we must hide ourselves. You must continue to live your lives, but do so in a way that draws no attention. Requires no light or motion. Shut down your lives, listeners, for fear of losing them. Remove all semblance of living to prolong a few more moments of that empty life. Be safe, Night Vale. I will do my best to keep bringing you the news.

**INTERN:** Hello, Cecil?

**CECIL:** Intern Andrew? How wonderful to hear from you again. Are you at the library?

**INTERN:** Yes, I've found my way into the library. It's very dark in here. The construction crew is standing over the collapsed scaffolding, poking at it with sticks and ordering it to put itself back together again. Their antennas are in the "nonaggressive" position, so I don't think they realize the danger they're in.

**CECIL:** Be careful, Intern Andrew. But also, be closer to the story. Be much closer, and tell us what you see.

**INTERN:** I am walking between the shelves. There are books all around me. I don't feel safe around so many books. There are small wallows here and there where a librarian has nested for the night. Some of them look quite fresh.

**CECIL:** Move quietly. There could still be a librarian arou———

**INTERN:** There is a librarian. It's seen me. It has me trapped in the biographies section. There are many books about Helen Hunt. I have no choice. I will have to fight my way out.

**CECIL:** You'd never survive. Just pretend you don't exist and hope the librarian shares your delusion.

**INTERN:** It's too late. I have my fencing sword in my hand. Say good-bye to my mother, wherever she buried herself after the mine closed, I'll do her proud!

**CECIL:** I will—

**INTERN:** And say good-bye to my best friend, Joann, and my second best friend, Jaime, and my tied-for-third best friends, Xerxes and Hassan. Wish them well on their artisanal upholstery business. Cover those chairs, my sweetest friends. Cover those chairs!

**CECIL:** Okay.

**INTERN:** And say good-bye to the Faceless Old Woman Who Secretly Lives in My Home. I don't know what I would have done without her. Probably mostly the same things I always did, because I didn't know she was there until she started running for mayor. And now I'm not clear how she's "secretly" living anywhere? How is it a secret at this point? Ask her that. Kind of smirk while you do. Lean back and cross your arms too. More. Great. Do that. For me.

**CECIL:** Okay, is that—

**INTERN:** And say goodbye to Cecil. Tell him his voice is like swimming in a clear, cold underground river.

**CECIL:** I'm Ceci———

**INTERN:** Tell him for me. All right, I'm going in. This will be a perilous and lengthy struggle. We will be intertwined in a gruesome embrace until one of us dies, maybe hours from now, maybe days. For Night Vale! Aaaaaaaaaa . . . [*sudden choking cut off*]

**CECIL:** To the family of Intern Andrew, he was a brave intern, although not very knowledgable about fencing swords and their complete inability to cut human flesh, let alone librarian exoskeletons.

And now, a public service announcement.

The Greater Night Vale Medical Community is calling on all citizens to give blood. There are always patients, unfortunate people, who need your help. Sometimes there is a great natural disaster like an earthquake or tornado. Or even a great artificial disaster like scissor fog. But don't wait these moments to give blood. Doctors need it every single day.

Never given blood before? It's easy. The Greater Night Vale Medical Community knows that many of you are afraid of needles, but there are so many non-needle ways to get your blood: court injunction, satellites, wolverines, a very carefully staged accident.

Put aside your rational fear of needles and pain, and give blood. This message has been brought to you by the Greater Night Vale Medical Community, which, oh this is weird, I'm sorry but I said I'd ask. The Greater Night Vale Medical Community wanted me to tell you that they, um, well, they think you're cute. Are you seeing anybody right now?

Because I told them you were. So no pressure, okay. They still wanted me to ask. They were very persistent. Okay, I'll tell them you are. No worries.

Listeners, the worst has just happened. We are getting reports that a librarian has entered a theater. Thankfully you are not one of those doomed souls who risked their lives for something as useless as live theater, but let us all, as an exercise in empathy, imagine what it would be like to be one of those unfortunates, in their last oblivious moments.

Imagine you are in a theater. Imagine rows of seats. Imagine a stage. Imagine amplification and a person a row behind you whispering to their friend constantly. Picture this. Picture yourself as you'd never be, in a crowd of listening strangers.

Now imagine the librarian in the theater, not yet spotted in the dark of the house. Imagine it slithering silently beneath the theater seats. What if, hypothetical theatergoer, it were under the seat you were in right now? No. Don't check. Don't check. If it knew you saw it, what would it decide to do to you? Don't check. Don't check. Okay, check. Ah. Nothing there. Good. So you are safe in your imagined theater seat. Or maybe the librarian anticipated your movement and slipped out of view just as you looked. That is a possibility too. What is wonderful about this world is that anything is possible. Anything that can eventually result in your death in this world is possible.

Was that a dry, scaled hand upon your shoulder? Oh, not that shoulder. Not that shoulder either. No, the other one. Oh, it keeps moving back and forth, doesn't it? You feel breath faintly on your neck, so faintly that you dismiss it, over and over, until it dismisses you for good. One by one people are disappearing from their seats, without a sound, just a flash of red and a dark stain, and your brain adjusts for this by remembering those seats as always having been empty and moist.

And then the screams start. First the left side of the theater. And then the right. The librarian is everywhere now. The entire theater is screaming. A person in the front row gets up, clutches their chest, and screams. Or, oh, several people in the front row. They tear at their hair. They scream louder than the rest of the theater combined. And then: silence. Utter silence. The front row sits down.

The silence is worse than the screams. No one is saying anything at all. No one is making the slightest move. The librarian is above them. Don't look up! The librarian descends. Perhaps on a web. Perhaps on great black wings. Perhaps with its tendrils wrapped around the walls and the beams. Its jaws open. It focuses in on a single person. Don't look up! There are only moments now. While that person waits, unknowingly, to get taken, I take all of you—safe at home, of course, not actually helpless in a theater—to the weather.

**WEATHER:** "Sepentine Cycle of Money" by Carrie Elkin and Danny Schmidt

Listeners, good news. I mean, the news was always good for you, safe at home with only a few hidden entities lurking around you and none of them so dangerous as librarians. But the news, surprisingly, is also good for those screaming victims trapped in a theater.

The librarians have been re-captured. Not by the Sheriff's Secret Police, not by Tamika Flynn and her valiant band of well-read child vigilantes, but by the librarians themselves.

We have learned that the initial escapee was named Randall. We have also learned that Randall was trying to leave his job as librarian. He was curious about all the other jobs in the world, as he was born a librarian and had only ever known the secret evils and dark magicks of library science.

Randall wanted to know what it would be like to work as a construction contractor, an auto body mechanic, a food co-op manager, a municipal park employee, a hooded figure. There is a whole world of occupations and opportunities in America. It is a free country, we explain to ourselves regularly without quite knowing what we mean. Randall even slipped into a theater to find out what it might be like to be a folk singer or an actor or an usher or just a regular audience member, just a human full of regret and worry, trying to find a moment outside of themselves by watching a live performance.

But the librarians, knowing that they are not human—far from it—found Randall and brought him back to the library. For while they are terrible, bloodthirsty pseudo-reptilians, librarians are also quite organized. Just as they would never want a highly researched nonfiction travel guide like Stephen King's *The Dark Tower* series to end up in, say, fiction, or a sci-fi fantasy comic book like Pat Conroy's *The Prince of Tides* to end up in religious studies, librarians also know that they should never be seen or felt or heard outside of a library.

Librarians know they cannot enter society and co-exist with humans without succumbing to immense hunger and curiosity, tearing us all into pink, pulpy piles of post-existence. So they dragged unhappy Randall from the theater (along with a couple of collateral audience members).

The people in the theater were filled with relief, and shaking with the echo of their terror. They each turned to a person near them, not even a person they came with, not a person they knew at all. They each turned to that stranger and they said, "You are alive for now." And then they said, "Congratulations." They shared a couple moments of eye contact to acknowledge the unlikelihood of this claim. One . . . two . . . and then they looked away, uncomfortable with all that eyeballs and vision imply. They mumbled, "Well, it was nice to meet you," And they all said, "My name's Amanda," even though very few of them were named that. And then the show went on, and that moment of exchange hung between the strangers in the audience, latent and invisible, perhaps to be reprised later or perhaps already only existing in the poor reconstruction of memory.

As usual, we had nothing to fear. And in saying that, I mean that we have everything to fear. Death is slotted for us all. Maybe many years from now in a soft bed surrounded by the soft eyes of those we love. Maybe not many years from now at all. We have every reason to be scared. But we should also put that fear aside. Like a library book, we sometimes need to check out our fear, read it, peruse it, study it closely, but at a certain point return it to its proper shelf and experience something else. Contentment, worry, calm, hunger, spine parasites, and a great deal of love of every kind. Put that fear in a place where you can find it again when it's useful, but don't carry it with you. Do not carry it with you.

Stay tuned next for a shuffling movement outwards, a dimming of lights, and a large hall left empty and silent until the next time it is not.

Good night, all of you listeners.

And good night, Night Vale. Good night.

# ABOUT THE AUTHORS

**JOSEPH FINK** created the *Welcome to Night Vale* and *Alice Isn't Dead* podcasts. He lives with his wife in New York.

**JEFFREY CRANOR** cowrites the *Welcome to Night Vale* and *Within the Wires* podcasts. He also cocreates theater and dance pieces with choreographer/wife, Jillian Sweeney. They live in New York.

# ABOUT THE CONTRIBUTORS

**CECIL BALDWIN** is the narrator of the hit podcast *Welcome to Night Vale*. He is an alumnus of the New York Neo-Futurists, performing in their late-night show *Too Much Light Makes the Baby Go Blind*, as well as Drama Desk–nominated *The Complete and Condensed Stage Directions of Eugene O'Neill, Vol. 2*. Cecil has performed at the Shakespeare Theatre DC, Studio Theatre (including the world premiere production of Neil Labute's *Autobahn*), the Kennedy Center, the National Players, LaMaMa E.T.C., Emerging Artists Theatre, and the Upright Citizens Brigade. Film/TV credits include Braden in *The Outs* (Vimeo), the voice of Tad Strange in *Gravity Falls* (Disney XD), The Fool in *Lear* (with Paul Sorvino), and *Billie Joe Bob*. Cecil has been featured on podcasts such as *Ask Me Another* (NPR), *Selected Shorts* (PRI), *Shipwreck*, *Big Data*, and *Our Fair City*.

**MEG BASHWINER** is a writer, performer, and producer. She plays the role of "Deb" and "Proverb Lady" on the hit podcast *Welcome to Night Vale*. She is the emcee and tour manager of the *Welcome to Night Vale* live show and has brought the live show to seventeen countries and almost all of the fifty states. She is the producer and cohost of the podcast *Good Morning Night Vale*. She is an ensemble member at-large for the New York Neo-Futurists, known for their popular weekly show *The Infinite Wrench*. She has toured productions of the New York Neo-Futurists' previous late-night show *Too Much Light Makes the Baby Go Blind* to the Edinburgh Fringe Festival, The Providence Improv Festival, and headlined the Out of Bounds Comedy Festival in Austin, Texas.

**KEVIN R. FREE** is a multidisciplinary artist whose work as an actor, writer, director, and producer has been showcased and developed in many places, including *The Moth Radio Hour*, Project Y Theater, Flux Theater Ensemble, the Queerly Festival (of which he is now the curator), and the Fire This Time Festival, where he served as producing artistic director, winning an Obie for his work in 2015. Recent directing credits include *Lady Day at Emerson's Bar & Grill* and *The Last Five Years* (both at Portland Stage) and *Topdog/Underdog* (University of Arkansas). New York City directing includes the Fire This Time Season 10 World Premiere 10-minute Play Festival; Okello Kelo Sam's *Forged in Fire*; Renita L. Martin's *Blue Fire in the Water* (Fresh Fruit Festival); *The First Time*; *Standing Up: Bathroom Talk and Other Stuff We Learn from Dad*; and *Poor Posturing*, all by Tracey Conyer Lee; Michelle T. Johnson's *Wiccans in the 'Hood*; and *Legislative Acts*, a sketch comedy show performed by New York City legislators. His full-length plays include *Night of the Living N-Word!!* (Overall Excellence in Playwriting, FringeNYC 2016); *A Raisin in the Salad: Black Plays for White People* (New Black Fest Fellowship 2012; Eugene O'Neill Semi-Finalist 2013); *Face Value* (Henry Street Settlement Playwrights' Project Grant, 2000), and *The Crisis of the Negro Intellectual, or Triple Consciousness*. His webseries, "Gemma & The Bear!," was an Official Selection of the New York Television Festival in 2016; and his latest webseries, "Beckys through History," received a creative engagement grant from Lower Manhattan Cultural Center in 2018 (more at www. MyCarl.org). He has worked as an actor across the United States and internationally, most recently appearing in New York City as Michael Curtiz in Reid and Sara Farrington's Drama Desk–nominated *CasblancaBox* (HERE) and as the Narrator of Lisa Clair's *The Making of King Kong* (Target Margin Theater). He is an accomplished voice actor as well as having recorded more than 300 audiobooks, and is the voice of Kevin from Desert Bluffs on *Welcome to Night Vale*. Twitter: @kevinrfree; www.kevinrfree.com.

**JESSICA HAYWORTH** is an illustrator and fine artist. She has produced a variety of illustrated works for the *Welcome to Night Vale* podcast since 2013, including posters for the touring live show. Her other works include the graphic novels *Monster* and *I Will Kill You with My Bare Hands*, as well as various solo and group exhibitions. She received her MFA from Cranbrook Academy of Art and lives and works in Detroit.

**ZACK PARSONS** is a Chicago-based humorist and author of nonfiction (*My Tank is Fight!*) and fiction (*Liminal States*). In addition to *Welcome to Night Vale*, he has worked with Joseph Fink on the website Something Awful and can also be found writing for his own site, The Bad Guys Win (thebadguyswin.com). You can call him a weird idiot on Twitter at @sexyfacts4u.

**KATE JONES** is a writer, performer, and wedding officiant from Howell, New Jersey. She is an alum of the New York Neo-Futurists and Degenerate Fox (UK). She plays Michelle Nguyen on *Welcome to Night Vale* and currently lives in Switzerland where she can often be found performing stand-up comedy, whether or not there is an audience. www.katekatekate.com or @QTPiK8 on Twitter.

**ASHLEY LIERMAN** is a professional university librarian and an occasional writer. Apart from contributing guest episodes to *Welcome to Night Vale*, she has written several stories for the chat fiction app Cliffhanger, contributed to two short-story anthologies by independent genre fiction press the Sockdolager (www.sockdolager.net), and has appeared as a guest on the podcast *I Haven't Seen That* (www.ihaventseenthat.com).

**ERICA LIVINGSTON** is a writer, artist, and full spectrum doula living in Brooklyn. She has two sons, a garden, and a deep belief in plants and people. She likes laughing above most things. She is an alumna of the New York Neo-Futurists, which is really the origin of how this bio even came to be here. At one point she was making lots of puppets and at another point she was more interested in handmade zines. These days she supports birthing people as they cross the threshold into parenthood. You can find her at birdsongbrooklyn.com.

One of the creators and cohosts of *We Got This with Mark and Hal* on the Maximum Fun Network, **HAL LUBLIN** also cohosts the popular podcasts *Tights & Fights* and *Good Morning Night Vale*. Best known for his work as one of the core WorkJuice players in *The Thrilling Adventure Hour* and as Steve Carlsberg on *Welcome to Night Vale*, Hal plays Wide Wale, Manolo and others on *The Venture Brothers* and several characters on Cartoon Network's *Mighty Magiswords*. His work runs the gamut from animated films and television programs to radio shows and video games for CBS, Happy Madison, Disney, SyFy, JibJab, *Wired*, and more.

**DYLAN MARRON** is an IFP Gotham Award and Drama Desk-nominated writer, performer, and video maker. He is the voice of Carlos on the hit podcast *Welcome to Night Vale*, an alum of the New York Neo-Futurists, and the creator of Every Single Word

(Tumblr's "Most Viral Blog" of 2015; Shorty Award Nominee), a video series that edits down popular films to only feature the words spoken by people of color. As a writer and correspondent at Seriously.tv Dylan created, hosted, and produced *Sitting in Bathrooms with Trans People*, *Shutting Down Bullsh\*t*, and the Unboxing series. He currently hosts and produces *Conversations with People Who Hate Me*, a podcast where he calls up the people behind negative comments on the internet. It was selected as a Podcast Pick by *USA Today* and *The Guardian*, named "the timeliest podcast" by *Fast-Company*, and won a Webby Award.

**DESSA** is a rapper, singer, essayist, and proud member of the Doomtree hip-hop crew. She's performed around the world at opera houses, rock clubs, and while standing on barroom tables. Her imaginative writing and ferocious stage presence have been praised by NPR, Billboard, *Forbes*, the *Chicago Tribune*, and the *LA Times*. As a musician, she's landed on the Billboard Top 200 as a solo artist (*Parts of Speech*; *Chime*); as a Doomtree member (*All Hands*); and as a contributor to *The Hamilton Mixtape*. She's been published by the *New York Times*, MPR, the *Star Tribune* (Minneapolis), literary journals across the country, and has written two short collections of poetry and essays. Her book of literary nonfiction, *My Own Devices: True Stories from the Road on Music, Science, and Senseless Love* (Dutton Books, Penguin Random House), is available now.

**JAMES URBANIAK** is an actor and writer based in Los Angeles. TV credits include the role of Arthur on Hulu's *Difficult People,* Grant on Comedy Central's *Review,* and the voice of Dr. Venture on Adult Swim's long-running animated series *The Venture Bros.* Films include *American Splendor* (role of Robert Crumb), *You Don't Know Jack* with Al Pacino, Todd Haynes's *Wonderstruck,* Richard Linklater's *Where'd You Go, Bernadette?,* and the Hal Hartley trilogy *Henry*

*Fool, Fay Grim,* and *Ned Rifle.* On stage he originated the title role in the original New York production of Will Eno's play *Thom Pain (based on nothing)* (Drama Desk nomination for Performance) and won an Obie Award for his role in Richard Foreman's *The Universe.* He created the scripted podcasts *Getting On with James Urbaniak* and *A Night Called Tomorrow* (cowritten with Brie Williams).

**MARA WILSON** is a writer, storyteller, and voice actress. Her voice can be heard on *BoJack Horseman* and *Big Hero 6*, and she both wrote for and voiced characters in the audio drama *Passenger List.* Her writing has appeared in *Vanity Fair, The Guardian, McSweeney's, Reductress, Cracked,* the *New York Times* and on Elle.com. She writes a weekly newsletter, Shan't We Tell the Vicar?, available on Mara.substack.com, and her first book, *Where Am I Now?: True Stories of Girlhood and Accidental Fame* is available from Penguin Random House.

# ACKNOWLEDGMENTS

THANKS TO THE CAST AND CREW OF *WELCOME TO NIGHT VALE*: MEG Bashwiner, Jon Bernstein, Desiree Burch, Nathalie Candel, Adam Cecil, Aliee Chan, Dessa Darling, Felicia Day, Emma Frankland, Kevin R. Free, Mark Gagliardi, Glen David Gold, Angelique Grandone, Marc Evan Jackson, Maureen Johnson, Kate Jones, Ashley Lierman, Erica Livingston, Christopher Loar, Hal Lublin, Dylan Marron, Jasika Nicole, Lauren O'Niell, Zack Parsons, Flor De Liz Perez, Teresa Piscioneri, Jackson Publick, Molly Quinn, Em Reaves, Retta, Symphony Sanders, Annie Savage, Lauren Sharpe, James Urbaniak, Bettina Warshaw, Wil Wheaton, Brie Williams, Mara Wilson, and, of course, the voice of *Night Vale* himself, Cecil Baldwin.

Also and always: Jillian Sweeney; Kathy and Ron Fink; Ellen Flood; Leann Sweeney; Jack and Lydia Bashwiner; the Pows; the Zambaranos; Rob Wilson; Kate Leth; Jessica Hayworth; Holly and Jeffrey Rowland; Andrew Morgan; Eleanor McGuinness; Hank Green; John Green; Griffin, Travis, and Justin McElroy; Cory Doctorow; John Darnielle; Aby Wolf; Jason Webley; Danny Schmidt; Carrie Elkin; Eliza Rickman; Mary Epworth; Will Twynham; Erin McKeown; Mal Blum; the New York Neo-Futurists; Janina

Matthewson; Christy Gressman; Adam Cecil; Julian Koster; Gennifer Hutchison; Kassie Evashevski; Chris Parnell; Amy Suh; the Booksmith in San Francisco; and, of course, the delightful *Night Vale* fans.

Our agent, Jodi Reamer; our editor, Amy Baker; and all the good people at Harper Perennial.

# BOOKS BY JOSEPH FINK & JEFFREY CRANOR

## MOSTLY VOID, PARTIALLY STARS
### WELCOME TO NIGHT VALE EPISODES, VOLUME 1

*Mostly Void, Partially Stars* introduces us to Night Vale, a town in the American Southwest where every conspiracy theory is true, and to the strange but friendly people who live there.

## THE GREAT GLOWING COILS OF THE UNIVERSE
### WELCOME TO NIGHT VALE EPISODES, VOLUME 2

In *The Great Glowing Coils of the Universe* we witness a totalitarian takeover of Night Vale that threatens to forever change the town and everyone living in it.

## WELCOME TO NIGHT VALE
### A NOVEL

"The book is charming and absurd—think *This American Life* meets *Alice in Wonderland*."
—*Washington Post*

From the creators of the wildly popular *Welcome to Night Vale* podcast comes an imaginative mystery of appearances and disappearances that is also a poignant look at the ways in which we all struggle to find ourselves...no matter where we live.

## IT DEVOURS!
### A NOVEL

"A confident supernatural comedy from writers who can turn from laughter to tears on a dime." — *Kirkus Reviews*

From the authors of the *New York Times* bestselling novel *Welcome to Night Vale* and the creators of the #1 international podcast of the same name, comes a mystery exploring the intersections of faith and science, the growing relationship between two young people who want desperately to trust each other, and the terrifying, toothy power of the Smiling God.

## ALICE ISN'T DEAD
### A NOVEL

"*Alice Isn't Dead* remains an intriguing complement, imbued with newfound soul—and romance. Alice has always known suspense, but as a novel it finds true love."
—*Entertainment Weekly*

From the *New York Times* bestselling co-author of *It Devours!* and *Welcome to Night Vale* comes a fast-paced thriller about a truck driver searching across America for the wife she had long assumed to be dead.